ON
LEFT
ALIVE

BOOKS BY HELEN PHIFER

ONE
LEFT
ALIVE

HELEN PHIFER

Bookouture

Published by Bookouture in 2020

An imprint of Storyfire Ltd.
Carmelite House
50 Victoria Embankment
London EC4Y 0DZ

www.bookouture.com

ISBN: 978-1-83888-849-7
eBook ISBN: 978-1-83888-848-0

This book is a work of fiction. Names, characters, businesses,
organizations, places and events other than those clearly in the
public domain, are either the product of the author's imagination
or are used fictitiously. Any resemblance to actual persons, living or
dead, events or locales is entirely coincidental.

This book is dedicated to all the amazing NHS workers and key workers who have kept Britain going throughout the 2020 pandemic.

I thank each and every one of you for your selfless acts of bravery.

CHAPTER ONE

Police Officer Morgan Brookes was driving around aimlessly, trying to get to know the vast rural area that she was responsible for until the end of her shift. Lifting her wrist, she looked at her watch: only another seven hours to go. She loved it here, was grateful she got to work in such a beautiful part of the Lake District. But God it was boring being on your own. She much preferred it when she was in company with another officer. Her colleague, Dan, had been her tutor since leaving her training at headquarters. They had spent hours in each other's company and become friends; despite his terrible jokes and sometimes blasé attitude, she missed his company.

A burst of static as the radio came to life made her jump.

'5129 we have an IR at Lake View on Easdale Road, Grasmere. A suspected suicide. There's a female hanging from a tree.'

Morgan felt a surge of blood rush through her veins, as the adrenalin kicked in. She hadn't attended a suicide on her own before, but she had been to several when she was completing her training and in company with a more experienced officer. She was ready for this.

'On my way. I'm single crewed though. Are ambulance travelling?'

'Yes, we'll get another patrol travelling as well. You're the nearest.'

She was glad to hear backup was coming, as she put on her blues and turned the van around, speeding through the lanes to get back to the road she hadn't long left. Morgan knew where Easdale Road was; she'd driven along it already today. Unsure which house was Lake View, she hoped it would have one of those fancy slate plaques outside the gates, which most of the wealthier houses in the Lakes had. She slowed the van so she could read each one. It was a nightmare; she couldn't see any house numbers and was relying on a name plate. Passing a cluster of houses without spotting the name or the female figure control had mentioned, she radioed back.

'Do you have me on ARL?'

'Yes, we do. According to this map you're about half a minute away, keep driving, it's the next house on your right.'

Putting her foot down, Morgan sped up until she found the sign for Lake View and turned into the long driveway. The van rattled as she drove too fast along the narrow drive. Just ahead, in front of the large house, she could see the body dangling from a tree and her stomach did a complete flip. A teenage boy was standing underneath, trying to hold the feet up with his shoulders and her heart felt for him. What an awful thing to find. A phone was clamped to his ear, and the look of relief on his face as she jumped out and ran towards him seared into her mind.

'Please help me, are you on your own?'

'Help is coming. They'll be here any minute. Who are you?'

One look at the woman hanging from the tree told Morgan that it didn't matter how long the other patrol took; there was nothing they could do for her. Her glazed eyes were staring blankly into the sunset; her small frame looked lost hanging from the branch of the large oak tree. There was a gentle breeze blowing her shoulder-length blonde hair across her face as her body swayed in the breeze. On the branch next to her was a worn child's rope swing and Morgan wondered if she had young children. It was desperately sad; she looked too young and beautiful to be dead.

'I'm Harrison.'

'Harrison, you're doing a great job. Do you know where there are any ladders?'

He nodded.

'I'll take over, you go get them. We'll need them to cut her down.'

She grabbed hold of the woman's legs and the boy ran towards an outbuilding. He came back moments later carrying a stepladder, his face red and eyes brimming with tears.

'Is this your mum?'

He shook his head. 'No, it's my girlfriend's mum. Oh God, why has she done this? Is she alive?'

Morgan couldn't be the one to call it even though she knew the woman was dead; she needed a paramedic to confirm it, and she didn't want him to think she wasn't trying to help despite the hopelessness of the situation.

'Harrison, I'm Morgan. I don't think she is, but the paramedics will be able to tell us for sure.'

The sound of an approaching siren filled the air and Morgan had never been so glad to see her colleague, Dan Hunt, in her life as he parked the van, leaving the flashing lights on, and ran towards her.

He took one look at the woman and shook his head, confirming what she already suspected.

Harrison had put the stepladder out. Dan climbed up it and pressed his fingers to the side of the woman's neck.

'There's no pulse. How long ago did you find her?'

Harrison shrugged. 'I don't know. It seems like hours ago, but probably ten minutes.'

Dan pulled a Swiss Army knife from his cargo trouser pocket and began to saw at the rope above the knot.

'Morgan, she's going to be a dead weight when she drops, can you both catch her?'

She looked at the boy. His complexion had lost all colour and his eyes were streaming tears now, but he nodded. They managed to catch hold of her. Dan grabbed her underneath her shoulders as the rope gave way and Morgan and Harrison took the weight of her legs and laid her gently onto the ground.

Harrison let out a loud sob. She put her arm around him, leading him to the van as the paramedics arrived in a first response vehicle and the scene became a flurry of activity. She heard Dan request a sergeant and being told the duty detective sergeant was already en route to attend the scene. Helping Harrison into the back of the van, where the windows were tinted, she sat him facing away from the direction of the tragic scene, where she could see the paramedic shaking her head at Dan. Morgan's heart felt heavy; this was terrible. Any sudden death was awful, but for this boy to be the one to find this woman was so unfair.

'Harrison you've been very brave. Can you tell me what that lady is called?'

He nodded. 'Olivia Potter.'

'How old was she?'

He was sitting with his head buried into his arms, which were balanced on his long legs, and shrugged.

'Not sure. Forties?'

'Is your girlfriend home?'

'No, I don't think so. The car isn't here. I didn't think anyone was home when I got here. I had a heart attack when I turned and saw Olivia like that. I didn't notice her when I arrived, I was checking my phone to see if Bronte had messaged back. Why, why would she do that? It's not right, is it? She was always so happy and chilled, not the kind of person who would do anything like that.'

He looked up at her, the tears were flowing freely again, and Morgan reached out to take hold of his hand.

'I'm so sorry, Harrison, that must have been a terrible shock for you. But I can't say. I don't know why she would want to do that.'

He nodded. 'Oh God, poor Bronte is going to be broken. She is really close to her mum.'

'Who else lives here?'

'Saul, Bronte's dad. Bronte, and her younger sister, Beatrix.'

'Do you have a number for Saul?'

He shook his head. 'I've got Bronte's.'

Morgan smiled. 'How old is Bronte?'

'Sixteen. She's not speaking to me because I liked Sophie Wood's Snapchat. That's why I came here to tell her it was only a like, it doesn't mean I want to run away with her and get married. She gets very jealous.'

Morgan nodded. 'Ah, teenage girls. It's a tough time being a teenager, isn't it. How old are you, Harrison?'

'Almost eighteen. What should I do? Do I message Bronte and tell her what's happened?'

'No, I don't think that's a good idea. I need to speak to Saul first; maybe you could find out where they are for me. Tell them you need them to come home, that there's been an emergency.'

'I can try; I don't really want to be the one to tell her. How do you tell someone their mum hung themselves from the rope swing?'

'That's our job, we'll take care of that. I just need you to try and get them to come back here, please.'

Another car pulled up and she recognised Detective Sergeant Ben Matthews from CID as he emerged.

'You stay here, I'll be back soon.'

Morgan crossed towards the DS, eager to introduce herself. She knew who he was but doubted he'd have a clue about her. She was probably just another name and number to him. As she got closer she heard him ask: 'Who was first on scene?'

'I was, Sarge.'

He turned to look at her and she felt her stomach tighten. She'd heard rumours that he was a miserable sod most of the time and didn't take too kindly to younger officers who were fresh out of training.

To her surprise, though, he smiled, completely disarming her. 'You are?'

'5129 Morgan Brookes.'

'Well, Morgan, talk me through what happened when you arrived, and *tell* me you didn't drop your lunch over there.'

He was pointing to a trampled KFC bag.

She shook her head.

'Not mine, sir, it must belong to the caller, Harrison Wright. When I got here, he was standing underneath the woman who was hanging from that branch.'

She pointed to where the frayed piece of rope was still swaying in the breeze.

'She was clearly dead, but we tried our best to hold her up and take away some of the pressure from her neck.'

'How did you know she was deceased, Morgan? Are you also a paramedic in your spare time?'

Morgan felt a burning sensation rush from her throat up to her forehead and knew she was probably the same colour as a cherry tomato.

'I, she looked dead. Her eyes were fixed; she didn't look as if she was breathing.'

Morgan could see Dan, who was standing behind the DS, grinning at her discomfort. He was such an idiot at times.

'How long have you been out on independent control?'

'This is my first shift on my own.'

'And how many sudden deaths have you attended?'

'Four: two suicides, one accident and a heart attack.'

'But this is the first on your own, yeah?'

Morgan wanted the ground to swallow her up. She hadn't done anything wrong. Why was he giving her a hard time?

'Yes, Sarge.'

He smiled again.

'It takes some getting used to, but you will. Look, all I'm trying to get at is we don't call death unless it's pretty obvious, like a body is missing a head or the person's brains are splattered all over the inside of a car. I've turned up to scenes where a body has smelt as if it's been decomposing for a week and then they've moved and still been breathing. Just, don't presume, okay? At least not until you've been doing this a lot longer than you have.'

She nodded, feeling embarrassed at his lecture, but determined not to let him see.

'Family?'

'Yes, Sarge, the woman is Olivia Potter. She has a husband, Saul, and two daughters, Bronte and Beatrix. The family car isn't here, and Harrison said there's no one home. He's sent Bronte a message asking her to tell her dad to come home.'

'Call me Ben, you can drop the whole Sarge thing. It's far too official for my liking.' He raised an eyebrow. 'Bronte and Beatrix Potter; I guess Olivia liked reading.'

Morgan smiled.

'Have you checked the house?'

'Not yet, I'll do that now.'

'What are your first impressions of the scene?'

'Is this a trick question? Am I supposed to answer or is it an excuse for you to tell me off again?'

Ben laughed out loud, then obviously realising how inappropriate it was he lifted his hand and pretended to cough.

'No, it's not a trick question.'

She shrugged. 'I don't know, she lives in this gorgeous house with her family, and Harrison described her as "happy and chilled". Not the kind of woman you'd expect to do this kind of thing. Not many women kill themselves by hanging, do they?'

'Not often, but some do. We need to locate her family and find out what her state of mind was before we make any judgement. It looks like a straightforward suicide to me.'

Morgan nodded and began to walk towards the house. She paused then turned to face Ben.

'How did she get up high enough to do it? There was no stepladder. Harrison ran and got that out of the shed.'

Ben shrugged. 'Maybe she was an excellent climber or used the rope swing. That tree doesn't look too difficult to get up to that branch. But I'll bear it in mind.'

Morgan left him and carried on walking up to the large detached house. It looked as if it had been recently painted the walls were so white, and the dusky pink front door made it stand out. Morgan loved it. It was modern yet quirky. There were pots of scented lavender and roses either side of the door and she inhaled the heady smell. It was such a perfect place to be able to call home. She tried the front door: it was secure. Then she walked the perimeter of the building checking the windows and other doors. All of them were shut tight and locked; there was no sign of life inside.

At the back door, Morgan turned and took in the view. She could hear a small creek at the end of the garden as it babbled along. The burning sun was setting against the backdrop of the Lakeland fells, giving out the last of its warmth. Olivia Potter lived in a beautiful place; she wondered what had happened to make her do such a terrible thing.

CHAPTER TWO

The bright flash from the CSI camera illuminated the darkened garden. The temperature had dropped along with the last of the sunlight and there was a chill in the air. Morgan couldn't take her gaze away from Olivia Potter; even in death she looked beautiful. Despite trying for the last hour Harrison hadn't been able to make contact with Bronte. Ben had asked for a PNC check of all vehicles listed for the address and it had come back with two: a brand new Jaguar F-Pace, in white, and a slightly older Mercedes C-Class. The Mercedes was parked in the garage, its engine cold, but there was no sign of the Jag. An ANPR marker had been placed on the vehicle to find out where it was last seen. It was strange that they couldn't find anyone to notify about Olivia, but it happened. For all they knew Saul could be on his way to visit family or take the girls somewhere and not even realise something was wrong. Morgan wondered if this was possible, that after being married for a long time like these two had been, for Saul not to have felt something at the moment of his wife's death? Harrison had said he was sure there had been no plans for the family to go away though. She couldn't stop the uneasy churning in her stomach that something wasn't right; she wished she knew what.

'Have you got a whammer?'

Ben's voice brought Morgan back to earth. She shook her head. 'Dan might, I'll go ask. Why?'

'There were no house keys in Olivia's pockets. I want to make sure everything is in order inside the house and see if we can find details of other family members. We need to find a next of kin for Olivia.'

She walked over to where Dan was sitting in the van with Harrison.

'Any luck getting hold of Bronte?'

He shook his head. 'She must be really pissed with me; her phone is going straight to voicemail now.'

'Is that usual, does she normally not answer?'

He shrugged. 'Yeah, well she ignores me when she's angry. She doesn't usually turn her phone off though, she's too addicted to Instagram. I'm getting a bit worried about her.'

Morgan didn't like it. Something was niggling away at her. Most people couldn't live without their phones, especially not teenagers. Why would Bronte not answer or turn her phone off? Perhaps it had run out of battery.

'Dan have you got a whammer in your van?'

Dan nodded. 'I'll go get it.'

Harrison stared after him and asked. 'What's a whammer?'

'A metal battering ram; we use it to put the door in when we need to gain entry to a property. Do you know if anyone might have a key? Have you got one?'

He shook his head. 'No, but Bronte sometimes left hers under a garden gnome for me so I could let myself in. Should I go and look?'

'Yes please, that would be great.'

She didn't ask him why he hadn't told them this earlier, putting it down to shock. Dan came over carrying the heavy metal bar.

'We might have a key.'

He rolled his eyes and let it drop onto the gravel drive with a loud thud.

Harrison came back holding a silver key in his fingers. He gave it to Morgan.

'Should I come inside with you?'

'No, you wait here. As soon as we've checked the house, I'll drive you home.'

'It's okay, I'm in my car.'

'You've had a shock, it might be better for one of us to drive you.'

'I need my car for work. I can't get to Kendal if I leave it here and I can't afford not to go in tomorrow. My supervisor is a right arsehole and I'm on my final warning.'

'I'll ask the boss and let you know.' Morgan pointed to the DS, who was chatting to Wendy, the CSI. She took the key over to Ben.

'Sarge, we have a key.'

'Great, you and Dan go and do a quick search. I doubt anyone's home; I'm pretty sure they'd have noticed us lot out here before now. But try and find anything with details for a family member we can contact. Undertakers should be here any minute to transport the body to Royal Lancaster Infirmary mortuary. Do you want to go with it and get it booked in?'

Morgan nodded, feeling sad that the woman who had been a living, breathing soul a couple of hours ago had now been reduced to an 'it'. She knew Ben wasn't being rude or impersonal; it was just the way it was. To him this was just another suicide, another body. He'd been doing it long enough that it didn't affect him; she hoped that the job would never become so matter-of-fact for her.

'Oh, I said someone might drive Harrison home.'

She turned and walked towards the house, Dan following behind.

Opening the door, she stepped inside, calling, 'Hello, this is the police. Is anyone home?'

They were greeted by silence. Inside the open-plan living area, she pulled out her torch and turned it on, shining it around. Nothing looked out of place and it smelt of fresh linen: no nasty, lingering smells to arouse their suspicion. Dan found the light switch and flicked it on, lighting up the whole downstairs.

'Wow, nice digs,' he said out loud.

She nodded. 'Nice indeed.' It was all very modern. No clutter. The entire lounge, kitchen, and diner was painted white, with different tones of grey picked out on feature walls. A set of keys dangled from a small hook behind the front door and Morgan wondered if they were Olivia's.

Dan headed for the kitchen. 'I'll do down here.'

Morgan made her way to the stairs tucked away at the back of the room. She turned on the light and went up the steps, calling out again, 'Hello, is anyone home? It's the police.'

There was no reply. She reached the first floor and admired the clean lines and clutter-free landing. Five doors came off it and she checked each room in turn. The master bedroom was as spotless and tidy as the rest of the house, with an en suite that sparkled. Morgan wondered if Olivia kept the house this clean or whether the family had a cleaner. She was almost afraid to touch anything for fear of leaving a mark. The next two rooms seemed to be spares. They were empty and decorated in the same style as the rest of the house. Morgan pushed open the fourth door and breathed a sigh of relief; this room looked as if it had been ransacked. The duvet was strewn across one side of the bed and there were piles of clothes on the floor. Make-up littered every available surface. She was glad the girls got to be typical messy teenagers in this immaculate show home. Walking towards the heart-shaped picture above the bed, she smiled to see a myriad of family photos in the frame. There were several of a dark-haired girl with her arm around Harrison; this must be Bronte. Other photos were of Olivia, a man she assumed was Saul and two girls in different locations. Morgan recognised New York, the Grand Canyon, Paris and Rome. They looked like the perfect, happy family and she felt her heart tear in two. Their lovely life was about to be torn to shreds. She felt a sinking feeling in the pit of her stomach for the girls who were about to find out their mum had taken her own life and left them alone.

'Morgan?'

Dan's voice echoed up the stairs.

'Coming.'

She tore herself away from the pictures and checked the last room, not quite as messy as Bronte's. Instead of bottles of expensive perfume and make-up this one was full of books. They covered every available surface and were stacked in piles by the side of the bed. She nodded in approval; Beatrix was a bookworm like her. At least she'd have the luxury of stealing herself away from the horror of her life into someone else's when it all got too much for her.

'Morgan.'

The voice was more demanding this time and irritated her.

'I'm coming, Dan. I had to check each room.'

'And?'

'Well they're all empty, obviously. What about down here? Did you find anything?'

He held up an address book and waved it in front of her.

'Guess who's getting the brownie points off Sergeant Moody?'

They went back outside where Ben was now sitting in the van talking to Harrison. Dan shut the door behind him, pushing it to make sure the door was secure. The body was being zipped into a black body bag and lifted onto the steel gurney. Morgan watched as the undertakers slammed the door of the private ambulance. The driver turned and waved.

'See you at the hospital.'

She waved back.

They drove away, leaving the garden looking like nothing had happened. Well, it would once the police vans had left. The only thing out of place now was the stepladder. When Saul and his daughters returned home, there would be nothing to show it had been a scene of such heartbreak that their lives would never be the same again. Morgan felt drained. She walked over to the van where everyone was congregated around Harrison. Ben looked at her, his steely gaze softened, and she felt a little better.

'Still want me to book her in at the mortuary?'

'Yes, please. Dan is going to follow Harrison home to make sure he gets there safely. Another patrol is on the way to wait here and see if the family turn up, to break the news to them.'

He stood up and got out of the van, followed by Harrison. Dan was already on his way back to his own van. Climbing into the driver's seat, Morgan turned on the engine, then whacked the dial on the heater up to full blast. Her hands had turned into blocks of ice and she was shivering. She waited for Harrison to leave, with Dan in convoy, before setting off.

About to drive away, there was a knock on the window. Jumping, she looked to see Ben standing there.

'I just wanted to say thank you, you did a good job.'

Before she could answer he turned and walked back to the white Ford Focus he'd arrived in. She smiled. Maybe he wasn't the ogre everyone had told her he was.

CHAPTER THREE

All the way to Royal Lancaster Infirmary, Morgan listened intently to her radio, waiting for someone to report that they'd located a relative for Olivia Potter. It was really starting to bother her that they hadn't. Three hours had passed now since she'd first arrived on scene and not one family member had turned up or been successfully contacted by the police. It happened, but unless Saul worked shifts, he should have been home by now. There was no obvious reason for the girls to be missing either. There had been no indicators inside the house that they'd gone away for a few days. Whenever she went anywhere her flat always looked as if a tornado had gone through it while she decided what to pack. Maybe she should have checked the storage cupboards to see if there were any suitcases around. She pressed Dan's four-digit collar number into her radio and waited for it to ring.

'*Yeah?*'

She rolled her eyes; he was so rude.

'Don't you think it's odd?'

'*What?*'

'That they haven't located anyone for Olivia yet.'

'*Who?*'

She paused. Was he serious? She was about to admonish him, when he answered.

'*Sorry, wasn't thinking. I don't know, not really. They could be at an afterschool club or dance class; they might even be at the cinema for all we know.*'

'Suppose so, but it's nearly eight.'

Are you fretting, Morgan? Don't let it worry you. They'll turn up; they can't be far, can they? Maybe they all had a big row and the dad took the kids away. Wouldn't be the first time some couple have had a big argument then one of them goes and tops themselves. It happens all the time.'

She ended the call. He was so matter-of-fact about everything, so unfeeling. Then again, she was the opposite; she took everything to heart and spent hours worrying. The shrill sound of her handset blasting broke the silence.

'Hello?'

'Why did you hang up? Look, what I meant was don't go seeing things that aren't there before we know the facts, okay. We're response officers; we're the first port of call for an emergency. We get there, take control, and make everyone feel safe, blah, blah, blah. Anything too complicated, it gets passed to CID and it's out of our hands. They get to be the ones to fret over it. If you get too involved, you'll end up wasting your time. You're not a detective; let them worry about the rest of it. You've done your part, time to move on to the next job. It's harsh, but that's the way it is, Morgan.'

'I know that, I get it. I just can't switch off like you can.'

'Well, you'd better learn to, or you'll end up batshit crazy.'

'What if there's something wrong though? What if something has happened to them?'

'Like what? The house was immaculate, no signs of a disturbance and it was all secure. Remember we had to get a spare key to get inside? Don't go overcomplicating things.'

She ended the call for a second time. She knew everything Dan had just said was true, but she also knew in her gut that something wasn't right with the whole situation. But who could she tell, or more importantly, who was going to listen to her, a rookie, with little experience and fresh out of company? They'd probably laugh at her.

The entrance for the mortuary came into view and she turned in. The hearse was already parked at the loading doors waiting for her.

The mortuary was housed in a bland, beige brick building. She parked the van next to the hearse and got out. The doors to the mortuary were opened by a smiling woman, dressed in blue scrubs with a long-sleeved thermal vest under them. As Morgan walked inside the hallway she was hit by a subtle chemical smell and how cool it suddenly was. She understood the need for the vest.

She'd been here only once before, with Dan. The first time she'd walked through the double doors into the examination room she'd been terrified, expecting to see steel tables lined up with rows of dead bodies on them and lots of blood. She'd been pleasantly surprised to see a couple of steel tables, but no bodies. It smelt better than she'd imagined as well. Clean. The pathologist had been very kind and taken his time to explain to her how everything worked and the process of what happened before a post-mortem could even begin. Like everything else it was lots of paperwork first.

The undertakers wheeled in the trolley. Olivia Potter's body didn't look very big inside the large black bag.

'Have you got some evidence bags?'

Morgan turned to look at the woman, who was still smiling at her. The ID card around her neck said 'Susie Quirk'.

'Right, shall we get her booked in then?' said Susie brightly.

Morgan left the mortuary with the bags containing Olivia Potter's jeans, linen shirt and her underwear and headed towards Rydal Falls. It was late enough that there wasn't too much traffic on the approach to the busy town, and she needed to return to the station to book Olivia's items into the property store. There had been no front door key in Olivia's pockets; in fact there had been nothing in any of her pockets. Not even a mobile phone, which was odd. When they'd removed her clothes there had been a couple of ligature marks around her neck, as if she'd tried it once then changed her mind, then tried again. Morgan wasn't an expert, she knew that the pathologist would be able to tell them more, but the alarm bells were ringing even louder in her head. There was something wrong with this case. She needed to speak to the DS and tell him, even if he did think she was interfering. There was no point even discussing it with Dan because he'd either tell her to back off or make fun of her like he usually did.

When she arrived back at the station it was like a ghost ship. The only person around was a PCSO going in for their break and the front counter clerk. Morgan went to see Brenda at the front office. She knew she'd help her book the evidence in.

'Thanks, Brenda. I've done it before with Dan, but there's so much to remember.'

She laughed. 'You'll get used to it. How are you getting on?'

'It's okay. Some days I wonder what on earth I was thinking, others I enjoy it.'

'It's not the easiest of jobs, but it can be very rewarding as well as stressful, but you already know that.'

Morgan turned to leave. 'Where is everyone? This place is dead.'

'All in The Black Dog no doubt, it's Mitch's leaving do.'

'Oh, I forgot.'

Brenda stood up. 'That's where I'm heading off to, are you going?'

Morgan usually avoided social occasions but she knew that everyone would be talking about her if she didn't at least turn up for one drink, and Mitch was a nice bloke considering he'd been a copper for twenty years and wasn't worn down or jaded by the job. He'd always been patient with her whenever she asked him questions about cases she was dealing with.

'As soon as I've updated the logs and submitted the Form 38, I am. See you there.'

Morgan went upstairs to see if the DS was still around. The large CID office was as deserted as the rest of the place. She was about to leave via the door to the smaller office at the back of the room when it opened and Ben walked out.

'Sarge, have you got a minute? Can I have a word?'

'Sure.'

She stepped inside, letting the door close behind her. 'I'm a bit concerned about the circumstances surrounding Olivia Potter.'

He pointed to a chair and she sat down. 'Do you want to tell me what's bothering you?'

'Have her next of kin been located yet?'

He shook his head.

'Don't you think that's odd? Surely by now someone must have gone home or tried to contact her and got no answer. She has two teenage girls; wouldn't they want picking up, or to know what's for tea?'

'I appreciate your concern, but we're doing everything to trace her family. I've got two detectives on their way to speak to her mother. Is that better? I've also spoken to a friend who is a teacher at their school. He said they didn't come in this morning and no one rang up to report their absence. They were picked up by their mum yesterday.'

Once more she felt her cheeks begin to flush. 'Yes, sorry. I'm not trying to tell you how to do your job.'

'Good, I hope not because I've been doing this for quite some time.'

'Sorry. I just think there's something not right with the whole situation. When we undressed her at the mortuary there were two different ligature marks around her neck.'

He let out a small laugh. 'Were you a pathologist as well as a paramedic before you joined the police?'

'No, actually, I worked at the outdoor education centre at Lakeside.' Morgan wanted the ground to swallow her whole, but she wasn't going to stop asking questions because of a little teasing.

'Well in that case we'll leave cause of death to the experts, shall we? Her post-mortem is scheduled first thing in the morning.

Hopefully by then we'll have located her family and broken the sad news to them. I think Saul has taken the girls away. Whether it's to visit family or friends that's anybody's guess. If not, you have my permission to go back and search the house again to see if you can find anything that might pertain to where they are. Is that okay with you?'

Morgan wanted to die, right now. She didn't know if he was being sarcastic or genuinely nice. She got the impression it was the former. Nodding, she stood up. 'Thank you.'

She left and went to the report writing room, where she logged on to the computer and began to update the log and fill out the forms she needed to, taking her time so she'd have to spend less time at the pub.

CHAPTER FOUR

The Black Dog was almost full; it was standing room only there were that many off-duty coppers milling around waiting to toast Mitch. Dan was at the bar ordering his fourth pint of lager. He carried it back to the table he was sitting at and squeezed into the tight space. It was loud and everyone was well on their way to being drunk. The door opened and in walked Morgan. He grinned and waved at her. She looked like a fish out of water, but she also looked cute. He hadn't seen her out of uniform before. She was dressed from head to toe in black; the little shorts she was wearing over a pair of fishnet tights showed off the tattoos on her thighs and not for the first time he wished he could take a closer look at them. Her copper-coloured hair was piled on top of her head in a messy bun and she had two perfect flicks of eyeliner. Not that he was an expert in make-up, but his last girlfriend used to spend more time trying to get her eyeliner right than anything else.

When Morgan finally got a large glass of white wine she walked over to where they were sitting. He squeezed up and patted the tiny space beside him. He was ready to be nice to her, give her a bit of a break since she'd had a rough day, but he saw the look which flashed across her eyes and a glint of anger sparked inside him. It was a look that said 'Christ, is that the best I can hope for' and it really upset him.

She squashed in next to him, their thighs touching. He didn't speak to her. Instead he carried on telling some loud story about a job he'd gone to yesterday. Morgan sipped her wine, listening. He knew she was here because she felt she had to be; she wanted to fit in. She smiled and made polite conversation when directly asked a question. Half an hour later, when she hadn't spoken a word to him, he brought the conversation around to this afternoon.

'Hey, did you realise our little goth here, Morgan, was a super detective.'

He felt her squirm next to him; still, he carried on, encouraged by the laughter that filled the room.

'Yep, been on the job five minutes and she was only telling that miserable git Ben Matthews how to do his job. Next, she'll be telling the DCI how to run a case. It was hilarious, you should have seen his face.'

Morgan smiled at the jokes he was making about her and lifted the wine glass to her lips, downing the rest of it in one gulp. Neither she nor Dan noticed Ben walk into the bar. He was ordering a double JD and Coke for Mitch while listening to Dan's little tale. The barman passed Ben the drink and he pushed it in Mitch's direction, who saluted his thanks. Then Ben turned around. Dan was still loudly telling everyone about Morgan, who looked as if she was going to burst into tears. There was a bit of a scuffle as she pushed herself up and squeezed past the table full of men who were laughing loudly at her expense. She walked towards the door and Dan shouted after her.

'Come back, Morgan, I'm only joking, you need to lighten up.'

She didn't look over her shoulder; instead, she kept her head high as she pushed her way through the doors and into the car park.

Dan stood up, regretting being quite so mean to her in front of everyone. The grin which had filled his face turned into a thin line when he realised that Ben had heard the whole thing.

Ben strode towards him and knocked the table with his knee, sending drinks toppling to a chorus of loud shouts.

He pointed his finger at Dan's chest. 'Morgan was obviously too polite to say anything, but I'm not. You are a complete wanker.' Ben, who towered over Dan, glared at him.

'It's just a bit of banter, nothing to get upset about.'

'Banter my arse, you're an idiot and you'd better apologise to her tomorrow or I'll be filing a grievance on her behalf against you for bullying.'

The barman came rushing over. 'Now then, lads, calm it down.'

Ben turned and left. Dan laughed, trying not to show how shaken he was. Ben was a much bigger guy than him; this could have ended up a lot worse.

Jonny, who was sitting next to him, ruffled his hair with his hand.

'You could have lost your shiny, white front teeth then, Danny lad. Ben is a bit of an animal when he lets loose. Better watch your step around him, either that or apologise to them both.'

He shrugged. 'No way, it was just a joke. If she's so uptight she can't take a bit of a laugh and he's so quick to defend her, let them stew. I'm not apologising, pair of losers.'

Jonny laughed. 'Your funeral, mate, Ben has friends in high places. It was funny though.' He raised his glass to Dan, then downed the rest of his pint and stood up. 'I have to go; my wife is on nights. See you tomorrow.'

Dan smiled, but it didn't reach his eyes. He was wondering if he should also call it a night or whether to drown his sorrows, along with his stupidity. He had nothing and no one to go home to. He decided to order another pint and drink himself senseless.

CHAPTER FIVE

Morgan stood on the pavement, wondering whether to call a taxi or walk back to her flat. It was a good ten-minute walk and the boots she was wearing weren't the comfiest. She set off walking along the main road. It was late but surprisingly quiet for a Friday night.

'Morgan.'

The deep voice bellowed her name and she turned around thinking that if it was Dan she'd tell him where to go. She saw Ben standing at the entrance to the small car park and thought, *Oh the shame, he just saw me get well and truly humiliated in front of most of my colleagues, as if today hasn't been bad enough.* Lifting one hand, she waved then turned and carried on walking, trying to put as much distance between them as possible so she didn't have to make polite conversation with him. Heavy footsteps pounded the pavement behind her and she hoped it wasn't some mugger about to take her out and end her day with a bang.

'Christ, I don't do running. Can you slow down a minute?'

She turned to see Ben, his face red and his breathing heavy.

'Sorry, I didn't realise you wanted me to stop. What's up?'

He took a couple of breaths. 'Nothing, I wanted to make sure you were okay. That Dan is such an arrogant little shit. I had to stop myself from ripping his head off.'

She nodded. Her eyes glistened with tears. *Don't you dare cry in front of him. You don't know him, sort yourself out.* She looked down at the floor.

'Look, I'm driving, can I give you a lift home, or wherever you're going?'

'Oh. Well yeah, if it's not too much trouble.'

'No trouble at all, I'll go get my car.'

'I'll walk back with you, thanks.'

They walked the short distance, neither of them speaking. She didn't want to make him feel obliged to make polite conversation. He pressed the key fob and the lights on an old VW Golf flashed. They crossed to it and Ben climbed inside, sweeping empty sandwich and crisp packets off the passenger seat.

'Sorry, it's a bit of a state. I don't usually give anyone a lift and I never have the time to clean it.'

'That's okay, I'm grateful for the ride. I take my car to the hand car wash at—' She stopped talking, not wanting to sound like she was telling him what to do, especially after Dan's comments about her.

'Where do you live?'

'Singleton Park Road. Do you know where that is?'

He nodded. 'Nice area.'

'I like it.'

They reached the turn-off and she directed him to the large house which was now split into three flats.

'I'll get out here, thank you.' Relief she was home flooded over Morgan. She wasn't in the mood for polite conversation.

'Are you okay?'

She nodded. 'Embarrassed, but I'll live.'

She got out of his car; about to shut the door, she paused, but couldn't help herself. 'I guess they haven't located Olivia Potter's family?'

He shook his head. 'Not before I left for the evening, but I'm sure section will trace them.'

Closing the door, she walked across the gravel to the steps which led to the pale green front door of her building. Opening the heavy door, she turned and waved, but Ben was already driving out of the gates.

Morgan went inside her ground-floor flat. The air was tinged with the smell of fresh paint and no hint of her ex-partner who'd left her when she told him about joining the police. She was happier on her own anyway; relationships were too complicated. Hers had been the first flat in the building to be refurbished. When the letting agent had shown her the brochure she'd fallen in love and knew she had to live here. The huge picture windows that overlooked the formal communal gardens were the perfect place for her to read on a rainy day. Inside everything was brand new; the white walls were pristine. It made the rooms look much bigger than they were. When she had some time off she was going to paint a feature wall in her bedroom: a splash of dramatic bottle green to match the gold accessories she loved to collect. The rest of the walls she'd leave white for the time being.

She kicked off her uncomfortable boots and went straight into the bedroom to put her pyjamas on. It had been a long day. She was tired but unable to switch off.

Her mind kept replaying Dan's words. They hurt. She'd thought they were friends and didn't understand why he would show her up in front of almost the whole of Rydal Falls police staff. It just reaffirmed what she already thought: that you were better off alone, no partner or friends to make you feel like crap. Tugging her hair from the bun, she let it fall over her shoulders and shook her head, rubbing her fingers through it where the bobble had been.

Taking a bottle of white wine from the fridge, she poured herself a large glass; it would help her to sleep. For a few hours anyway. Carrying the glass, she took it to the only chair she had in the living room. It was an oversized, worn leather armchair which looked out of the floor-to-ceiling windows onto the gardens. Sinking into it, she curled her feet underneath her and sipped at the chilled wine and stared into the blackness outside. She liked the dark, always had since she was a child. There was something very comforting about seeing the moon against the inky sky. Her mum had nicknamed her Selene after the Greek goddess of the moon, and on her fifteenth birthday she'd given her a rose gold necklace with a crescent moon that had a tiny diamond set in the middle. It was Morgan's most treasured possession and the only thing she had apart from one photograph to remind her of her mum now. Sipping the wine until she felt relaxed enough to switch off her busy mind, she placed the glass on the floor and closed her eyes, letting her mind drift and a dark fog settle over it.

*

Hammering on the front door to the flats woke her with a start and Morgan blinked awake. It was still dark outside. Who could that be? As far as she knew the other two flats in the building were still being refurbished and hadn't been rented out yet. She stood up, rubbing her eyes. Grabbing her phone from the kitchen side, she checked to see if she had any missed calls, but there weren't any. It was almost one a.m. Keeping hold of her phone, Morgan opened the door to her flat and crossed the large entrance, barefoot, to the front door, where she peered through the spyhole and let out a gasp, dropping her phone. She wondered how he'd found her. The pounding on the door resumed again and echoed around the hallway.

With a deep breath, she unbolted the door and pulled it open.

'What the hell are you doing here?'

'Hey, Moggy, is that the way to greet your old dad?'

'How did you find me, Stan?'

'It's not rocket science, Moggy, a friend of a friend said you were living around here. It's cold out, aren't you going to invite me in?'

'No.'

She pushed the door, but he was too fast. His foot was already there, stopping it from shutting.

'Seriously, go away.'

'Aw, come on. I've got nowhere to go, just let me in until the morning. I haven't got enough money to stay anywhere.'

'Go back to Carol.'

'I can't, she threw me out.'

She shook her head. 'I wondered how long it would take her to see sense.'

'Please, I fell over, I've hurt my head and feel dizzy. It's dark along that road.'

Waving her hands to activate the motion sensor hall light, Morgan looked at her father's face. He did have a graze on the side of his head and some scratches on one hand, but they didn't look fresh. They were a couple of hours old. His hair was fully grey and he looked more dishevelled than the last time she'd seen him. It had been at least a year. They'd rarely spoken in the five years since her mum's death. She'd blamed him for everything.

Against her better judgement, she opened the door and took a step back.

'You're a good girl, Moggy, you always were. Feisty, but kind.'

'You can come in for tonight on one condition.'

'What's that, love?'

'You don't call me Moggy. I'm not a flipping cat. It's Morgan.'

He lifted his fingers to his lips and mimed zipping them shut. 'Sorry, Morgan.'

She pointed towards her open flat door and watched him stumble towards it, the smell of cheap whisky permeating the air around him. It was so strong she waved her hand in front of her nose to waft it away. A sinking feeling inside made her wonder if she was going to regret this dutiful act of kindness tomorrow.

CHAPTER SIX

After dropping Morgan off, Ben had driven straight home to his empty four-bedroomed house. It was untidy, and he couldn't remember the last time he'd dusted. Maybe it was time to get his act together; Cindy had been gone over three years now. Her stuff was still all around the house; he hadn't been able to touch it, although he had moved the awful faceless figurines she'd insisted on collecting. They were the only things he'd boxed up so he didn't have to look at them. When she'd been alive the urge to draw faces on them whenever they argued had been strong and difficult to suppress. He'd managed to resist, though, and always imagined this small feat had earned him brownie points with whoever was watching over him. Not enough points to save Cindy though.

He felt sad and in dire need of a treble shot of something strong. Suicides always left him this way. No matter how many he attended it was always the same; it was something he could never get used to. Didn't want to get used to if he was honest. Accidents and murders, even terminal illness were all tragic and devasting, but these people didn't die by their own hands. They didn't willingly wake up and decide that today they'd swallow fifty paracetamol and put a plastic bag over their head because they could no longer take the pain inside that being alive caused them.

In the kitchen, he opened the freezer and pulled out the bottle of vodka he kept in there. He took a glass from the cupboard and filled it with ice and neat vodka. Sitting at the kitchen table, he stared at Cindy's fluffy dressing gown on the back of the chair opposite him. It no longer smelt like her; instead it smelt of bacon grease and dust. He knew he should eat something. He hadn't had anything since a bacon buttie that morning. Downing the vodka, he got up and opened the fridge door. Two eggs, some crusty cheese that looked as if it was growing its own penicillin and half a tin of chopped tomatoes greeted him. He grabbed the tomatoes, looked inside the tin and gagged. They were green and furry. It would have to be eggs again, and he didn't want eggs. Opening the cupboard, he found a packet of chocolate digestives that would have to do. Refilling his vodka glass, he took that and the biscuits upstairs with him to the bathroom. He would have a shower, finish his drink and eat as many biscuits as he could before sleep overtook him.

As he stood under the spray of steaming hot water, he cast his mind to Olivia Potter, wondering if section had located her husband and what it meant if they hadn't. Was Morgan right to raise concerns, or was she being overzealous because it was the first sudden death she'd attended on her own? When he'd towel dried himself and was dressed in clean boxers and a long-sleeved T-shirt he felt better. Walking past the master bedroom, he stared through the open door at the super king-size bed. He hadn't slept in that either since Cindy had gone. It reminded him of how lonely he was. Instead, he'd taken to sleeping in one of the spare rooms which doubled up as a home office. The single bed was comfortable, a bit of a squeeze but he managed.

Finishing his drink, he tossed the packet of biscuits on the small chest of drawers next to the bed and threw himself onto the mattress. Days like this wore him out; mentally, emotionally, physically, coming home to this empty house which was like a shrine to his dead wife exhausted him. Memories he didn't want to surface always did after a suicide, and there wasn't anything he could do to stop them. He sat on the bed and opened the biscuits, slowly making his way through half a packet as he looked down at the paunch which protruded over the top of his boxers. He needed to sort his life out. Once upon a time he'd have cooked a healthy meal, been up for a run before work, maybe even gone for one at the end of his shift. He wouldn't be living off crap and vodka. What would Cindy do if it had been him who had died? He smiled; she definitely wouldn't be living like some weird hermit, that was for sure. His stuff would have been boxed up and donated to a charity shop the day after his funeral.

So, what are you holding on to, Ben? This stuff is just stuff; your memories are inside your mind and in your heart. He lay down and stared up at the ceiling; there was a large crack running from the light across to the wall above his head. If he didn't get a builder in to look at it the whole ceiling could come down. He closed his eyes, and like he did every night, determined that tomorrow he would find a builder and tomorrow he would get some boxes to pack away Cindy's stuff.

CHAPTER SEVEN

Morgan's eyes opened wide; the room was dark, but she didn't need to look at her phone to see the time was 04.25 because that was the exact time she woke every single morning. It didn't matter how tired she was, how late she went to bed, if she'd been drinking, if she was ill. It never made any difference. For the last five years, since the worst day of her life, her brain had somehow convinced itself that she needed to be awake at this godforsaken hour and so she was. As she lay there, she heard a loud snore coming from the direction of the living room and groaned, pulling a pillow over her head to muffle the noise. She was hoping it had been a bad dream, that her useless father hadn't really turned up late last night and was now drooling and snoring on her one and only chair. Forcing herself to get out of bed, she pulled her dressing gown around her, pushed her feet into the big, furry slippers she'd bought herself on her last shopping trip to Primark, then went into the living room to shake his shoulder. Bad enough he was here, in person, stinking out her lovely flat; she wasn't going to listen to that awful noise which sounded like a cross between a chainsaw and a hoover. Grabbing his shoulder, she shook it. He didn't flinch, so she used more pressure.

'Stan,' she hissed into his ear.

He didn't stir and she felt her blood begin to boil. Grabbing her headphones from the laptop, she pushed them into her ears and selected a playlist of nineties dance music to drown him out. Then she set about making herself a bacon sandwich. She didn't really want to make him breakfast, didn't want to give him anything, but she had been brought up better than that. Her mum had taught her to be a kind, selfless girl with good manners. So, she made him one, covering it with tin foil.

She wrote 'Stan' on a Post-it note. Not 'Dad'; it was never 'dad'. Not since her mum's death. Setting the coffeemaker going, she went into the bathroom, showered then came back in to eat her sandwich. Filling her travel mug with fresh coffee and screwing on the lid, she looked in disgust at the crumpled mess that was still snoring in her chair. She left her bedroom door open while she dried her hair, hoping the noise would wake him. Then she stamped around as she dressed in her uniform, tugging her black Magnum boots on so her footsteps echoed even louder. She was raging by this point; she didn't want to leave him in her flat. She looked at the clock on the wall: it was now 5.45; she didn't start work until 7.00. But she couldn't stay here, she needed to see what was happening with Olivia Potter; she was desperate to know if the family had been found and told the news. Better to go into work early; at least she could sit in peace before the rest of her shift came in, and catch up on the logs. She set about writing him a note.

Stan,

Breakfast is on the kitchen worktop. Do not be here when I come home, there is nothing of value for you to steal. Don't forget where I work. I'll report you then hunt you down if you take so much as a hair slide that belongs to me. If you have nowhere to go, then you'd better get yourself to the homeless shelter on Ann Street and see if they can help. If not, go find one of your friends to stop with. This flat is not big enough for the both of us and I'm not risking my tenancy by letting you stay here another night. It's not your new crash pad, I don't want you here.

Morgan.

She pushed it into his hand, so he'd find it when he woke up and prayed he'd be long gone by the end of her shift. Just in case he did get any ideas, she grabbed her laptop and stuffed it into a tote bag along with her purse and headphones.

Leaving the flat, she let the door slam but doubted it would have made him stir. She was seething at not being tougher with him. She should never have let him in and now she hadn't been able to kick him out.

The station was almost empty, aside from a couple of officers from the nightshift in the report writing room. Not wanting to give anyone the excuse to ask why she was in work so early, she headed upstairs to one of the offices she knew would be empty, at least until the start of her shift. She didn't want to explain to anyone about the insomnia that had plagued the last five years of her life. That was too personal.

There was one empty room next to the large CID office with the door open, so she took her coffee inside. Firing up the computer, she waited for it to let her log on, sipping her coffee while she waited. When her home screen filled the monitor, Morgan quickly brought up the logs to see the latest update on Olivia Potter. In the notes it stated that several visits throughout the night had been made to the address, but it was all in darkness. No contact had been made with her husband by the police. Her mother, Helen Taylor, had been informed late last night, but there was no mention of Olivia's father. Enquiries were still ongoing to locate husband and daughters. That was it, nothing more. Morgan exhaled while reading the update. Something was definitely wrong, she was sure of it. None of this was normal. Last month a woman had died in a car accident and her daughter had been travelling in Australia. It had taken a few hours, but they'd managed to track her down and break the news to her. She was over the other side of the world; why couldn't they find Saul Potter when he lived on their doorstep?

'What are you doing here so early?'

Startled, she looked up to see Ben standing there, holding a paper coffee cup.

'I couldn't sleep.' She didn't tell him it was an everyday occurrence.

'Me neither. Put me out of my misery then, have they located her husband yet?'

She shook her head. 'I'm not trying to tell you what to do, but it's all wrong. Very wrong.'

'I never said you were bossy, it was that arse, Dan. Anyway, I woke up early thinking about it and I think you're right. Do you want to go back to the house and check it again? Take the keys from the sergeant's office, see if there's any sign the husband's been back or if something got missed yesterday.'

'Yes, I do. Thank you. Should I go now?'

He shook his head. 'No, it can wait until after morning briefing. I don't think another forty minutes will hurt; Olivia Potter isn't going anywhere.'

'Thanks, Sarge.'

He turned and walked into the office. Morgan checked her emails, then logged off and headed down to speak to the sergeant and get the keys for the Potters' house. This was her job; she didn't want Dan coming in and taking over. He could sulk all day if he wanted; she wasn't working with him and if they got paired up she'd be the first to say it wasn't an option.

By the time everyone arrived, had made mugs of tea or coffee and all filed into the briefing room, Morgan was itching to go. It would take her a good twenty minutes to get from Rydal Falls to Grasmere, traffic permitting. She could have told Sergeant Madden she needed to leave, but there was no way she was giving Dan any more fuel to add to his already low opinion of her. It still smarted that he'd turned on her like that. She'd wait patiently and offer to be the cover for Grasmere and surrounding areas.

The briefing was over quickly. The main topic of conversation was for observations for the missing white Jag F-Pace. She wouldn't know what an F-Pace was to look at but Mads, the nickname his team called Sergeant Madden, circulated the registration number, which was much easier to identify. An automated number plate recognition marker had been placed on it, meaning when it passed an ANPR camera it would ping and notify whoever was in the control room, so they could get the car stopped. Mads allocated areas and gave Morgan the same one as yesterday. She couldn't stop herself from grinning. Dan frowned, but she ignored him. It would be some time before she bothered speaking to him, even if he apologised. Friends didn't make you look like an absolute idiot, especially in front of the people you worked with, and she was starting to realise that perhaps they had never been friends at all.

She left first, eager to get to the house and give it a thorough search. Not that they hadn't yesterday, but there was a nagging feeling that they had rushed, that they had missed something.

CHAPTER EIGHT

Ben read through the notes on the log again. It was odd they hadn't found Saul Potter; Morgan had been right to be concerned. He wasn't sure what was going on, but it didn't make sense that the rest of Olivia's family seemed to have disappeared. It would be interesting to see what the post-mortem results brought back. Yesterday he had been a hundred per cent sure it was a straightforward suicide. Today, he wouldn't like to say. Part of him wondered if he should go back and search the house with Morgan.

The office door opened.

'Ben, can I have a word?'

He looked up to see Detective Chief Inspector Tom Fell. He was smiling, so it wasn't bad news. Ben stood up, following Tom out into the corridor and into his own office, closing the door behind him.

'Morning, sir, everything okay?'

'Yes, just a couple of things really. Have we really not located that poor woman's family?'

'No, we're on it though. Husband's car has a marker on it now and the officer who was first at scene has gone back to check the property and see if she can find anything that might have been missed yesterday.'

He nodded. 'Good, that's what I'd do. Look, I'm sorry to say that we're losing Ian. He's going through to Barrow. So with him gone, Mitch's retirement and Des still on long-term sick leave, we're short-staffed. Can you put out a shout to see if anyone wants to come off section and do an attachment for three months? It would give us an extra set of hands.'

'Actually, boss, I think I know someone. She's pretty new, though, just out of company.'

'You mean she might be a bit green? I was thinking someone more experienced. Who applied last time?'

Ben thought back to the last set of emails he'd received and grimaced. Dan was always emailing him for a placement, but there was no way he was working with him. There was a clash of personalities between them; no matter how hard he tried not to let it, Dan's lazy attitude towards the job annoyed Ben. There had been more than a couple of crimes that should have been solved with a bit of hard work and common sense. Dan had a knack of not following up on enquiries as efficiently as he should and Ben's team had stepped in and got the result Dan should have in the first place. The other officer who had shown an interest was now on maternity leave.

'Leave it with me. Would you have a problem if it *was* someone relatively new?'

'Not at all, as long as they're keen and can follow orders. We both know the key qualities are to listen to what they're being told and be of some use.'

Ben wasn't sure if Morgan was going to fit the bill, but she was definitely keen and willing to work hard. He would speak to her about it later, see if she was interested.

His phone began to vibrate in his pocket. He took it out, to see 'Dr Death' flashing across the screen, excused himself from Tom and darted out.

'Morning, Declan.'

'Morning, Ben. I've just done a preliminary examination of the body brought in last night and had to suspend it until I spoke to you. I found something of interest I thought you might like to know before I carry on.'

'I'm listening.'

'There are horizontal ligature marks as well as the mark of the noose. At this stage it's impossible to say whether that means it took her a couple of attempts, or someone else strangled her and hanged her to make it look like suicide, but it makes both a possibility.'

'I'm on my way, can you wait for me?'

'Yes.'

'Thanks, Declan, I appreciate you phoning. I think Morgan is right, something has been off about this from the start.'

He hung up, berating himself for not looking closer yesterday at the scene. Morgan had said there was no sign of a step, that the ladder was brought over from the shed. He'd been too eager to dismiss it as suicide; he'd been to a couple of hangings from trees in public areas where the deceased had climbed the tree to get high enough to do it. You didn't normally carry a stepladder with you on these sorts of occasions. He went back into the office, which was still empty; everyone had gone straight out to follow up on their enquiries after the briefing. Christ, this place was like a ghost ship.

CHAPTER NINE

Morgan pulled into the driveway of Olivia Potter's house; it was a different scene today from the chaos that had formed on the perfectly landscaped gardens yesterday. She had half expected when she arrived to see a car parked outside and find the missing family had returned from wherever they'd been. But there was no car; it was eerily quiet. She parked the van and got out, her gaze falling on the tree where Olivia had been found. It was so sad, and she didn't think she could ever get used to it no matter how many suicides she attended. She took the key from her pocket and opened the door once more; it didn't smell quite so pleasant as when she'd gone inside yesterday. She could still smell the plug-in air freshener, but there was another darker, heavier scent beneath it.

She didn't announce her arrival this time. The house looked exactly the same as it had yesterday when she'd checked. There were no trainers or school bags in the hall, which you'd expect if two teenagers were here. She ran upstairs, checked each room in turn and this time she opened wardrobe and cupboard doors. There were different-size suitcases in a cupboard. So, they hadn't gone away.

Downstairs she checked the kitchen; there was a door next to the American-style fridge-freezer. Dan must have assumed it was the adjoining garage door yesterday. To be sure, she slid the bolt across and tugged it open. Blackness enveloped her eyes and a strong, earthy smell filled her nostrils. How had they missed this? It definitely didn't lead to the garage, rather to a basement of some sort. Tugging the torch from her body armour, she turned it on, shining it around to look for a light switch. A pull cord dangled to the left of her and she yanked it, causing a small bulb to flicker on and illuminate the steep, wooden steps.

The hairs on the back of her neck prickled. She had never liked cellars. Bad things happened in them. She'd read a book once, *The Ghost House*, and had been scared for days over the goings-on in that cellar. The smell she detected when she'd first walked into the house was coming from down there. It was much stronger. Like rotting meat. She crossed her fingers that maybe a freezer had defrosted. She thought about calling for someone to come and back her up and realised that Dan was in the other van and probably her nearest patrol. She'd rather run into the depths of hell and face Satan than have to rely on Dan to be her backup today. She could do this on her own. If he turned up and there was nothing down here, that would be another round of ammunition for him to fire her way. Spurred on, she began to walk down the wooden steps. The smell was getting stronger the closer to the bottom she got and she wondered if there might be a dead animal in here. Maybe a cat had got trapped, or a squirrel.

Still shining her torch around despite there being some light from the bulb, Morgan stepped onto the concrete floor and turned slowly to take in the large space. There were the usual things you'd expect to find in a cellar: stacks of boxes, shelves containing tools and tins of paint. Nothing out of the ordinary. As she moved around the beam from her torch illuminated a jumble of clothes in the far corner.

The light hit two small circles and reflected back towards her.

She screamed so loud it echoed around the cellar as she realised two eyes were staring at her.

Jumping back, it took her mind a few moments to process what she was seeing and then she felt her legs begin to quiver. Her hands tried to grab the radio to press the talk button and missed. She tried a second time.

'5129 to control, I need urgent assistance.'

Her voice was barely a whisper.

'5129, you're very faint, can you repeat the last?'

'Urgent assistance. I've found the missing family from the suicide yesterday.'

'Are they kicking off?'

She shook her head. 'No, I think they're dead.'

'Where are you?'

'Easdale Road, the same address as the suicide.'

Morgan could hear the radio burst into life as patrols began to shout up they were on their way. She took a pair of blue nitrile gloves from her pocket and slipped them on, painfully aware of the need to preserve the scene, but also mindful that she needed to make sure there wasn't anything that could be done for them. She remembered the DS's harsh words yesterday about not being medically trained to call death.

'Control, I'll need ambulance travelling.'

'How many casualties are there? Ambulance will need to know.'

'Three, I think, one male and two females.'

She crossed the floor and knelt down by the side of the man who she assumed was Saul Potter. His face was covered with a piece of white cotton that was heavily bloodstained. The adult male was only wearing a once white T-shirt and pair of shorts, no socks or shoes. He had a shaved head and stubble on his chin that she could see underneath the piece of fabric was stained with dark, red blood. There was a pool of blood around him and the left side of his head was a strange shape. It looked like a deflated football it was so caved in. She placed two fingers to his carotid artery to see if she could feel a pulse. Nothing; he was cold and hard to the touch.

A slight moan behind him stopped her in her tracks though. The other two bodies looked as if they could be the girls from the photographs in the bedroom. Both of them looked so tiny lying there. Neither of them had socks or shoes on either. They were so close together they were almost touching. She tried to stay silent, to hear which had made the noise, or had she imagined it? Then it happened again, and she realised that one of them was breathing. It was very shallow; she had a similar head injury to who Morgan assumed was her dad. But there were signs of life.

'Control, I need that ambulance now. There's a teenage girl unconscious, breathing very shallow; she's lost a lot of blood and has a serious head injury.'

Morgan's breath was coming fast. Shit, should she put her in the recovery position? She decided against it. Unzipping her body armour then the black fleece jacket she was wearing, she shrugged it off and used it to cover the girl as best as she could. It was so cold down here, she could see a cloud of white vapour every time she exhaled. It was a wonder the girl hadn't died of shock and hypothermia. She noticed another piece of the white fabric on the floor next to this girl. She must have moved enough for it to have slid off.

'It's okay, honey, I'm a police officer. Help is on the way. We'll get you to the hospital. Just hang on.'

Another faint moan spurred Morgan on; she had to save this girl.

Morgan stared at the other girl lying behind this one. Her face was covered in a piece of the same white material stained with dark, congealed blood. She didn't need to lift the cloth to see that the right side of her face was all caved in: she could tell by the flattened shape the cloth was sticking to. There was so much blood pooled on the floor around the bodies. She stared at the thick, dark clots that had formed. She felt as if she was knee-deep in it. She breathed deeply through her mouth so she wouldn't inhale the strong odour. If she passed out, she would be letting the girl down, but the room was starting to go a little fuzzy around the edges. What if the killer came back? She was here on her own. God knows how long it would take other patrols to arrive. The smell was cloying, sickly and unbearable. Her stomach was doing some weird thing and the back of her mouth was filling with water. God, she'd better not puke. She focused on her breathing, slowing it down in time to the motion of stroking the uninjured side of the girl's head. She took hold of her hand, unsure if she was helping or making things worse, but knowing that if their places were reversed and she was close to death, that she would want someone to be there for her, giving her some comfort in her final moments.

Her brain could barely process what these poor girls had been through. Who would do something like this, and why?

CHAPTER TEN

Ben reached the roundabout at junction twenty-six, about to take the turn-off for the M6 Southbound, when Amy slapped his arm and shouted.

'Shit, boss. You need to go back, don't take the slip road.'

He swerved and carried on back towards the Kendal exit, a symphony of horns blaring behind them.

'Jesus, what the hell's the matter with you?'

Detective Constable Amy Smith had been parking up as he left the station and had the misfortune of running into him while getting out of her car. Ben had asked her to accompany him to the mortuary. She'd shrugged and got into his.

'They've found bodies at the house.'

'What house? You need to give me more than that. I didn't swallow my psychic pills this morning.'

'The suicide from yesterday.'

'Turn the radio up, I can't hear.'

'See, this is why you should pay more attention.'

He glared at her and she grinned.

He listened to the panicked voices as officers shouted up and the control room operator gave orders out.

'Can you ring Morgan? I sent her there on her own; I need to know she's okay.'

'Who's Morgan, what's her number? I haven't had my psychic pills today either, boss.'

'Crap, I don't know her collar number. She was the one who found Olivia Potter yesterday. Bloody hell, they went in and searched the house. How the hell did they miss three dead bodies?'

'No one is perfect. Hang on, the bodies are in the cellar, ooh, one's still breathing.'

He stole a glance at her to see if she was being sarcastic, but she was just giving him a running commentary.

'Who, who is still breathing?'

'I think it's a girl, I missed the start of that part.'

He reached out and took the radio from her. 'This is DS Matthews to the officer at scene.'

'Go ahead, Sarge.'

'Are you okay, Morgan?'

'Yes.'

'What have you got?'

'Adult male with a serious head injury; teenage female with a head injury: both appear to be dead; sorry, foxtrot. Paramedics are on the way. One teenage female with serious head injuries, breathing, unconscious. I'm sorry, they were in a cellar that must have been mistaken for the garage. It was bolted from the outside.'

Her voice almost broke on the last sentence and he felt bad for her, bad that she'd gone in there alone to discover this. Bad that she was going to blame herself for not finding them yesterday, and he wondered where this sudden influx of empathy had come from. He'd spent the last three years being a miserable, tetchy git who didn't really give a shit about anyone, and now this.

'I'm on my way.'

Amy looked over at him and arched an eyebrow.

'What?'

'Nothing.'

'Then why are you looking at me like that?'

'"I'm on my way."'

'I am on my way.'

She nodded. 'Yep, you are. Super cop Matthews to the rescue.'

'What's that supposed to mean?'

'Nothing.'

She turned and stared out of the window; they drove in silence until she finally broke it.

'Do you like her then? You know, as your colleague I need to know this stuff. It's part of my job description to keep the boss on the straight and narrow.'

'Jesus, Amy, I only met her yesterday. She had a crap first day on independent patrol, then at Mitch's leaving do that idiot Dan made fun of her in front of everyone in the pub. Now this. I think she deserves a little bit of compassion.'

She leant across and placed the back of her hand on his forehead. 'Just checking you're not coming down with something. And I'm shutting up right now.'

She smiled at him and began to look at her hand-held device to see what the latest updates were on the log they were heading to. Ben knew she was only joking and he didn't mind, but he was questioning himself. Did his team really think he was a bastard who didn't care about anyone? Why else would she be so shocked at him being nice? Maybe it was time to shake things up a bit. He glanced in the rear-view mirror. His hair was in desperate need of a cut; he had a beard that was more homeless-guy-who-doesn't-have-a-mirror than trendy. As for the double chins, he cringed. Christ, he'd really let himself go. Cindy would be horrified to see him looking like this. Time to get his act together.

'I still can't believe the whole family are dead. Who would do something like this? It's horrific.'

'Not the whole family, didn't she say one was still breathing?'

'Yeah, but if she's been left for dead it doesn't sound too good.'

He put his foot down and began to drive as fast as he could without sirens. He needed to get there and see the carnage for himself.

*

By the time he arrived there were already two ambulances and a first responder vehicle parked up, two police vans, and an unmarked car. He motioned to Amy they should get kitted up. He didn't want the scene getting contaminated any more than it already had been. Two paramedics came out of the house with the unconscious girl on a stretcher. They loaded her into the back of the van and began working on her. He saw Morgan follow them out of the front door. She was pale, her bright yellow body armour was stained red and for want of a better way to describe it, she looked completely shell-shocked. He saw Dan trying to speak to Morgan, but she didn't acknowledge him or even look at him; in fact, she looked as if she was about to pass out.

Amy nudged him. 'Your new bestie needs a hand before she hits the deck.'

Ben could see that, but he didn't exactly want to be the one to rush to her rescue because he'd never live it down. Yet, he couldn't stand there and watch it happen. He pushed Amy towards her.

'Go grab her arm, bring her to the car and get her in the back seat. We can pretend we're interviewing her, give her five minutes.'

Amy was already walking in her direction.

'Hi, Morgan. I'm Amy, one of the DCs. DS Matthews would like a word with you. We need to get the details of what's happened.'

Not waiting for a reply, she grabbed Morgan's elbow and guided her in the direction of the car, where Ben was zipping up the pale blue paper suit. He opened the back door and watched as Amy expertly got her inside without making a scene.

Amy turned to him. 'You owe me one.'

He nodded. Then turned to look at Morgan. 'How are you doing?'

She stared at the back of the ambulance. The doors were open and they could clearly see the two paramedics working hard to stabilise the girl so they could drive to the hospital.

'I think it's Bronte, she looked older. I didn't know she was there. I let her down; she was still alive and I could have found her yesterday.'

'You did find her though. If it wasn't for you insisting something wasn't right, we all wouldn't be here right now. She wouldn't be in with a chance of survival.'

Her head moved in slow motion, up and down.

'I need you to focus, Morgan. I need to know exactly what happened. Have the paramedics confirmed death of the other victims?'

'Yes. They did a quick assessment, said if you want them to run a heart strip they will. But it's quite clear they've been dead a while.'

'No, I don't need them to do that. What about you, did you think they were dead?'

'You told me off yesterday for making that assumption.'

'I know I did, disregard that. I was trying to give you good advice; this is a desperate situation. What was your first impression?'

'That they were all dead, then I realised one of the girls was still breathing. I got scared. I didn't know if the killer was still in there or if…'

He nodded, encouraging her to continue.

'Maybe it was Olivia? She might have killed them all then killed herself.'

'We don't know anything yet, but it's a possibility. Thank you, Morgan. Stay here for a little while. When you're ready you can go out and face the others.'

She looked up at him. 'I'm okay. I don't need to take time out. There's a door in the kitchen, it leads down into the cellar. That's where they are. Can I go to the hospital with Bronte?'

Morgan was already out of the car and on her way to the open ambulance.

'Of course, it's all hands on deck back there. You might be able to help out.'

He'd slipped on two pairs of blue nitrile gloves while they'd been talking and some shoe covers. Amy was dressed the same. He looked at her and she gave him a thumbs up. It was time to meet the rest of the Potter family.

He just wished it was under better circumstances than this.

CHAPTER ELEVEN

Over the years he'd been in the police, Ben had attended some pretty tragic crime scenes. The worst had been a house fire where two children had died. Thankfully the smoke had got them and when he'd pushed his way in – despite being told not to by his superior – and found them, they had looked as if they were asleep. He'd been to some terrible accidents, a fair few murders and suicides, but this, however, was by far the most horrific. He went down the wooden steps first, Amy following behind.

Standing at the bottom step, Ben took in the scene in front of him. On first observation it looked like any old cellar, apart from the strong odour of blood and decomposition, and then when his eyes fell onto the bodies in one corner it was hard to believe what he was seeing. It looked like someone had discarded a pile of clothes there, until he realised the clothes had body parts attached to them and stained cloths covering their faces. Immediately he thought that whoever had done this knew the victims, their guilt causing them to cover their eyes so they weren't looking at them. Judging by the pools of blood on the floor they had been killed down here.

He shone his torch at the walls and ceiling, sucking in a deep breath. There was blood spatter everywhere. Whoever did this must have been covered in blood. He took his time scanning the rest of the cellar, but there was no obvious sign of a murder weapon.

'Bollocks.'

He heard Amy whisper the word behind him and he had to agree it was definitely bollocks. He crossed towards the two remaining bodies. There were discarded packets where the paramedics had ripped open necessary medical equipment to save the girl, which meant this crime scene had been contaminated, but for the greater good; preserving life took priority over anything else. Although he wasn't sure, judging by the head injuries inflicted on the remaining members of her family, whether she was going to thank them for it. There was a good chance she'd have sustained some serious brain damage, not to mention losing her entire family in one go. If she came around, would she rather they'd left her to die? He shook himself out of it, not going any further.

'We need this documenting by CSI before anything else gets disturbed. What the hell happened down here?'

Amy didn't answer, which was unusual. He turned to look at her. Eyes wide and taking deep breaths through her mouth – this wasn't like her; she was usually as tough as he was. It only reaffirmed to him just how bad this crime scene was. He pointed to the stairs and shoved her gently in that direction. She turned and didn't pause, mounting them a lot faster than she'd come down. He followed suit, and the pair of them exited the house into the fresh air. Although the smell in the cellar wasn't as bad as it could have been, it was enough to have permeated his nostrils and it lingered in the back of his throat.

The ambulance was gone, he saw, along with Morgan. That was good; at least she was out of here for the time being. He'd need to get a full statement from her later. The CSI van was now parking in the space the ambulance had vacated, and behind that was the DCI's battered Land Rover. Tom lived on a remote farm with his wife, Christine, and never went anywhere without his trusty steed as he called it. He watched as Tom waved him over and he opened the door, climbing into the passenger seat.

'What have we got?'

'A pretty big mess, sir. Two bodies in the cellar, both with their heads staved in, and pieces of cloth over their faces. Another victim has been taken to the RLI by ambulance.'

'Shit. Is there a reason we didn't find them yesterday? Wasn't the house searched?'

'Yes, it was. There are no signs of anything untoward happening in the house; it's clean. The cellar door was bolted from the outside and, to be fair, it looks as if it's the adjoining garage door. The garage was checked from the outside; rookie but very easy mistake to make.'

He nodded. 'But there's one still alive; if we'd have found them yesterday...'

He didn't finish his sentence; he didn't need to. Ben was painfully aware of the consequences of such a mistake.

'It's done, it is what it is. We need to focus on the scene now.'

'Anything unusual I should be aware of?'

'Well apart from an entire family turning up dead and their faces being covered, not really. According to the pathologist, Olivia's hanging is looking suspicious, so I did consider whether the father may have murdered his family. Perhaps he hanged Olivia, then took his daughters into the cellar and killed them and himself.'

'Only that story doesn't add up. How did he cover his own face and lock the cellar door?'

'True, sir, maybe Olivia killed them and couldn't take the guilt so took a couple of attempts to hang herself?'

Tom nodded. 'That seems more feasible, unusual but not entirely unheard of. Who found the bodies?'

'The officer I was going to offer the attachment to.'

'Seems like a good shout. There's nothing like being thrown in at the deep end to learn how to swim. Do you think she'll be interested after this?'

'Hard to say, but quite possibly. I get a feeling she'd like to see this through to the end.'

They both got out of the Land Rover. Wendy, the duty CSI, was gathering the equipment she needed from the back of the van. Hoisting her camera case over her shoulder and picking up the heavy bag she needed, she set off towards the house. Ben followed.

'Do you know where you're going?'

'Cellar, I hate cellars. They're always full of creepy shit, not to mention creepy crawlies.'

He smiled; for a tough crime scene investigator whose job involved bodies that were crawling with insects, she really had a dislike of them. It made him feel better, though, when she was trying her best not to puke into her face mask while he was doing the same behind her.

'You're safe, no insects that I could see. Not sure about close up though. I didn't go too near. But they weren't covered in flies, which is always a good sign, although there could be lots of spiders.'

She turned and looked at him. 'Thanks.'

He shrugged. Took out his phone and scrolled through his contacts to the name 'Dr Death'. Declan answered on the second ring. Ben heard his voice vibrate and knew he was on loudspeaker.

'Did you get the message?'

'I did, I'm on my way. Is it as bad as it sounds?'

'Yeah, probably a lot worse. Paramedics have called it; CSI is in here now. You should be good to go when you get here.'

'Cheers, pal, glad you send the good stuff my way.'

The line went dead and he smiled, knowing that Declan loved it and was a fantastic pathologist.

CHAPTER TWELVE

Morgan had held Bronte's hand the whole way here while the paramedics had worked on her. Relieved now they'd reached the hospital, it had been some journey as the ambulance had sped through the narrow, rural roads of Cumbria to the entrance of the RLI in a busy city. Jumping out, she stepped to one side as the paramedics unloaded the girl and rushed her through the double doors into resus. She followed them through, unsure whether she'd be allowed in the room or not. The receptionist pointed to a small room to the side which said 'Police'.

She nodded and stepped inside. There were a couple of chairs and a small table with some yellowed magazines on it, along with two empty plastic coffee cups. All in all, it was a bit grim. Sitting down, she wondered what to do. Not having been in a situation like this before, it wasn't long before the door opened and one of the paramedics who'd been working on Bronte walked in. They hadn't had time for introductions earlier at the house, but he looked to be around ten years older than her, with a shaved head and stubble that reminded her of Jason Statham.

'They're working on her. She needs a CT scan but they have to stabilise her first. Then she'll be going to intensive care if she doesn't need surgery to relieve any swelling on the brain.'

'Thank you, do you think she'll come around anytime soon?'

He shook his head. 'Not my call to make, but it's possible she won't. Did you see the side of her head?'

'Yep, it's a mess.' She swallowed the lump which had formed in the back of her throat as she relived the shock of finding Bronte alive in that dark, foul-smelling cellar.

He reached out his hand. 'I'm Luke, and you are?'

'Morgan.'

'Thanks for helping us out and driving the van. Are you okay, can I get you anything, a coffee?'

She smiled. 'I'm good, thanks for asking. It was a bit of a shock finding them all like that. It's so sad.'

'I've been doing this for nearly ten years and I've never seen anything like this.' He sat down and smiled at her. 'How long have you been in the job?'

'Just over six months, I've only been out on independent patrol for two days. Yesterday I went to a suicide at the same property where I discovered the bodies today.'

Luke let out a whistle. 'Crap, talk about being thrown in at the deep end.'

A laugh erupted from her lips and she felt better, lighter. He joined in; she knew one of the absolute necessities of working in jobs like theirs was the ability to make light of the most terrible situations. It kept you sane and smiling when really you wanted to scream and shout.

His radio crackled as the ambulance control room asked if they were clear to attend another job. He told them negative.

'I'd best go clean out the van ready for our next customer. Thanks again, Morgan, hope I see you around sometime.'

'You're welcome and yes, that would be great.' Passing him the keys, she pulled out a card with her contact details on. 'If you're ever at a loose end you could call me. Anytime.'

Grinning, he pocketed the card.

As the door closed behind him, she wondered what had just happened. She'd never given her number or blatantly asked someone to call her. Of course, the fact that he was older had a lot to do with it. She'd always had a bit of a crush on older men.

Finally the door to the small waiting room opened and a nurse hurried towards her.

'You can come through, she's stable for now.'

'Is she awake?'

She caught the eye roll the nurse gave her as she led her into resus and realised that was a stupid question.

A woman wearing a pink stethoscope crossed the room towards her.

'Doctor Andreas; are you the one who brought her in?'

'Yes, I'm the officer who found her. Is she awake, or likely to be anytime soon?'

'No, I'm afraid not. She slipped into a coma on the way here. Her head injury is severe and she scored three on the GCS which is the lowest you can get.'

'GCS?'

'Glasgow Coma Scale, it's what we use to assess the severity of a brain injury. Three is the lowest, chances of survival are generally small, I'm afraid.'

'But there is a chance?'

'There's always a chance; she's young. We're sending her for a CT scan so we'll know more then, but there's no point in you waiting here. It could be days, possibly weeks before she regains consciousness or, I'm sorry to say, if she does.'

'I'll leave my details at the desk. Could you put on her file that if she does wake up police will need to speak to her immediately? And Doctor... would it have made a difference if I had found her yesterday?'

Doctor Andreas smiled at her kindly. 'Impossible to say, but perhaps not; her head trauma is severe. We can add the details to the file though, and we can set up a safe word so you can check on her progress without going through the hassle of trying to explain to everyone why you want to know.'

Morgan asked the control room to get the DS to contact her. A few seconds later her radio was ringing.

'Sarge, the hospital suggested a safe word. Is it okay to proceed?'

'Yes, absolutely. How is she?'

'Serious, she slipped into a coma on the way here.'

'Tell them we'll use the word campervan.'

She frowned, not sure why, but not wanting to question him. 'Okay, thanks.' She passed the information on to Doctor Andreas.

'Make sure you tell the receptionist to add it on her file.'

The doctor turned around. Two porters had arrived to take the bed in which Bronte lay down to the X-ray department. Morgan stepped out of the way and watched as the doctor, nurse and two porters expertly pushed the bed and equipment attached to it along the corridor. She left her contact details, that of the duty sergeant's office back at the station, and a number for DS Matthews with the receptionist.

Walking outside, she suddenly realised she was stranded in Lancaster with no van or car to get back to the station. Unclipping her radio, she took it off her body armour and scrolled through the menu to find the list of recent calls, dialling the one the DS had rung her from.

'Go ahead.'

'Sarge, it's Morgan. Is there more I can do here?'

'Actually, I need you to stay with her until CSI get to you. We need to take her clothes and samples for forensic analysis.'

She felt her face turn red.

'Oh, I'm sorry. I didn't realise.'

'It's okay, you're not supposed to know all this stuff on day two. I've called the late shift CSI in early to come straight to you. As soon as I'm not needed at the scene, I'll also be coming to talk to the doctors, so you can grab a lift back with whoever is finished first.'

'Thank you.'

She ended the call, turned around and walked back through the automatic doors in search of the X-ray department.

CHAPTER THIRTEEN

Ben watched Declan from the bottom step of the basement stairs, giving him room to work. He'd taken samples, body temperature, room temperature and bagged both victims' hands up. Not touching the faces, he turned to Ben.

'Can I remove these cloths?'

Ben nodded. 'Yes, they've been photographed. CSI will bag them up. I just wanted you to see them in situ before they were removed. What do you think?'

Declan didn't answer. The light in the cellar wasn't that good. He was crouched next to Saul Potter's face; with one hand he shone a torch onto it while with the other he lifted the corner of the material to take a look underneath. He let out a long, low whistle.

'What a mess; it's overkill and I'm leaning towards it also being personal. Whoever did this meant business, they wanted him out of action and fast.'

While Ben pondered this, Wendy came down, clutching an assortment of both plastic and brown paper evidence bags and crossed towards Declan, holding a plastic one open for him to drop the cloth in. He did and she sealed it shut, then placed it into a brown bag, sealing that, too.

'I'm thinking they were killed down here, so whoever our killer is managed to lure them down somehow. Not sure how they managed to kill all three without there being a fight though. He's a pretty big guy; how do you take him out when you're threatening his family?'

Ben nodded. 'Maybe by threatening his family the killer had complete control, either that or they were drugged. Any signs at all of them being attacked upstairs and moved down here, Wendy?'

'I've made a quick check of the house, where I found a bucket under the kitchen sink with some white cotton cloths inside that I've bagged up to send off; they look similar to the ones on the victims' faces. There are no signs to suggest a break-in. Whoever did this must have known the family or at least they trusted them enough to let them inside.'

Ben was rubbing his hand across his stubble. 'Whoever did this must have been covered in blood. Can you take a close look at the sinks, bathrooms for any forensics? They had to have cleaned themselves up before leaving. Unless you think there is a chance he could have killed his wife, made it look like a suicide, managed to get his daughters down here, killed them then himself?'

Declan looked at the compression on the side of Saul's skull. 'It's a significant injury; it would be difficult to do that to yourself, and also would need a heavy weapon, like a wooden bat or club. Did you find anything like that near to his body, Wendy?'

'No.'

'There's your answer, Ben, that's a no. You're looking for something heavy enough to do this amount of damage. It will be bloodstained, hair, skin should be visible on the end of it, and some other person has clearly taken it with them. Although, can you help me roll the bodies? You never know, they could be lying on it.'

Ben knelt down and between them they rolled Saul onto his side, but there wasn't anything underneath him. They did the same with Beatrix.

'Well there's your answer: whoever killed them knows enough about forensics to take the weapon with them.'

Ben's mind was working overtime. Olivia was the obvious suspect. Could she have killed her family then hanged herself, wracked with guilt? There were so many possibilities and the only person who could tell them exactly what had happened was Bronte, who had slipped into a coma.

They gently rolled Beatrix onto her back and Ben felt his heart tear a little at the terrible way this young girl had had her life taken away from her. He stood up, the creaking sound from his knees echoing around the room. He felt much older than his forty-five years this morning.

Declan began to put the samples he'd taken into his case then snapped it shut.

'I'm happy for the bodies to be moved to the mortuary now, unless you need to keep them in situ a little longer.'

Ben wasn't sure what he wanted to do. Wendy had called in a crime scene manager from headquarters to come and assess the scene. He decided to leave them where they were until this had been done. There was no rush: better to have triple-checked the scene for every shred of evidence than to rush it.

'Wendy, I'm going through to the RLI to speak to the doctors about the surviving victim. You don't need me, do you?'

She shook her head. 'Nah, I'll ring if I find anything you need to know about.'

He went upstairs and outside, not realising how clammy and smelly it had been in the cellar until he inhaled deeply and took fresh air into his lungs.

The DCI was still on his phone, but had managed to get suited and booted.

He crossed the driveway towards him as he ended his call.

'Sir, I'm going to the hospital to see the victim. There's not much we can do at the moment until the crime scene manager has been to assess the scene.'

Tom nodded. 'I'll go take a look, but happy to go with your instructions. Should we all meet back at the station for a briefing at' – he lifted his wrist to check the time – 'four. Will that give you enough time to get back from Lancaster?'

'Plenty. Boss, it's pretty bad down there.'

Ben knew Tom didn't have the strongest of stomachs when it came to messy crime scenes.

'I believe so, but I'd better take a look. Thanks.'

He left him walking at a snail's pace towards the front door of the house, a small smile playing across his lips. Everyone had their weaknesses: Wendy disliked insects, Tom wasn't good with blood, and from the scene earlier, he guessed neither was Morgan. He only hoped Tom made it out into the fresh air before he puked or passed out.

Stripping off his protective clothing, Ben bagged it up and placed it in the back of the van for Wendy to take back to the station with her. Amy had come outside already and was leaning against the side of the house, smoking. He walked over to her.

'I thought you'd packed it in?'

'So did I until I had to look at that. Jesus, who would do that?'

'I guess that's where we come in. I'm going to Lancaster to visit the surviving victim. Can you stay here and make sure everything is taken care of? Let me know if you need me, and I'll come straight back.'

'I can, although I don't really want to have to spend any time alone down there with them. It's sad, and creepy.'

'It's not a Netflix horror movie, Amy, they're definitely dead and not about to get up and chase you.'

'I know that, I'm just saying.'

He laughed. 'Lunch is on me.'

'Cheers, Sarge, but surprisingly my appetite has vanished.'

'Well, when it returns, I'll buy your refs. I won't be long, it's just a formality really since she's slipped into a coma. I just want to see what the doctors have to say about her condition.'

'Fine, is your new protégé there still?'

He looked to see if she was taking the piss; she wasn't laughing.

'Yes, and I reckon she's stranded. She drove the ambulance while the crew worked on the vic.'

'All right, go rescue her, but then you'd better get your arse back here and rescue me.'

'Yes, *boss*.' He emphasised the 'boss' and this time she did laugh.

CHAPTER FOURTEEN

Greg Barker saw the dark blue BMW parked in his 'Reserved for Mayor' space and felt his blood pressure begin to rise. That self-serving arsehole, Jamie Stone, thought he ran the whole town; he actually thought the whole parish council revolved around him. Well, it bloody didn't. Jamie was nothing; all he ever did was attend meetings and talk about himself and his ideas. Ideas which most of the time were completely irrelevant to what the meeting had been called for. Just because Stone was obsessed with bringing in more modern recreational amenities to the town, everyone thought he was God's gift. Why the hell did Rydal Falls and the surrounding villages need a skate park? It was unheard of; was there any point encouraging local children to try and break their necks when the nearest hospital was at least a thirty-minute drive? He didn't think so. He'd like to take a skateboard and shove it up Jamie Stone's arse.

He got out of the car and slammed the door, bending to check his reflection in the wing mirror. His thick head of freshly trimmed grey hair made him look much younger than his seventy years. There were a few more lines around his brown eyes and forehead than he liked, but for a pensioner he was fitter than most twenty-year-olds thanks to his eight-mile runs and fell walking. He was in pretty good shape and age was just a number, it didn't mean anything.

'Afternoon, Mayor, glad you could make it.'

Greg turned and saw the man himself striding towards him, holding a large box, and felt his fists clench.

'Jamie. Look, I've been meaning to talk to you about this for some time now.' He pointed at the parking space.

'You after a new car, mate? It's about time you upgraded and got yourself a decent ride.'

Greg had dreamt about being mayor for a long time and now that he was, it was nothing like what he'd expected. He'd pictured people being in awe of him, bowing down to him and grovelling. Imagined local business owners falling over their own feet to get in favour with him, bending over backwards to get his approval. Admittedly some people did all of that, but most of them didn't, especially Jamie, and it irked him more than he'd like to say.

He stared at the much shorter man standing in front of him. What he lacked in stature, though, he more than made up for in confidence. As Greg stared at him, he imagined drawing back his fist and punching him square in the nose. How satisfying it would be listening to the cartilage crunch.

'Why would I need a new car? This is a classic Aston Martin DB4. I doubt very much you could ever afford to buy the tyres.'

'Look I can't stand around chatting, sorry. I have to get back to the office. Apparently they've found bodies at a house on Easdale Road and I need to get someone out there as soon as possible.'

Opening the boot of his car with his key fob, he threw the box inside, pressed a button for it to glide shut and climbed in. Sticking his head out of the window, he shouted: 'Soon as I have a spare ten minutes I'll take you out for a spin. You can have a test drive and see what you think.'

Greg lifted his hand, stepping out of the way as Jamie began reversing towards him.

'I'd rather chop both my legs off and shove hot pins in my eyes.'

'What?'

'Yeah, that would be great.'

He watched as Jamie roared into the distance, driving way too fast. Another example of how bloody selfish the man was. Part of him wanted to return to his car and move it into the reserved parking space, but the other didn't want anyone to know how much it bothered him, in case they all started to park there on purpose to annoy him. After a moment's debate, he continued on into the town hall.

Inside the building, which functioned as a magistrate's court, council chambers and a women's centre, he made his way upstairs to his office. Wondering what had happened on Easdale Road, he went into his office, closing the door behind him, and sat down behind the large mahogany desk. The chair was old and comfortable, if a little creaky. The oak-panelled walls had various portraits of the previous mayors along the walls. It looked more like a rogue's gallery to Greg. Despite the ornate gold frames surrounding them, they looked a right bunch.

Picking up the phone on his desk, he dialled the direct number to the police station he had for Chief Superintendent Adrian Quinn.

He answered on the first ring. *'Greg. What can I do for you?'*

'Adrian, hi. I've heard there have been bodies found on Easdale Road. I know you can't tell me much but I'd appreciate a heads-up on what you know.'

'An entire family have been found dead. Well, almost: one of them is still alive, just.'

Greg let out a whistle. 'Accidental?'

'Not from the information we have up to now, but you know I can't say. It's all still hush-hush at the moment.'

'Jamie Stone already knows and is on his way to the scene. Thought I'd give you warning.'

'Christ. When I find out who is passing information on to the press, I'll have them on suspension before they can hand me their badge.'

'Well, as our esteemed editor of the local newspaper, maybe you should ask Jamie who his contact is. But about the bodies, is it anyone I know and is there anything about it that will put tourists off? You know what the local businesses are like, any whiff of a scandal and they're up in arms.'

'Greg, I don't know if you're acquainted with them. An entire family are dead, dying. I don't care what the owner of Rocks and Socks thinks. All I care about is finding out what happened to them and why.'

'Can you at least tell me where on Easdale Road?'

'A property called Lake View.'

Greg felt the room begin to swim; he knew that house. He knew the family who lived there. His palms became clammy and he felt as if he had tunnel vision.

'By the way that's confidential until a press release has been issued.'

'Oh, yeah, of course.'

The line went dead as he pushed his chair back from the desk and leant as far forwards as he could, bending his head down. The horror sinking in, he stayed that way, unable to lift his head up for fear of passing out.

CHAPTER FIFTEEN

Morgan had no idea how long a CT scan should take, but it was longer than she expected. She caught a glimpse of Bronte as the doors finally opened, and they began the intricate task of wheeling her out. The girl looked as if she was clinging onto life.

'Where is she going?'

'Theatre, we need to remove a part of her skull. There's a large hematoma pressing against it.'

'I need her clothes, and we need to swab her hands. A CSI is on the way, is this possible?'

The nurse nodded. 'It will take a little while for the theatre to become available.'

She let out the breath she'd been holding; thank God she hadn't entirely messed up. She wanted to impress Ben, show him she was made of the stuff detectives were. Up till now, though, she'd felt she was on a steep learning curve. They didn't cover any of this stuff in training at headquarters.

As she followed the porters back to a cubicle in the emergency department, she saw Ben walk through the doors, followed by a male CSI. Morgan's shoulders dropped and the knot in her stomach loosened at the sight of them both. She waved them through, holding the double doors open for them to slip inside.

'How you holding up?'

'I'm good, although I'm not going to lie. Much better now that you two are here.'

Ben smiled. 'Why don't you go grab a coffee, take a break. The afternoon shift is in briefing; as soon as they're finished someone is coming to relieve you. While I'm here and Mark is doing his thing, you can have some time to think.'

'Thanks, but if it's okay with you I'd rather stay. Then I know what to do for future reference.'

All three stood outside the cubicle waiting for the doctor's permission to set about taking the relevant forensic samples and seizing Bronte's clothing. A nurse assisted Mark to take the fingernail scrapings and remove her clothing, taking time to gently dress her in a hospital gown. Ben stepped outside, taking Morgan with him to give Bronte some privacy.

Morgan looked back. 'That poor kid, it's horrific. Why would someone do that to her, to them?'

'That's what I intend to find out. Listen, I know you've had a rough ride and it's early days, but what are you wanting to do career wise? Are you wanting to stay on response, or do you think you might want to pursue a career in CID at some point?'

'I want to be a detective, it's all I've ever wanted. That's why I joined really. I don't think I'd want to spend the next twenty years driving around the country lanes aimlessly waiting for the next job to come in. I want to be the one putting the clues and evidence together, helping to solve crimes.'

'You've given it some thought then?' A small laugh escaped his lips.

Once more she felt her face begin to flush and wondered if he thought she was far too enthusiastic.

'Sorry, that sounded…'

He held his hand up. 'Look you have to stop apologising if you're going to be working for me, I can't take it. I'm miserable, grumpy, and I moan a lot but I'm not a complete bastard. You won't get any extra pay, it's much longer hours and you'll have to go on the national detective development course at HQ and work with a tutor DC eventually. But I'm offering you a three-month attachment if you want it, so you can see if you like it or if it's what you thought it would be before you decide. If you hate it, you can go back onto response. At least you'll have given it a shot, though, and will know one way or the other if it's the right career path for you.'

Morgan screwed up her face. 'I don't quite know what you mean?'

'Don't frown like that, you'll end up with a face like mine. I need a hand. I'm desperately short-staffed and this is a huge case. There are lots of enquiries that need fixing up. Amy and I will take the lead, but you will be given tasks from the both of us to complete. You're keen, you've been involved from day one and I think you'd be an asset to my team, eventually. What do you think, would you like to move up to CID? At least you won't be driving a van around all day.'

Morgan let out a squeal. Grabbing hold of Ben, she threw her arms around him and he stiffened up. Realising she'd overstepped her mark, she let go, her hands dropping back down to her sides.

'Sorry. Yes! Is this real? You're being serious and not making fun of me?'

He shook his head.

'Yes, yes, yes please. Oh my God, I can't believe it, I thought I'd have to wait years for a chance to work in CID.'

Laughing, Ben shrugged. 'To be honest you've kind of fallen on your feet because I'm so short-staffed; normally I wouldn't get within a hundred feet of a rookie.'

'Oh.' The excitement deflated as fast as it had arrived.

'I don't mean that in a horrible way, it's how it is. Circumstances have dictated otherwise though, and I know you'll work hard and fit in with my team. So, you're in?'

He held out his hand. She stared at it, noticing for the first time the smooth ring of skin where his wedding band should be. Grabbing hold of it, she shook it.

'I'm in. Do I get to wear my own clothes?'

'You certainly do.'

The curtain opened and Mark stepped out with a couple of paper evidence sacks in one hand, his case in the other.

'All done. I think she's going down to theatre soon.'

'Cheers, Mark.'

Morgan stepped back into the cubicle, and Ben went to speak to the doctor in charge. If she'd thought that Bronte looked frail before, she looked even smaller now in the cotton hospital gown that drowned her tiny frame. Unable to stop herself, she reached out and took hold of her cold hand.

Clasping it tenderly, bending down, she whispered, 'Keep fighting, Bronte, I'm going to find who did this to you and your family. I promise you.'

CHAPTER SIXTEEN

Neither of them spoke much on the way back to the station, and Morgan was desperate to change out of her soiled uniform. As if reading her mind, Ben parked up, saying, 'You can go get changed, shower then come up to the office.'

'I'd better go and speak to my sergeant, tell him where I'm going. They might be short on patrol if I come up now.'

'You sort yourself out, and I'll speak to Mads. He won't mind; the DCI requested we ask you as soon as possible.'

That wasn't strictly true, he knew. He'd requested Ben find someone ASAP. He hadn't specifically requested Morgan, but she didn't need to know that.

She went in the direction of the women's locker room, and he headed to the patrol sergeant's office. Knocking on the door, he walked in without waiting to be asked.

'Mads.'

'Ben, how's it going? Is Morgan with you, is she coping okay? It's a bit much for your first independent patrols.'

'She's fine; at least she seems it. Look, I need some help. We're desperately short-staffed and Tom said to find someone today. I've asked her and she's happy to come up and do a three-month attachment. It will be a massive help.'

'What? It's her second day. Don't you want someone slightly more experienced and who's willing to take on the extra caseload? Dan has been wanting to come up for months. He'd be more than happy to.'

Ben shut the door and lowered his voice. 'Dan's difficult; I can't work with him. Not at the moment. This is the biggest murder case I've ever worked on, and I need to be focused. I can't afford to spend all day wasting my effort trying to keep him in line. Morgan's keen and has been on the case from the moment it was called in. I think she'll be okay.'

'I think she won't, she's inexperienced.'

'Yes, but she's confident and I have faith in her. Don't forget, you owe me one.'

Mads squinted at him; he did owe him one. Ben had saved his arse when his wife had come looking for him at the Christmas party after he'd left early with one of the PCSOs.

'Christ almighty, you know this is going to cause a shitstorm with Dan. He won't be happy about it.'

'Tough, he's a big boy and he can have the next place that becomes available; besides, if she's crap and it isn't working out, I'll send her back down and he can come up. I can't get fairer than that.'

'You know this could go to professional standards if he finds out he was passed over just because he gets on your nerves. We'd both be up shit creek without a paddle. Not to mention it's unheard of to give someone so inexperienced this kind of opportunity.'

'Yeah, I'm aware of that possibility. However, he's not going to find out about this conversation, is he? Just like your missus isn't going to find out where you really were on the work do.'

Mads glared at Ben, who felt bad that he'd resorted to blackmail to get what he wanted. But it was Morgan or nothing; there was no way on this earth he was working extra-long days with Dan. He wanted to solve these murders, not spend his time resisting the urge to punch his cocky little face every time he opened his mouth.

'On your head be it; this is nothing to do with me. Don't say I didn't warn you when it all goes wrong.'

'Why would it go wrong? She seems okay. At least she's keen and isn't worn down and feeling jaded yet like most of the response officers. Thanks.'

He opened the door and saw Dan hovering around outside. He didn't even look his way. By the time he'd reached the stairs he heard

Dan go into Mads office and ask if he could have a word. Which just proved to Ben what a sneaky little shit he was. Let him go to professional standards with a complaint; he'd tell them about the way he bullied new officers. Two could play that game.

*

Amy was sitting at her desk, sipping a large mug of tea. She nodded at him.

'You have some visitors.'

'Who?'

'Some bigwigs from HQ. They're in your office with a brew and biscuits. You can thank me later.'

He went into his office to see a DCI and a DC he vaguely knew from the Murder Investigation Team.

'Morning, ladies.'

'We've been sent down to lend a hand.'

'By whom?'

'You know the protocol, anything big and they call us in. Look, as far as we're concerned you have everything under control. We can help get extra officers in to run the HOLMES system: they can input the information onto the system to be collated and pass out the relevant tasks it generates. Help with enquiries, that kind of thing. It's not a pissing contest; there's a dead family.'

'I'm well aware of that, thank you. Well, your help would be great. How does it all work then?'

Both women looked at each other. They'd obviously thought he'd put up a fight.

'I'm Detective Chief Inspector Claire Williams and this is Detective Constable Abigail Walsh. We can run the HOLMES from HQ, and one of us can come down here and work to oversee the investigation. Feed back into it, offer you support. Come up with an investigative plan: everything you do, but it comes under the remit of the Murder Investigation Team.'

'Sounds fair enough.'

Again, they glanced at each other; obviously not used to such a warm welcome, he thought to himself. He didn't care. He could do his own thing. Morgan would do what he asked, and Amy rarely listened to anyone. She was always doing her own thing. The rest of the team could take up the slack and keep these two happy. As long as the three of them worked together on his little squad it would be fine.

'There's a briefing in the blue room in' – glancing at his watch – 'in an hour, that should give CSI a chance to get back. Is that okay with you both?'

They nodded.

'Help yourselves to desks, whatever you need. Amy will sort you out.'

'Thank you, that's great,' said Claire, the older-looking of the two.

If Ben had to choose, he'd say that Abigail would get the short straw and have to work down here with his team. Claire would pull rank, make the younger detective drive here every day.

He stood up. 'Can I get you another drink?'

They both shook their heads.

'Excuse me while I go make one then, I need coffee.'

He left them in his office and walked back into the larger one, where Amy was staring at Morgan, who had arrived, hair damp and out of uniform.

'You found us then, bet you feel better after that shower.'

Amy swivelled her head to look at him.

Morgan smiled. 'I do. I don't like the smell of blood, especially when it's dried on your clothes and every time you inhale it's there.'

'Amy, Morgan is going to be working alongside you for the foreseeable. She's on a three-month attachment.'

'I'm so excited to be able to work with you. I always wanted to be a detective.'

Amy glared at Ben. He was doing a great job of upsetting everyone he spoke with today.

'Morgan, the first job, and probably one of the most important, is to learn where the brew cupboard is. Mine's a strong coffee, two sugars. Help yourself to whatever. Amy drinks tea by the bucket, strong with no sugar.'

'Amy, do you want a fresh drink?'

'No, I'm good thanks, Morgan. I'll show you where we keep our stuff. And he might be in charge, but he's capable of making his own drinks, aren't you, boss?'

'Of course I am.'

'So, only make him one if you want one yourself.'

Amy stood up and led Morgan out into the corridor to where the small kitchen was. He gave them a couple of moments then followed.

'Look, I wanted you out here so I could tell you what's happening without those two listening.'

'And what's that, boss?'

'Those two are going to be running the investigation: one from HQ, the other from here.'

Amy crossed her arms, a look of anger flashing across her face. 'What about us?'

'We'll do what we usually do, and then feed back to them. It's complicated, so I'm not going to argue with them. I'm not stupid enough to turn down any extra help when we're so thin on the ground, but you run everything through me first before you go to them.'

'Fine by me.'

He looked at Morgan, who looked even more perturbed than she had earlier. 'Morgan, is that okay with you?'

'Yes, of course, Sarge. I don't know what I'm doing though.'

Amy laughed. 'To be fair neither do we. We've been winging it for years. You'll be fine, as long as you use your common sense.'

'Ah, well I have that in buckets. Thanks, I'll give it a go.'

They left Morgan making two mugs of coffee and went back into the office where Claire and Abigail had set themselves up at desks with their laptops.

CHAPTER SEVENTEEN

Morgan followed Amy to the blue room, which was actually painted an unusual shade of pink, and took a seat at the large table. There was a huge television screen, and a camera which kept moving around the room. Abigail, Claire and Wendy filed in, followed by everyone else and took a seat. The room was mirrored on the television screen. Morgan hated seeing herself on camera, she rarely took selfies, so every time it swung around to her she bowed her head, feeling self-conscious. Her hair was frizzy after her shower; there was only a hose in the ladies' changing rooms to dry your hair with and it didn't give it the smooth, straightened effect she preferred. Ben came in last, walked straight over to the camera and turned it off. Her shoulders dropped, and she breathed a sigh of relief.

'No need to scare ourselves with that, it's bad enough looking at you all in the flesh.'

Laughter filled the room. Amy had her laptop open and was logging herself onto the system.

'For the benefit of today's new additions to the team I'll do a brief introduction.' He went around the room and let each person speak.

'This all started yesterday with the report of a suicide out at a house called Lake View, on Easdale Road. PC Brookes was the first officer on scene. It all looked pretty straightforward. I attended and didn't think anything was untoward. I should have looked closer, but I didn't. I hold my hands up and the lesson has been learned; no matter how long you've been doing this job never take anything at face value.

'The body was taken to the RLI, where the pathologist wasn't happy that this was a straightforward suicide. Fast forward to today: unable to trace Olivia Potter's husband or children despite ANPR markers being placed on his car and the reg being circulated countywide, there were no sightings. Morgan went back to the house this morning and found the grim discovery in the cellar.'

Amy brought up the crime scene photos and slowly clicked through them. Claire sat forward and Abigail let out a small gasp. Morgan didn't need to look at them: they were forever imprinted in her mind in all their bloody, technicolour glory. Not wanting anyone to think her squeamish, she stared at the screen. It didn't look real in the photographs. The carnage and devastation didn't hit home like it had in that cellar which smelt of damp and blood.

'Saul Potter, and his youngest daughter Beatrix, were both dead on the scene, massive blunt-force injuries to their heads. Both faces were covered with white cloths. Bronte, the older sister, was found by Morgan barely alive and rushed to the RLI, where she is currently undergoing surgery to remove a clot from her brain. The safe word when speaking to staff for updates is "campervan".'

Everyone scribbled it down onto their notepads, and Morgan did the same.

Ben continued talking and, listening to his soothing voice, her eyes began to feel heavy and she had to pinch her arm under the table to wake herself up. She'd never live it down if she fell asleep in her first murder investigation briefing. Ben would send her back down to response faster than she'd come up. But she was tired, beyond tired. Her dad's late-night visit had disrupted her routine. The usual feeling of swallowing a lead ball settled in her stomach at the thought of him being in her apartment. She didn't trust him; she was sure he wouldn't have left like he'd promised and he'd have eaten what meagre food she had in her fridge.

She felt a sharp dig in the side of her stomach and glanced around to see Amy staring at her. With a start she realised her attention had drifted off and she mouthed 'sorry'. She brought her attention back to Ben, who was staring at her, and she realised he'd asked her a question. Only she had no idea what.

'Sorry, can you repeat that?'

'I said that you were going to be responsible for CCTV enquiries at surrounding properties to Lake View. Is that okay?'

'Yes, Sarge.'

'Good, the houses along that stretch of Easdale Road are expensive. Which means they're likely to have good security systems with a possibility of CCTV. At least that's what I'm hoping for. It would be a bit of a miracle if they all worked or had cameras which covered the road.

'Amy, you are in charge of background checks on the family. I've already asked Intel to do the more in-depth stuff. I want you to get me their Facebook accounts, friends list, et cetera.'

Morgan raised her hand.

'Yes.'

'Teenagers don't really do Facebook any more. They tend to go for Snapchat or Instagram; TikTok is very popular at the moment.'

Ben repeated. 'Tick tock, what the hell is that?'

She shrugged. 'Not too sure, I just know a lot of them use it.'

Abigail nodded. 'She's right, studies show it's more our age group that use Facebook.'

'Well then, there's a good chance Saul and Olivia are on Facebook. Just see what you can find. Wendy, can you give us an update on the evidence at the scene?'

Wendy began to talk them through what she'd found.

When she'd finished Claire asked, 'What can you tell me about the cloths covering their faces?'

'That's a good question. When something of this calibre, using extreme violence, happens, it often leads to a family member or someone close to the family. Ashamed because of what they've done, they cover the faces. You said there are doubts surrounding

Olivia Potter's hanging; is there any chance this is a murder–suicide? Maybe she killed her family then killed herself. Or could the surviving daughter have done it then injured herself, but not severely enough to kill herself? What about Saul, is there any chance he could have done it?'

Ben shook his head. 'All very real possibilities, but no, Saul, isn't the perpetrator. I agree we need to look into Olivia a little more closely, and Bronte; we need to see if either of them had motive. I do agree it's either one of them or someone close to the family. There were no signs of forced entry, so whoever it was had a key and knew them all well enough to get into the house without arousing their suspicion.'

Abigail asked, 'Who found the first body?'

Morgan answered. 'Bronte's boyfriend. He rang it in when he found Olivia hanging in the front garden when he arrived to see Bronte.'

Claire and Abigail both said, 'Bingo,' in unison.

Ben looked at Amy.

'Let's bring him in: what's his name?'

Morgan spoke before Amy had chance to look at the incident report on the laptop.

'Harrison Wright. He'd been at work though; he had a bag of KFC with him when he arrived.'

'How do you know he'd been at work?'

'He had a red shirt with KFC embroidered on the left side of it and he told me he had.'

Amy grinned at Ben. 'Ah, well, it's not him then, is it, if he clearly has an alibi like wearing a uniform.'

Ben frowned at her. 'Bring him in for a friendly chat. I want to speak to him myself. Let him stew for a bit in interview room A. Claire, Abigail, should we go and take a look at the scene? I'd appreciate your advice as to whether we can get the bodies moved to the mortuary.'

Morgan realised Amy was being sarcastic and scolded herself for being so gullible. Ben ended the briefing; everyone had a set of tasks to complete. She was no longer sleepy: she was determined to show everyone how capable she was of carrying out the role she'd been given. She would scour the CCTV footage for any clues no matter how long it took her.

CHAPTER EIGHTEEN

Ben pulled his vibrating phone out of his pocket; it had been going on and off the whole time during the briefing. It was Declan. 'What's up?'

'I'm ready to continue with Olivia Potter's post-mortem. I want to get hers out of the way before the rest of her family arrive. Are you free now?'

'Can you give me an hour? I have two visitors from the Murder Investigation Team and was going to take them to the scene. I can show them then come to you.'

A loud crash in the background almost deafened Ben.

Declan shouted down his ear, *'For the love of God, can you just be careful with that, it's evidence. If you smash my samples to smithereens you can go in front of the judge and explain what happened to them.'*

He lowered his voice. *'I swear to God I have the clumsiest assistant you could find. Lovely, hardworking, but a bloody liability. One of these days she's going to end up dropping someone's brain all over the tiled floor. I'll hold on for you then, come straight down.'*

Another loud noise and more cursing from Declan filled the air then the line went dead.

Ben looked at Morgan, who was tugging on a coat.

'Hey, you can come with me if you want. While I'm showing the bosses the crime scene you can go check for CCTV at the nearest properties.'

He didn't tell her that once he was done, they were going to watch a post-mortem. She looked a bit overwhelmed and he didn't want her running back down to Mads begging to go back on response after only being on his team for an hour. He did wonder if this was taking the whole throwing someone in at the deep end a touch too far. Then decided that if he was giving her a baptism of fire he may as well get the worst of it over within the first twenty-four hours. After everything she'd been through, she would relish the simplicity of tasks such as house to house or CCTV enquiries.

She didn't answer but nodded her head. That would do for him. He'd go easy on her tomorrow if she was struggling.

He was heading out of the station with Claire, Abigail and Morgan when his phone vibrated again. It was a message from Amy this time.

Who knew you'd have an entourage of women at your disposal, never thought I'd see the day ☺

Holding the door open, he waited for everyone to leave then turned and gave her the finger. As the door shut, he heard her loud laughter following them down the corridor and couldn't help but smile.

*

He drove to the house with Morgan. Abigail and Claire followed in the car behind.

'Ben, do you think a woman could have done this? I just don't see either Olivia or Bronte resorting to this level. I've read a lot about violent crime and it doesn't sit right with me.'

He glanced at her. 'I agree, personally I think our suspect when we apprehend them will be male, but we can't rule anything out. Harrison is looking viable at the moment. He knew where there was a key to the property, and he's in and out all the time. A familiar face that they all seemed to trust.'

'He's so young though.'

'Is there a minimum age for murder? We'll see what happens when he's interviewed. If he has a cast-iron alibi then we're back to square one.'

There was a PCSO guarding the entrance to the drive and a man in a flashy blue BMW was talking to him, blocking his entrance. He didn't look as if he was about to move.

'What's this clown doing?'

Ben beeped his horn, but the car still didn't move. The PCSO looked towards him and shrugged. Ben got out of his car, striding over to the BMW, about to drag whoever was being an arsehole out of the driver's door.

'Is there a problem here?'

Ben recognised Jamie Stone, the editor of the local paper, but wouldn't give him the pleasure of acknowledging him.

'Yes, there is. I want to go up to the house.'

Ben crossed his arms. 'Why? Are you family or a close friend?'

'No, I'm the editor of—'

'I know who you are. You say you're not anything to do with the family who live here?'

'No, I'm a reporter. The public have a right to know—'

He cut him off again. 'A right to know what exactly?'

'About this?' he finished lamely.

'At this moment in time, neither the public nor you have the right to know anything. This is an ongoing case which has nothing to do with you. So, I suggest you move your car out of my way before I arrest you for police obstruction. As the editor of that piece of crap paper, you should know that all enquiries into serious incidents are run through the constabulary press office.' He lowered his voice. 'So, piss off out of my sight before I arrest you.'

'Hey, you can't talk to me like that.' He radiated a sense of anger towards Ben.

Ben turned and waved Morgan over. 'Have you got your cuffs on you and pepper spray?'

She jumped out of the car, a pair of cuffs dangling from her fingers and began to walk towards him.

Ben leant in and grabbed the guy's collar.

'You can't do this. It's police brutality, I'll have you reported.'

A red mist fell over Ben's eyes and if it hadn't been for the voice of DCI Claire Williams behind him he'd have dragged the arrogant man out of his car and cuffed him. He let go of his collar and stepped back.

'What is the problem here? You are indeed obstructing a police officer, so I'm going to ask you kindly to move your vehicle. I like to think I'm a reasonable person.' She looked at the Apple Watch on her wrist. 'So I'll give you ten seconds and then I'll be arresting you.' She smiled the whole time she spoke, and the driver of the car shook his head.

'You wait, you won't hear the last of this. I'm good friends with the Crime Commissioner.'

'Are you really, then you'll already have his number. I won't need to give it to you. Ten, nine, eight, seven.'

The car engine roared into life and he drove away, the whole time shaking his head.

Ben stared at Claire; his opinion of her had just gone from okay to awesome.

'What a prick; I wouldn't worry about the Crime Commissioner either.'

'Why?'

'I'm married to him.' She winked at Ben, who laughed.

They drove up to the house where another PCSO was standing outside the front door, holding the pale green crime scene booklet for them to sign in.

Ben opened the boot of his car. A box containing every piece of protective clothing they needed was filled to the brim. Carrying a small box of blue nitrile gloves, Morgan got out of the car, a reluctant but determined expression on her face. But he decided she didn't need to go back in: he wasn't that mean.

'Do you want to sign us in, Morgan? Then you can go and make a start on the CCTV enquiries at the houses nearest.'

He wasn't sure, but he thought he heard her release the breath she must have been holding in.

She took the booklet from the PCSO and wrote their names, asking for Claire and Abigail's surnames as they filed into the property one by one. Ben led the way.

Reaching the closed door to the cellar, he turned and announced, 'It's bad.'

Claire nodded. 'They usually are, at least the ones we attend. They are much worse than a fight that's gone horribly wrong.'

He knew that, of course, but he felt it was his duty to warn them. He would have said it to a seasoned detective with thirty years' experience. Opening the door, he began to make the descent into the now floodlit cellar, which smelt distinctly worse than it had a couple of hours ago.

At the bottom of the steps, Ben stood to one side, letting Claire and Abigail take in the scene for themselves. They stared at the masses of dark red blood spatters covering the walls and ceiling.

Claire stepped towards the bodies. She pointed to the ceiling.

'Impact spatter is significant, along with the cast-off spatter. Every time the assailant swung the weapon back it flung blood onto the nearby surfaces. I think the victims were already lying down when they were attacked.'

Wendy came down the cellar steps. 'I think so, too; the blood-stains are circular, which suggests a ninety-degree angle of impact.'

Standing behind Saul, she motioned swinging her arms backwards then forwards.

Claire bent down to look at the bodies then turned to Ben.

'Do we know where the cloths are from which covered the faces? Did they match any of the towels or bedding in the rest of the house, cleaning cloths, that kind of thing?'

Wendy nodded. 'I found some white rags in a bucket under the sink and think they may be a match. Forensics will tell us for definite.'

Ben spoke. 'Whoever did this had intimate knowledge of the house if they knew where to find the cloths without disturbing anything.'

Abigail began to look around the shelving and boxes in the cellar. 'The weapon hasn't been located yet?'

'No, once the bodies have been moved the search team are going to do a full sweep of the house and grounds.'

Claire snapped photos on her phone of the bodies in situ, and then the surroundings. 'Please can you show me where the body was found yesterday? I'm happy for these two to be moved if you're finished processing them.'

'Yes, of course.' He led them back upstairs and out into the garden, where a late September sun was shining.

Abigail sighed. 'Such a beautiful house and gardens. On first impressions you'd think they had everything made. What a terrible ending for a lovely family.'

Claire shook her head. 'Yes, tragic. However we can't assume they were a lovely family. You know that, Abi. For all we know they were up to their necks in debt and beat their children. Until the financial checks and witness statements have been taken from friends and colleagues, we actually know nothing about them.'

Abi turned to Ben and shrugged. 'Sorry, I know. It seems on the surface they were.'

Morgan was walking back up the drive.

Ben waved her over. 'How did you get on?'

'The house nearest was empty. I caught the cleaner from the house a little further along just before she left. She said that they do have CCTV, but she has no access to the system. The owners will be home after seven. She also said that the Potters were a lovely family. Olivia wasn't working. She told her employer that she'd sold her hair and beauty business in Manchester for a nice profit so they could move down here. Saul had sold his construction company as well, so they were financially stable. Saul was in the process of starting another company, but there had been a few complications.'

Ben smiled. 'Brilliant, I love it. You can always rely on hired help to have the low-down on everyone. I take it she didn't see anything yesterday?'

She shook her head. 'No, but she said she did notice Saul's car parked in a lay-by yesterday afternoon. It's near another house she cleans on Fell Road.'

'Brilliant, I'll get a patrol to check it out.'

He walked back to the car, asking for a control to check for Saul Potter's car in the location they'd just been given. His head was pounding. He needed a drink, probably water, but he hated the stuff so it would be a large coffee with an extra shot and probably a large, gooey, sticky cake to go with it. Sitting inside, he watched as Morgan pointed to the tree where Olivia Potter had been found hanging and wondered if she really had killed her family before killing herself. They would find out soon enough; next stop after the nearest coffee shop was the mortuary.

CHAPTER NINETEEN

Ben had left Claire and Abigail at the house. He parked on the double-yellow lines outside The Coffee Pot, a small café that brewed the best coffee this side of the Lake District. Morgan had gone in clutching the £10 note he'd passed to her. The hazards were flashing, and he didn't care if a parking warden busted him; he was desperate and, judging by the look of exhaustion on Morgan's face, so was she. She came out a few minutes later with two large, pale pink coffee cups and a paper bag. She got in and he had to stop himself from snatching the cake from her fingers, he was so jittery and desperate for something sweet. As she passed him the bag, he peered inside. 'There's only one sticky toffee muffin in here.'

'I know, it's all they had.'

Gingerly he held the bag in her direction, hoping she said no. She shook her head.

'You sure?'

'Yes, I'm good. Thanks.'

He didn't give her a chance to change her mind. Ripping the wrapper off, he took a huge bite and half of the ginormous muffin disappeared into his mouth. He knew she was staring at him in horror and he didn't care. Swallowing it down with a swig of coffee, he pushed the rest of it in.

'What?'

'Nothing, I'm impressed.'

'Guy's got to eat, I'm starving. You must be hungry; it's been a long day.'

'I don't know what I am, ready for a large glass of wine or a shot of vodka perhaps. Not food though. I'm not ready for that. So where are we going, back to the station?'

He didn't usually care what anyone thought of him, whether he was heartless or worked them too hard. But for some reason it bothered him if she thought he wasn't being fair to her, and the fact that he hadn't told her his plans to take her to Olivia Potter's post-mortem was making him feel bad.

'I need to go back to the RLI.'

Morgan perked up. 'Are we going to see Bronte? Has she woken up?'

The look of joyous expectation on her face made him feel even worse.

'Unfortunately, no. I have to go see the pathologist. He wants me present at the post-mortem for Olivia Potter, which kind of means you're going to have to be there too.'

He focused on the road ahead, forcing himself not to steal another glance at her face. He didn't know what effect she was having on him; he couldn't decide if he was treating her as if she was his daughter or whether he was ready for a new friendship like he had with Amy.

'Oh, I haven't been to one of those yet.' Her voice was quieter than before, and he realised she was probably feeling a little daunted at the thought of it.

'To be fair, there's not much call for it. Back in the day when I first joined it was a standard thing, everyone had to attend one. Now it tends to be only for suspicious deaths and murders. I'd let you wait it out in the car, but it can take a few hours—'

She cut him off. 'I don't need to wait in the car; before we continue can we get one thing straight?'

He nodded.

'I might be new, young, inexperienced or whatever you want to call me. But, I'm not some delicate flower. I'm here to learn. You said I could work alongside your team. I only want to do that if you treat me like a part of it, not some outsider who's along for the ride to only do the easy jobs.'

He'd just taken the biggest gulp of coffee he could while driving and began to choke on it as he tried not to laugh. When he'd finished coughing, and was sure he wasn't about to crash the car, he turned to her.

'Sorry. From now on you get the shit jobs like the rest of them without so much as a care whether you're happy or not. I can be an utter bastard; ask Amy, she'll vouch for me. That's good, I'm glad we've cleared that up; in that case you can scribe for me at the post-mortem.'

'Thanks.' Her reply was curt.

The drive took a while because the traffic in Lancaster was getting busy, but at last the hospital came into view.

'I've hardly been here before in my life, now it's my third visit since yesterday. Don't we have a hospital a little bit closer than this?'

'Yes, we do, but it doesn't perform post-mortems. Our hands are kind of tied.'

He drove around to the rear of the nondescript building with a small blue sign that read 'Mortuary'.

'You know I always thought a mortuary would be a bit scarier than this.'

'It's not scary at all, more sad than anything else.'

Parking in one of the two spaces, they got out of the car. Ben pushed the doorbell and they waited for someone to come and let them in.

The door was opened by the same woman who'd let Morgan in with Olivia yesterday. She was in blue scrubs, her pink hair tied back in a tight ponytail. Ben flashed his warrant card. 'Declan is expecting me.'

'He is; just so you know he's in a bit of an arsy mood.'

She turned and led them inside. Ben looked at Morgan and shrugged his shoulders. He'd never seen her before and never in the years he'd worked with Declan had anyone described him that way. He guessed this was who Declan had been complaining about on the phone. She didn't look much older than Morgan; maybe they'd both acquired new protégés at the same time.

His phone began to vibrate, and he recognised Amy's number. 'Amy.'

'Good news, a patrol located the missing car. It was parked in a lay-by on Fell Road.'

'Brilliant, I want a full forensic lift.'

'I already told them that.' She ended the call.

He smiled at Morgan. 'Saul's car has been found; hopefully there might be something of evidential value inside it.'

CHAPTER TWENTY

Greg Barker sat in his office scrolling through the newsfeeds on his phone. He needed to know what was happening at the Potters' house on Easdale Road. He felt bad; the police would no doubt want to talk to him once they discovered that until a few months ago he and Saul had almost been business partners on a new housing development on the outskirts of Rydal. It never took off and hadn't ended particularly well; there had been an argument more than once, over the money needed to get it off the ground, planning delays and Olivia. Greg had got a little too close to her, been a shoulder to cry on when things had been tough between her and Saul. And now they were all dead. The girls too. How did that even happen? What was certain, though, was that once Jamie Stone learned the connection, he would make sure fingers were pointing towards him. It was ridiculous. Had he put too much strain on Saul with the stress of starting this new project and he'd flipped, killing them all? He hoped not. That would be an unfortunate chain of events. But at the end of the day not his problem, until the police came knocking and decided that it was. Considering an entire family had been wiped out, there was very little information about it. He picked up the phone. It rang for some time before the voice on the other end answered.

'*Hello.*' The voice was curt.

'It's me, I need a favour.'

'*Like what? I'm busy now; in fact I'm up to my neck in it to be precise.*'

'What happened on Easdale Road?'

'*You know I can't tell you anything.*'

'Yes, I think that you can. I don't want all the details, just what's happening with the investigation. Where's it going?'

There was a slight pause. *'It's nothing to do with me, I'm not working it. They gave the student I trained the placement in CID. I've been waiting a couple of years for that opportunity and I was passed over for an inexperienced woman whose face must be a better fit than mine.'*

Greg could almost taste the bitterness it was so palpable.

'You have access to the logs though, and must know people who are.'

'Why are you bothered anyway?'

'Why wouldn't I be, I knew them.'

'I'll see what I can find out and get back to you. Don't phone again.'

The line went dead. He swore under his breath. That arsehole Dan needed to be a bit nicer; he knew Greg could make his life a misery if he decided to.

The door opened and in walked Mary Jane with five women who looked even older than her, and she was ancient. Mary Jane stopped when she saw him.

'Sorry, Mayor, I didn't realise you were in. Just giving the newest recruits to the Friends of Rydal Falls a tour of the building before our meeting.'

He didn't tell her that, if she'd bothered to look, the sliding sign on the door said 'engaged'. Instead he pushed the feeling of heaviness in his stomach caused by the Potters' deaths to the bottom and stood up. Crossing the room towards the group, he held out his hand and shook each of theirs in turn. Except for Jamie, he never failed at winning someone over; usually women and men fell at his feet eager to please. And judging by the pink cheeks and huge smiles, his track record wasn't going to be broken today.

Greg began his usual spiel about his role as mayor and they listened intently, hanging on to his every word. He liked it when his audience was this interested in what he had to say. When he'd finished he asked, 'Any questions?'

'Yes, what are you going to do about that terrible murder on Easdale Road? It's terrifying to think that an entire family have been killed in their beds.'

He looked at the woman who spoke. It seemed she knew more about it than he did.

'I'm afraid that's not my problem to sort out.'

Her eyes narrowed and he realised that he'd been a bit abrupt.

'What I mean is, I have no jurisdiction over that terrible tragedy. It's the police who are dealing with it. It has nothing to do with my role as mayor.'

'We're not safe in our own houses though, are we?'

Mary Jane looked aghast. 'Bertha, come on, this is hardly the time or place, is it? That awful mess is not the mayor's concern.'

Bertha's eyes narrowed to thin slits as she stared at him. 'Well it should be. This concerns everyone. I don't want to wake up with a killer standing at the bottom of my bed ready to knock my block off and steal my family jewels.'

The other women turned to look at her and began whispering amongst themselves. Greg wanted to tell Bertha to get the fuck out of his office; instead he smiled at her.

'I'll be working with the police to ensure there are more patrols. I don't think there's some madman breaking into houses and killing people. I mean we live in rural Cumbria. The worst crimes around here are sheep rustling and thefts from farm outbuildings. There's very little violent crime, especially against strangers.'

'Well that makes it even worse then, because it could have been someone they knew, someone we all know.'

A burning sensation began to rise up his throat and he wanted to grab hold of Bertha and throw her out of his office before she said another word.

Mary Jane had gently taken hold of the woman's arm and was tugging her out into the corridor.

'Come on, ladies, the mayor is a very busy man. I think it's time for coffee and cake.'

A murmur of excitement went around the small group and they all began to push to get out of the door.

As she left Bertha turned to him. 'Well I hope they catch whoever did this before anyone else dies.'

Then they were gone, and he flopped back into the ancient chair, loosening his tie. What the hell had just happened? He'd be damned if he knew, but whatever it was it had left him with a bitter taste in his mouth and a strong desire to throttle Bertha if he ever set eyes on her again.

CHAPTER TWENTY-ONE

Even in death, Olivia Potter was hauntingly beautiful. Her sun-kissed skin and perfectly shaded silver-blonde hair made her look much younger than her age of forty-six. Morgan stared at her body, knowing it would be hard to ever shake the image of her lying on the cold steel table with the huge Y-shaped incision running from her collarbones to her pubic bone. Butterflies filled her stomach and she focused on the dead woman's face. She looked healthy, almost like she was in a deep sleep and not dead. Morgan would bet that she was the type of woman to go running and do yoga. She tried to wrap her head around the fact that just yesterday, this woman had been a living, breathing person with a beautiful family and home. She would have woken up and eaten breakfast. Morgan hoped she had enjoyed it; she'd probably had a better breakfast than Morgan usually made.

She didn't want to watch as Declan worked fast on the autopsy, his assistant following his orders, but at the same time, she couldn't look away. He began to fold the skin, fat and muscles away, exposing Olivia's internal organs. As he began to explain that he was cutting into the sac surrounding the heart, Morgan looked away. In between taking notes she focused back on Olivia Potter's face and began counting the smattering of freckles across the bridge of her nose, anything to keep her mind busy and not thinking about what Declan was doing.

When Declan walked Ben and Morgan out of the pathology lab, after he'd finally completed the post-mortem, the churning of her stomach finally began to subside. Fingernail scrapings had been taken along with other forensic samples, to send off for analysis. Morgan was feeling a bit out of it; thankfully she hadn't been sick or fainted, though, which had been her biggest fear. She wanted to prove to Ben that she could hack everything he threw at her, and then some. She was, however, exhausted, and wanted to go home for a long soak in the bath with a very large alcoholic beverage of some kind.

'I messed up big time yesterday, Declan.'

This statement from Ben brought her back to the present; he sounded disappointed with himself.

'I took it on face value it was a straightforward suicide.'

'And usually they are, Ben. How often have you come across something of this calibre? In Grasmere no less.'

Ben let out a heavy sigh. 'Never.'

'Exactly. You weren't to know about the bruising around the neck. It was hidden by the rope. You had no way of knowing that the trauma to the back of the tongue had been caused until we did the PM, or even that the rest of her family were dead.'

Morgan kept quiet; none of this was anything to do with her. She wanted to say that not all of her family were dead, but she didn't. Declan let them out and they walked to Ben's car.

'Should we go and check on Bronte while we're here?'

He shook his head. 'Not now, it's been a long day and Amy texted me before the post-mortem to remind me about speaking to Harrison. I need to go back and see what he has to say for himself. He's had a good few hours to stew now.'

'Are you allowed to keep him that long when he's not under arrest?'

'Yes, because he hasn't been detained. He's free to go whenever he wants. For all I know he might have already walked out.'

'But you don't think he has.'

He shook his head. 'Not if he's got any common sense. His girlfriend is on life support and her family are dead. He discovered her mum's body, so I should think he'll want to cooperate fully unless he has something to hide.'

'And do you think he does? I don't know how I feel about him. He was so distraught yesterday when I arrived on scene. He looked genuinely shocked at discovering Olivia's body. He's an excellent actor if he is.'

'I don't know, usually there's some connection between the victims and the killer. The way their faces were covered suggests it was someone who knew them, someone who didn't want to look at them after they were dead. But if that's the case, I just don't know why they staged Olivia's murder to look like a suicide.'

'Maybe she came back later than the others and he panicked? Perhaps by hanging her the killer was trying to throw us off-guard, give themselves enough time to get their act together. Sort out an alibi, get rid of any evidence that could be linked to them?'

He nodded. 'You're pretty good for a rookie, you know. I think you'll be okay at this.'

'Cheers, I appreciate that vote of confidence, Sarge.'

*

By the time they arrived back at the station it was hours after Morgan's shift had finished for the day. As they went inside, Ben looked at his watch: it was almost nine. It was also a good few hours after the end of his shift.

'There's not much for you to do now, so it's up to you. If you want to go home you can, or you can see how the CCTV enquiries are going.'

Morgan wanted to go home; she was tired and every now and again she caught the awful, lingering smell of death, which seemed to have attached itself to her. She wanted a hot bath, but wasn't sure if they'd think she was wimping out by leaving.

'I'm okay for now. How long a shift do you normally work under these circumstances?'

'Twenty-four, thirty-six, sometimes forty-eight hours with the odd kip and shower in between.'

'Oh, then I'm good.'

He nodded. 'You crack on with viewing CCTV then. There was an expensive camera around the Potters' property. The hard drive should have been seized by the search team and booked in by now. If you go and see John in the video-imaging unit he'll show you how to access them. For starters, I want to know everyone who came in and out of the property in the last forty-eight hours before they died. Then we'll go back further.'

'Fine.'

She left him and went in search of the video-imaging unit. She could do this.

John showed her to a small room with a monitor inside and how to work the equipment. Realising she needed something to eat first, she went to the canteen and got herself a coffee from the vending machine along with a couple of bars of chocolate and a flapjack. Stopping off to grab a notebook from the stationery cupboard, she went back to settle in to watch the hours of footage.

There was no recording from the external camera the day Olivia Potter's body had been found; it was all fuzzy. She made a note to get someone to check the outside camera and see if it had been tampered with. Dan was on shift tomorrow; she would email him and ask him to check for her. There was footage of the day before, though, and Morgan sat through it, her eyes brimming with tears as she watched the beautiful, seemingly happy family go about their business.

The girls had gone out to the car in the morning with backpacks on, Beatrix in her uniform, Bronte in jeans and a hoodie. The camera was very clear, and Morgan found herself leaning forward on her elbows, engrossed. Saul came rushing out of the house and got into the front seat of the car, and Olivia waved her family off from the front door. He forgot something, got back out of the car and walked back towards his wife, who he pulled close and kissed on the lips. There was no sound, but the girls were leaning out of the car windows pulling faces and shouting at their parents. Morgan's heart felt as if it was about to tear in half. How sad. This was obviously a very happy family who loved each other deeply and now they were all lying dead. Except for Bronte, but she might very well wish she was if she ever woke up. Who knows what kind of brain damage she was going to have after such a violent, vicious assault?

As the car made its way along the drive it stopped at the bottom. A figure came into view, but it was difficult to make out who it could be until they began to walk along the drive. Morgan let out a small gasp as her hand lifted to her mouth. *Surely not, why would he be there?* It took forever, but the slightly hunched, shuffling figure finally became clear on the monitor in front of her. Morgan felt the blood begin to rush into her head as her heart started pounding and her hands began to shake. It was Stan, her father; there was no mistaking him.

Pushing her chair back, she stood up and rushed to the nearest toilet, dry heaving into the toilet bowl. When she was done, she went to the sink and splashed cold water against her cheeks and ran her wrists under the tap *You're completely overreacting; so what if he was there. It doesn't mean he killed them. Does it?*

When she felt composed enough to face Ben, she stood up and went straight to his office. It was empty. There was no one in CID either, and she realised they must be talking to Harrison Wright. The best thing to do, she decided, was to go home and speak to Stan, ask him what connection he had with the Potter family. For the first time ever, she hoped he hadn't done what she'd asked and had stayed in her flat. Once she'd spoken to him, she'd approach Ben and tell him: that was the best thing to do. It made sense; there was no point dragging Stan into it unless she'd found out why he was there.

Morgan wasn't sure what to do: did she book off with the control room or did she just go home when she was tired and exhausted? Going back into Ben's office, she scribbled a note on a yellow Post-it.

Gone home. If you need me ring and I'll come straight back. No CCTV of the day Olivia was found hanging. Camera malfunctioned. Morgan.

She peeled it from the pad and stuck it to the top-left-hand corner of his computer monitor.

CHAPTER TWENTY-TWO

By the time she arrived home her stomach was a mass of knots and she had a dry lump in the back of her throat. She'd been through every scenario possible and had managed to convince herself that Stan was involved in the whole sorry mess. She'd lose her job if this was true; the shame and embarrassment would be too much to bear. Dan would love it if she was thrown out after one day working in CID. When she'd seen him earlier, he'd stared right through her, ignoring her as if she was the one who'd upset him. It didn't matter that he'd belittled her in front of most of the station at Mitch's leaving do. She'd thought they were friends and now it felt as if they were arch enemies. It didn't make any sense to her that he was being like this with her. He'd been fine when he arrived at the Potters' house the day before.

The flat was in darkness, and she prayed Stan was still there in a drunken stupor because he'd finished off the bottle of vodka she kept in the small freezer compartment and the three bottles of wine in her rack. When she opened the door to her flat, she called out, 'Stan.' Her voice fell flat; it didn't seem as if he was here. Reaching out, she flicked on the switch; the open-plan lounge and kitchen filled with light. He wasn't slumped in her chair like she'd been expecting. She looked around and felt a ball of anger fill her chest.

'The cheap, lying, stealing bastard.'

Her flat had been ransacked; every drawer and cupboard were open. Her papers and clothes were strewn everywhere. Morgan felt a surge of anger towards the man who had brought her up and done the shittiest job he could. She should have known not to trust him. She didn't know what to do. The place was a mess.

She rushed into her bedroom. 'Oh no, you *didn't*.'

But he had.

Her bedside drawer was wide open and lying on the bed was the empty black velvet box which should have contained her most prized possession: the rose gold necklace her mum had given to her. It was too much and Morgan felt hot tears begin to fall down her cheeks. She didn't care that he'd taken the emergency cash she kept in the tin in the kitchen drawer. Neither did the missing wine bottles bother her, but it hurt her that the thing she treasured most was now probably in some Cash for Gold shop, sold for twenty quid when it meant the world to her and was irreplaceable. Clutching the empty box, she felt herself begin to slide down the wall, tears of frustration and exhaustion flowing from her cheeks.

'Morgan!'

Ben's deep voice shouted from the entrance door to her flat and she wanted to curl up in a ball and die right where she was. Could this day get any worse?

'Morgan?' This time it was higher pitched, concerned. 'I'm coming in, are you here?'

She heard his footsteps as he walked around the polished wooden floorboards, taking in the mess.

Wiping her eyes with her sleeve, she stood up just as he came through the bedroom door.

'Jesus, are you okay, what's happened?'

Don't cry, don't you dare cry the voice screamed inside her head. She opened her mouth and managed to let out a sob so loud it filled the entire room. Before she could do anything, he was there, his warm arms around her holding her close and patting her back awkwardly as if he was petting a dog he was a little bit afraid of. She should have pulled away and dried the tears; instead she cried even harder.

'It's okay, let it all out, you'll feel better.'

Eventually she did pull herself away from him, and he bent down to retrieve a fallen box of tissues, handing them to her. She took one and wiped her eyes, then blew her nose.

'Better?'

She nodded.

'What's happened, have you been burgled?'

'Sort of. Stan, my dad, turned up in the early hours this morning. He was drunk and said he had nowhere to stay, so I let him in. I'm so bloody stupid. I knew he'd do this, but I felt bad. Anyway, I came home and found this. He's taken a necklace that my mum bought for me. It's all I have to remember her by. He burnt nearly all the family photos after she died. I came home from school and there was a bonfire in the back garden; he was throwing all her stuff onto it.'

'That's terrible, Morgan. Let me ring it in. We'll get CSI here.'

'No, I don't want to report it. What's the point? I just want my necklace back.'

'But you can't let him get away with this. I know he's your dad, but he's clearly an arsehole, as well as a thief.'

'I'm already a laughing stock with my shift, thanks to Dan, and if he gets wind of this it will make things even worse; the shame of being burgled by my own dad. Please, Ben, I don't want it reporting.' Her voice was higher pitched than usual and she'd spoken so fast she wondered if he'd listen to her plea or call rank.

He sighed. 'It's up to you, I won't say anything if you don't want me to.'

She shook her head.

'Can I help you clean up then? Although if you saw the state of my house it's debatable just how skilled at cleaning I am.'

She laughed. 'No, I don't need any help. Thanks. Did you want me?'

'I just wanted to let you know that we've let Harrison go; his alibi checks out and he seems like a good kid. A patrol found Saul

Potter's car in a lay-by along the road the cleaner you spoke to informed you about. It's been forensically lifted and taken to be examined. I also wanted to make sure I hadn't pushed you too hard.'

'Back to square one then with suspects? That's good news about the car, maybe something will show up inside that links back to the killer. Oh and no, you definitely didn't. I'm enjoying this, at least I think I am.'

He laughed. 'Yes, for the time being. Harrison is still on my list. I'll leave you to it then.'

She walked him to the door.

He turned to her. 'If Stan comes back you have to ring the police or me; do not let him inside. You don't deserve to be treated like this.'

He left and she closed the door behind him, turning the key in the lock. He might be grumpy, but he seemed to care underneath that rough exterior and she liked him even more.

*

Morgan ran the bath she'd been promising herself all day. She put in some lavender oil, pink Himalayan and Epsom salts, then lit the scented pink candle she kept in the bathroom. A little self-love ritual that her mum used to swear by might make her feel a little better after the crappy two days she'd had. She was unable, though, to pour herself the wine to go with it because her idiot dad had taken everything that contained a drop of alcohol. Instead, she made herself a cup of lavender and lemon tea. The kids at school had taunted her, saying her mum was a witch; Morgan didn't see it that way. Her mum had been a herbalist; she grew and collected an assortment of herbs which she would then use to make teas and bath oils to soothe worries, aches and pains. There was nothing remotely witchy about her, apart from her love of nature and natural healing.

As Morgan slipped into the steaming water, which smelt divine, she closed her eyes and lay back. Inhaling the lavender, she felt her entire body begin to relax. By the time she'd sipped her tea and let the water go lukewarm she was ready to get dressed in a pair of fresh cotton pyjamas and climb into bed. She'd picked the drawers up and tidied her bedroom so it didn't look as if it had ever been violated.

Climbing under the soft duvet, she waited for sleep to come. She didn't think about the long, horrific day she'd had; instead she lay breathing deeply in through her nose and out through her mouth, counting backwards from one hundred until she let out a gentle snore.

CHAPTER TWENTY-THREE

Morgan's eyes opened wide. She didn't need to look at the clock; she knew it was 04.25. The same time she had woken every morning without fail since her mum had died. She missed her more than she could put into words. They'd had a loving friendship that had soothed her soul. It wasn't a typical mother/daughter relationship; Sylvia had treated her like an equal and not a child. She had never forced her to do homework, insisting that life skills were far more important and weekends were spent gardening, cooking, making batches of herbal teas. Looking back she realised she'd been lucky to have had Sylvia in her life, even though it had only been for the first eighteen years, and she wouldn't change a second of it. Morgan wished her mum could have talked to her about what was happening in her life instead of deciding to end it.

Considering she'd climbed into her bed just before midnight, she felt refreshed for a change. Perhaps it was the tears she'd cried at the loss of her treasured necklace or the soothing bath she'd had before bed. Whatever it was, she felt better and ready to face the day. Getting up, she began cleaning up the rest of the mess Stan had left behind. It wasn't as bad as it had first looked last night. It must have seemed worse because she'd been exhausted. Once everything was put back and tidy again, she set about making herself a pot of coffee and some toast. If yesterday was anything to go by, today would be just as long and busy, if not worse.

The smell of burning toast brought her rushing back to the kitchen. She'd forgotten to turn the dial down. Her dad always ate his toast burnt to a crisp. The thought of him made her fingers curl into tight fists. The shock of seeing the mess he'd left had totally thrown her, and she'd forgotten the reason she'd rushed home to see him, to ask him what he'd been doing at the Potters' house the day before they were murdered. Crap. She needed to tell Ben, who would probably say it was a conflict of interest and she couldn't work on the investigation because of it. If that happened, she would be furious, not to mention mortified. If she thought Dan's teasing was bad now, it would only get worse once he found out what a disaster the last twenty-four hours as a detective had been.

Taking her coffee and toast, she sat at the small table where she took her laptop out of her bag. As she ate her toast she wondered how many murders there had been in the area. Probably not that many; it was a quiet town in the Lakes after all. She set about searching the internet, which brought up a couple of recent murders in Keswick and Kendal. Neither victims were killed by strangers: it had been partners or ex-partners. Perhaps Ben was right: the killer was someone who knew the family. But who would bear such a grudge against them to do this? It was too horrific to comprehend. Morgan stared at her laptop screen. There at the bottom of the page was a grainy black-and-white photograph of a house that looked familiar, with the heading 'Family Slain'. She clicked on it and waited for the article to load. It was from the local paper, which had changed its name since this had been written, a whole forty-five years ago. As it loaded, she sucked in her breath and didn't let go.

It was the Potters' house, she was positive.

An entire family were murdered in their beds at a rural property on Easdale Road last night. The O'Brien family only moved in recently after renovating the property which had lain empty for years. Jason O'Brien and his wife, Jennifer, were found bludgeoned to death in their double bed. Their two daughters, Anna and Melissa, were found in their bedrooms. Police have cordoned off the entire area and are asking for anyone who may have seen anything to come forward.

Morgan let out a gasp; how could this happen *twice* in the same house? She began to scribble notes on a pad.

Did the O'Briens' killer get caught?
Where are the case files?
Did the Potters know about the murders when they bought the house?
Is there any connection between both families?
Did Stan also know the O'Briens?

A sinking feeling in her stomach as she reread the last line made her feel like throwing up. Pushing away the remainder of her breakfast, she rushed and got dressed. She needed to get to work now, log on to the computer and try to find any information on this case.

As she drove into the car park, she had to look on the bright side; at least coming to work this early had its benefits. There was no need to worry about a parking space, she had her pick. By the time the early shift started in another hour they'd be fighting to get parked. It felt strange not getting her kit on and going into the downstairs report writing room, where the response staff worked before going out on patrol. Instead, she carried on upstairs to the CID office.

It was empty. She looked at the desks: some of them had photos on, mugs with sarcastic slogans on them containing days-old tea or coffee. While waiting for the computer to load she gathered all the mugs and took them out to the small kitchen, where she tipped their offending contents out and filled the sink with steaming hot water and a good dollop of washing-up liquid. Leaving them to soak, she went back and sat down at the desk in the corner of the room, nearest the back wall. There were no personal items on it so she didn't feel as if she was encroaching on someone's work space. She logged on to the computer and began searching. She tried everything, but nothing brought any results up. How on earth was she supposed to find anything out? It was ridiculous. All the systems were new and the records didn't go back very long. Even the older systems, which ironically were much easier to navigate, only went back to the nineties.

Frustrated, she gave up and went to wash the cups. Her arms elbow deep in soapy water, she didn't hear Ben, who came up the back stairs.

'Do you ever sleep?'

She screeched. 'Jesus, you scared me.'

'I don't look that bad, or do I?'

She laughed. 'Not really, I never heard you. I found something really interesting, but I'm stuck. I've tried everything to bring up the old case files.'

'How far back are you trying to go?'

'Forty-five years.'

'Forty-five years, blimey. What's that, 1974?'

'Close, 1975.'

'Then you'll need to get Kenny, the caretaker, to let you into the attic. There are boxes and boxes of files up there from before everything was digitized. Even if it was on the computer, it's so long ago there wouldn't be any need for it to be on the system. What is it?'

'The Potters aren't the only family to die in that house. I was searching the internet before I came to work and found an article from the local paper about a family who'd recently moved in who were all killed.'

Ben stared at her. 'You're having me on, is this some kind of joke?'

She shook her head. 'Why would I joke about something so horrible?'

He shrugged. 'I guess I've been working with Amy too long; she would.'

They went back into the office and she pulled up the report she'd discovered earlier, sending it to the printer.

'Where's the printer?'

'Down the corridor; we share one with admin.'

Morgan rushed to go and retrieve it. She came back in and handed it to Ben, who read it.

'I didn't know anything about this. Shit, as if this wasn't complicated enough, now this. Did they catch anyone? Because it might give us a lead to go on. They'd possibly have been released to go back and kill the next family. Christ, it's like a Michael Myers movie and we're smack bang in the middle of it.'

He loosened the tie he'd not long put on. Taking the printout from her, he began to walk towards his office.

'Sarge, there's something else.'

He turned to look at her.

'My dad.' Morgan felt her throat constrict it felt so dry. She couldn't get the words out; they were stuck in the back of her throat, giving her a bad taste.

Ben waited for her to continue.

She let out a small cough.

'Stan, he... He was on the CCTV I viewed from the Potters' front camera the day before the murders. He's talking to Saul Potter then he comes up the drive.'

'What happened next?'

'I didn't carry on watching. I was so shocked I paused the recording and went home to confront him. That's when I discovered he'd ransacked my flat.'

She couldn't look him in the eyes. It was better to get it over with now. She could re-join her shift. They'd be coming in soon – maybe she could tell them she hated CID; it was not for her. She didn't have to let them know she'd been kicked out so soon.

'This kind of complicates things, doesn't it?' she asked him.

He reached out, taking hold of her arm and led her into his office, closing the door behind him.

'Have a seat.'

She sat down, still unable to look him in the eyes.

'Thank you for your honesty. This can't have been easy for you but you're doing the right thing. I'm going to have to look into him now, and he's going to have to be brought in for questioning. We might be able to rule him out. What's he do for a living?'

'You mean when he's not being an alcoholic petty thief? Not much. He's a bit of an odd-job man, does a spot of gardening. Nothing much.'

'So, there's a good chance he might have worked for the Potters.'

'Possibly, he wouldn't have a reason to be at their house if he didn't know them. Look, I know this is awkward, but I really don't want to go back down to response. I want to stay involved; I want to catch whoever has done this.'

Ben began to rub his hand across his chin. 'No, I don't want to lose you. I think I can swing it that you stay up here. Look, you're the one who has brought this to my attention. You could have tampered with the evidence or neglected to tell me the man was related to you. You haven't, though; you've been open and honest, which I really appreciate. What will happen is that you will continue working up here, but I'm going to task you with looking into the first set of murders. You will probably have to spend hours up in the attic looking for the files. I'll clear it all with the DCI. Tom will agree to it. Is that okay with you? Right, you'd better show me this footage before I speak to the boss.'

'Yes, of course. Thank you.' She wanted to high five him, but wasn't sure if he'd appreciate it.

She led him to the CCTV viewing room she'd run from last night. The light was still on but the television monitor had turned itself off. When she pressed the button it fired to life, still paused on the zoomed-in image of Stan. Her throat felt dry as she reached forward to press rewind. Ben watched in silence.

She left him to it and went to see if she could find Dan.

She saw him going into the locker room and followed, calling, 'Dan.'

He turned to face her.

'Morgan.'

'I sent you an email. I just wanted to mention it.'

'Very good, what about?'

The hairs on the back of her neck bristled. He was being so offhand with her and she didn't get why.

'To ask if you could check the external camera outside the Potters' front door and see if it had been tampered with.'

He put his hands in his pockets.

'And why can't you?'

A burning rage began to build inside her chest at his attitude.

'Because I'm tied up with enquiries for a murder investigation. Look, Dan, I don't understand why you're acting this way. I thought we were all a team, that we worked for the same side. I guess I got that bit wrong, but you get paid to do this stuff, so why don't you do it instead of acting as if it's all some huge inconvenience?'

He shook his head and turned his back on her. Morgan stormed off before she completely lost her temper with him. At least she could continue to work with CID. She was mortified about the possibility that Stan could be involved, but she had a new feeling inside her. A steely determination that she could do this. She would research the first murders and prove to Ben and Dan that she had what it takes to make a first-class detective.

CHAPTER TWENTY-FOUR

Ben watched the man on the screen as he shuffled up to the house. He waited until Morgan left the small room and was out of earshot. Then he phoned Tom to tell him they had a suspect that needed bringing in. He explained about Morgan and was relieved when Tom agreed with his plan.

'Do you think this Stan Brookes is good for the murders, Ben?'

'Too early to say, boss, but he's as good a place to start looking as anywhere. He knows the property, and knew the Potters.'

Ben ended the call. He looked at his watch and grinned. Not a bad start to the day and it wasn't even seven a.m. He couldn't wait to get his hands on Stan Brookes. He was looking forward to teaching him about family values and not stealing from his daughter. Of course, he wouldn't let Morgan know about any of that. He didn't want to embarrass her more than she already was with such a loser for a father. Up to now she was having the shittiest first week anyone had probably ever encountered and yet here she was at the crack of dawn ready to work a long shift for no extra pay and not much thanks.

Amy was right: he might be getting soft in his old age but to him it felt as if she'd woken him up from a three-year sleep. Since Cindy had died, he'd been on autopilot. His home life was a cycle of eat, drink too much and sleep. Work was… well, it was work. He'd plodded on doing his best to solve crimes and getting the results without putting too much effort in. Olivia Potter's death had changed all of that; his sloppiness had resulted in Bronte Potter almost dying in a cellar next to the bodies of her family. He should have been more thorough and now he would have to shoulder the burden of that for the rest of his life: another thing to add to his list of things he'd well and truly fucked up. There might be an internal investigation into the mistakes made at accepting her death as a suicide, but until that happened and he got kicked off the job he was going to do his best to bring the killer in and get justice for the Potter family. Amy could accompany him to the post-mortems of Saul and Beatrix; he would send Morgan to the hospital for an update on Bronte. He'd noticed that she'd been desperate to go and visit yesterday.

He wondered what Claire Williams would think when he rang her with an update on the latest news. Hopefully she'd be happy with Morgan continuing to work on researching the early murders. If not he'd be willing to put up a fight to keep her; he felt as if he owed her something now that her life had gone so spectacularly to shit.

By the time the office began to fill up Ben was raring to go. Morgan was nowhere to be seen and he assumed she'd gone on the hunt for the old case files. He didn't know anything about that case or who had worked it. Once she had some information to go on he might be able to put her in contact with the original detectives, although they'd have been retired a long time. Fingers crossed they were still alive. He decided that now was as good a time as any for a briefing. Claire and Abigail were both here; he could update them all at the same time and save repeating himself.

'Right then, should we go to the blue room for an update?'

He led the way.

The blue room was in a strange place tucked away on the first floor down a tiny corridor. There was a staircase before the corridor which led up to the attic; Kenny was coming down it.

'Morning, Kenny, is Morgan up there?'

'If you mean that young lass, then yep. Who did she upset to get that job? Have you been up there lately? It's a shithole with boxes strewn everywhere not to mention pigeon crap. Rather her than me.'

Ben wondered if he should get someone to help her try and locate the files, but he didn't have anyone to spare. She was on her own for now, though he doubted she'd care.

He sat down at the oval table and waited for everyone else to join him so he could give them the latest updates.

CHAPTER TWENTY-FIVE

Morgan stared at the haphazard stacks of cardboard boxes strewn around the attic space and groaned. She could hear the gentle cooing in the eaves from the pigeons and there were feathers and droppings everywhere. Not exactly the most hygienic place she could spend her morning. A shiver wracked her entire body; there were large holes in the roof where the wind was blowing through and it was freezing. She closed her eyes. *You can do this. Isn't it what you want? How many rookies get this kind of chance, Morgan? Woman up, all you have to do is find a stack of boxes with the right year on.*

Her eyes opened. Dan hadn't spoken to her properly since she'd been given the chance to work alongside Ben. Considering he'd been her tutor, he was such a child at times; he had the mentality of a seventeen-year-old. She wasn't going to give up this opportunity for anyone, let alone him. Ben had said they needed extra bodies, and she knew if she said she couldn't cope he'd replace her in a heartbeat, and there was no way she was giving him a chance to make her look as if she couldn't do the job. She'd show them all he had made the right decision by giving her this opportunity.

An hour later, she found a box labelled 'O'Brien Murders Unsolved'. A whoop of delight escaped her lips. It didn't matter that it was right at the bottom of the biggest stack of boxes in there. She began to lift each box off and restack them into a pile, wondering how many cold cases there were up here. Maybe if she did a good job on the O'Briens, Ben would let her work them. It would be fascinating and a good way to learn. When the last box was there for her to inspect, she felt a small tingle of excitement: this box was much bigger than the others. But of course, there was an entire investigation of a murdered family in here. It was heavy as well.

She dragged it to the stairs where there was more light than in the shadowy attic space. Sitting on the top step she lifted the lid off, and inside were stacks of files, some brown paper evidence bags and a folder. She pulled the smaller folder out and opened it and a stack of photos fluttered to the floor. Staring down at them, she realised she was looking at some of the worst crime scene photographs she'd ever seen. All the books, documentaries, films and television shows she'd watched over the years were nothing compared to these small photos of complete violence and devastation.

Footsteps coming up the stairs startled her from the daze she was in and her heart skipped a beat.

Ben appeared around the bend, almost running into her.

'Christ, you scared me sitting there like some little ghost; you look as white as one.'

She held up a stack of photos. 'I found the box.'

He looked over her shoulder at the stacks of boxes. 'You deserve a medal, well done. I'll help you carry it down, although I don't want that box in the office; it might have some kind of pigeon disease. You can take it in the empty room that used to belong to CCTV operators. In fact, it might be a good idea to turn that into an office for you. You're going to need lots of room to go through this without getting it mixed up with the current investigation. I'll ask Kenny to set you a computer up and a couple of whiteboards.'

'Thanks, that will be great.' She stood up, wiping her hands on her trousers. She felt grimy and wanted to shower, change into fresh clothes. These were minging now. She placed the photos back inside the box and he stooped down to pick it up.

'I can manage, you know.'

'I know you can, but it's the least I can do after you've spent all this time up here looking for it.'

She followed him down to the first floor; he walked past the CID office and carried on towards the far end. Pushing open a door with a 'Knock Before Entering' sign, she followed him inside a large, empty room. There was a bank of old television monitors along one wall with a set of controls to operate the cameras.

'Wow, those are practically antiques.'

Ben laughed. 'Careful, I remember when they installed them. They were top of the range back then.'

'Oh. I didn't mean…'

'It's okay, Morgan, I'm older than you and I'm joking.'

He placed the box on a large table. 'What do you think, are you okay to work from here? I'm only down the corridor. I'll be popping in to check where you're at with everything and you can come see me whenever you want.'

'Yeah, I mean it's a bit outdated but it's good. Who'd have thought I'd end up with my own office so soon after joining your team? I don't know whether to take it as a compliment or an insult.'

He reached out and took hold of her arm. 'It's definitely not an insult. I'm not trying to get rid of you. I want you on my side, but things have got a little complicated and I can't jeopardise any ongoing investigations. You understand that, don't you?'

'Of course I do. Have you picked him up yet?'

'Not yet. Officers are on their way to a couple of locations where there might have been sightings of him.'

She nodded, finding it difficult to find the right words to say. Her entire life had been turned upside down in three days. How she wished she had someone to go home to and talk about it with. She didn't even have a cat. Her last boyfriend had dumped her when she'd told him she'd been offered a place in the police, which told her all she needed to know about his character. What she'd give, though, to have someone to share a bottle of wine with and tell them what a rubbish day she'd had. Although she was fiercely independent she still liked company.

Ben left her to go and find Kenny, and she went in search of the cleaners' cupboard. There was no way she was going to spend ten hours or more a day cooped up in an office which hadn't been dusted or cleaned in at least three maybe four years.

By the time Ben came back in an hour later with two mugs of coffee, the whole place smelt of lemon and beeswax. She had dragged everything out, polished, hoovered and put everything she needed into a more suitable workspace. She'd even cleaned the grime from the windows so daylight could filter through. Kenny had set her a computer up and was in the process of drilling two huge whiteboards onto the wall.

'Wow, I like what you've done with the place. It's like the television show where they get sixty minutes to makeover a house.'

She grinned. 'Do you watch much daytime TV then?'

'God, no. Absolutely not, I've seen it advertised.'

Amy followed him in. 'That's an outright lie. He watches all the crap when he's on lates, then spends the next eight hours filling anyone in who might listen to him. He's right, though, you've done a good job. I might move down here. It's better than our office and not full of people.'

'No, you're not. You need to be back there so I can see where we are and what we're up to.'

She shook her head. 'He doesn't trust us, do you, boss?'

'No, you've been doing this too long. You know how to flaunt the rules. Morgan is new, she's keen, and I imagine she wants to get jobs done and learn how to do stuff. A bit like you ten years ago, before you decided you didn't like working for a living.'

Amy walked out tutting and Morgan felt awkward. She didn't want to be responsible for bad feeling between the pair of them. Ben must have noticed the concern on her face.

'Don't worry, we're always like this. She'll be in a mood for around six minutes then snap out of it. Kenny, can you give us a couple of minutes?'

'I'm done now.' Kenny turned to Morgan. 'If you need anything else you know where to find me.' He left them to it.

'I just wanted you to know an arrest team is being assembled to go bring your dad in. He's supposed to be on his way to Ann Street. I'll be the arresting officer and interview him.'

'Oh, I thought he was a person of interest not a suspect.'

He paused. 'He is, but he's also the last person up to now to have seen them alive, and you said yourself when he turned up he had some scratches. The DCI has decided it's better to bring him in under the Police and Criminal Evidence Act and get him questioned. He's only going to clam up and ask for a solicitor if we ask him in for a friendly chat. We might as well do it in one shot before he has a chance to. Oh, I was wondering if you'd mind going to visit Bronte. See what the hospital staff say about her condition?'

'Yes, of course and thanks for telling me.'

She sat down. Her knees felt like they couldn't hold her up. He passed her the mug of coffee and she gripped it tight, afraid her fingers were going to start trembling and she'd spill it everywhere.

He opened his mouth to say something else, thought better of it and left her alone.

CHAPTER TWENTY-SIX

The hospital was a hive of activity. It was far bigger than the one nearest to Rydal Falls and the corridors went on forever. Morgan followed the signs to ICU. She wasn't sure if she'd be allowed in or not and had a feeling that Ben had sent her here to get her out of the way while Stan was being brought in. As she reached the entrance to the unit she bumped into the ward manager, who was coming out.

'I'm Morgan Brookes from Cumbria Constabulary.' The woman looked at her as if to say 'and?'. Morgan wasn't sure if she was to call herself detective or officer. 'PC Morgan Brookes; is it possible to visit Bronte Potter?'

'She's already got a visitor and a police guard, but I suppose you can for a short time. It's only two visitors at a time and usually just close relatives.'

'Thanks, where is she?'

'Through the double doors. There's a private room at the end. You can't miss the copper sitting in the doorway.'

Morgan covered her hands in sanitiser and pushed open the door. The sound was almost deafening from all the different machines and monitors beeping and buzzing. She saw the room at the end and yes, there was a huge copper sitting on a chair: one she recognised.

She smiled at Tony, who waved back, and crossed towards him, trying not to stare at the patients hooked up to life support machines and their visitors. He stood up, opening the door for her and she stepped inside.

Bronte still looked tiny in the huge bed. Harrison was sitting on a chair next to the bed holding her frail hand in his. He didn't even look her way.

'Hi, Harrison, how are you doing?'

'How do you think I'm doing?'

Tony pointed to the door, and she followed him out of the room.

'I know he's upset, but he's an arrogant little tosser. There's not much point even trying to make conversation with him. I've given up.'

'He's had a bit of a shock. It can't be good. How long has he been here?'

'They only let him stop two hours and then they kick him out. Don't think the nurses like him either. Anyway, look at you, why are you in your scruffs?'

'On attachment with CID.'

'No, you're not.'

She nodded.

'But, you're only just out of company. I thought we had to have two years' experience?'

She shrugged. 'No idea, I think they're short-staffed and I was probably in the right place at the right time to be honest.'

'Well I never, what do you think, do you like it?'

Morgan stared at him. It was a simple enough question yet she couldn't answer because she had no idea if she did. It was all a bit of a blur; she didn't know where she fit in yet or if she ever would.

'It's early days and long hours. Has Bronte woken up at all?'

'Nope, not even twitched.'

'Thanks, I'll go speak to the nurse.'

She turned around to walk the short distance to the desk.

'Sorry to bother you, I'm PC Morgan Brookes. Could you give me an update on Bronte?'

The nurse looked up from her paperwork. She studied her for a couple of seconds. Morgan noticed the name on her ID card read 'Kimberley'.

'What's the password?'

For a moment her mind went blank; she knew it, of course she did. 'Caravan.'

The nurse laughed. 'Close enough, but it's "campervan". The surgeon is happy with the surgery to remove the clot; the swelling has gone down significantly. He's going to start reducing the anaesthetic later on and see how she reacts; hopefully she'll wake up. But there's no knowing how serious the brain damage is at the moment.'

'So, you think she could wake up? That's great news.'

The nurse smiled. 'We're hoping she'll wake up, but we won't know until we try and she might have complete amnesia.'

'She won't remember what happened?'

'I'd say there's a good chance she won't, but you never know. She's young and obviously very strong-willed or she wouldn't have survived this long.'

'Thank you. I'll pass it on to my boss.'

She went back to the room where Harrison was still staring at Bronte.

Tony shrugged.

'Harrison, I need to have a chat with you about some stuff. How about we go grab a coffee and you can have a breather?'

He shook his head, still not making eye contact with her.

'Please, it's important. It's me, Morgan, I was first on scene when you called 999. You can either speak to me or I'll have to take you back to the station and I think you've spent long enough in there already.'

He stared at her and a flicker of recognition sparked in his eyes. Grunting, he pushed his chair back and stood up. She took this as a good sign.

'You lead the way, I have no idea where the café is.'

He walked out, head bent and hands tucked into his pockets. She followed him.

*

He led her to the stairs and down to the next floor, where he strode towards what she hoped was the dining room. Down here was much quieter than upstairs; it was darker as well. A cold shiver ran down her spine; they were pretty secluded down here. What if he was the killer? He could turn around, drag her into a side room and no one would know about it.

Then she spied the dome of the CCTV camera on the ceiling in front of them; well, hopefully someone would. The air filled with the sound of clanging cutlery and loud voices. Harrison turned left into the wide opening and she followed suit. Considering the corridor had been so deserted, the café wasn't: it was almost full to capacity. They got in the queue and she picked up a slice of peppermint crunch cake.

'Are you hungry, get what you want. I'll pay.'

He shook his head. 'Just a Coke, please.'

'You go find us a table and I'll get them.'

He began walking towards an empty table in the corner of the room and she picked up another cake, just in case he changed his mind. She remembered what it was like to be a teenager all too well; you never accepted anything an adult offered. God, was that what she was now: an adult? It was strange to think that she was probably only five or six years older than him, yet here she was trying to solve the murder of his girlfriend's family. And what if it had been Stan? How would she explain that to the angry teenager sitting staring into space?

Using her phone, she paid for the drinks and cakes, and carried the tray over to where Harrison was chewing at the skin on the side of his thumb. She sat opposite him, passed him his can of pop and nudged the slice of millionaire's shortbread his way. She sipped her latte and took a bite of her peppermint crunch, taking her time to eat, not wanting to rush him. His stomach growled so loud she heard it.

'You might not have much of an appetite, but you need to keep your strength up for Bronte's sake. She's going to want to see you when she wakes up, and it's no good if you've made yourself ill and can't be here, is it?'

'Suppose so.' He picked up the cake and demolished it in three bites.

'Can I get you something else, sandwich, hot meal?'

'No, thanks. So, what do you want with me? I already told that arsy copper yesterday it wasn't me. I was in that stuffy room for hours when I should have been here, by Bronte. I had nothing to do with any of this.'

That was two people who'd called Ben arsy; why did she not see it?

'I guess I wanted a chat. I want to know more about the family. How long they've lived in the house, when they bought it, general stuff. I don't want to try and blame you, I'm just trying to piece together what their lives were like. Can we talk about that?'

Sipping his drink, he stared at her for a few moments then nodded. 'Yeah, we can.'

'Good. Thank you, Harrison.'

She retrieved the large hardback notebook, which she'd taken from the stationery cupboard, out of her handbag and placed it on the table in front of her, so he could see what she was writing. There was so much at stake here and for the first time she got the feeling that she was way in over her depth. Was she able to do this? She gave herself a mental shake. Of course she was, and Ben must think so also or he wouldn't have wanted her on the team. Either way she knew she had a huge responsibility and there was only one thing she could do: prove to everyone that she could do this on her own.

CHAPTER TWENTY-SEVEN

Morgan gave it a few more minutes then picked up her pen.

'Do you know when the Potters moved into the house?'

'End of March, beginning of April.'

'This year?'

'Yes, it had been empty for ages before they bought it. Saul had builders in for weeks plastering the walls and fitting new bathrooms. They lived in a caravan while the work was done.'

'On site?'

He nodded.

'That must have been a squeeze. How did they all get on?'

Harrison let out a huge sigh. 'Amazing, they got on really well. I mean Bronte and Bea argued a lot, but sisters do that. My sisters practically kill each other on a daily basis.'

She laughed. 'I'm an only child. I used to long for a sibling to argue with. Have you been going out with Bronte a long time?'

'Almost a year, so yeah that's a pretty long time for me. I really like her though, she's fun and not afraid to take risks. Bea was a lot quieter. She read a lot, didn't go out much. Every time I went around she had her nose in a book. Not like me, I hate reading. I'm more of an Xbox or Netflix fan.'

'How did Saul and Olivia seem to you, were they happy?'

'I think so, they were always hugging and kissing. A bit embarrassing really, but it was their house, you know.'

'Did you get along with them?'

He nodded. 'I liked them, they were pretty cool. Well apart from the kissing.' His breath caught in the back of his throat and he lifted his hand to wipe his eyes. 'It's hard to imagine that I won't see them again. I just can't believe they're gone, all of them.'

'Not all of them, Bronte is still here and fighting to stay by the looks of things.'

He sniffed.

'Did they have lots of friends come to the house? They seemed like a pretty popular couple.'

'Some. I know Saul's friend came around a lot. They were talking about starting a new business, but it fell through. I think he had a bit of a thing for Olivia; he was always wanting to hang around with her.'

'Did Bronte know about this? Did she ever talk about him?'

'She said she saw more of him than her own dad, but she was only messing.'

'What's his name?'

'Gary or Greg, not sure to be honest. His surname might have been Ryder or Barker;. I didn't take much notice of him. He's a bit of a creep if you ask me.'

'That's okay, I'll find that out. Thanks, you've been very helpful. Oh, one last thing, did you know about the previous murders at the house, or did Bronte?'

He looked confused. 'What previous murders?'

'A family was murdered in that same house back in the seventies.'

His eyes almost popped out of his head they opened so wide, and his mouth fell open. 'No way, you're having me on.'

'I'm being serious.'

'No, I mean no. How did they die? Are you sure it's the same house?'

'I have very few details on it to be honest, but I'm serious.'

He sat back in his chair and put his arms behind his head. 'That's crazy, wait till Bronte finds out they moved into the Amityville Horror House. She'll go insane.' He stopped talking.

'One last thing, do you know this man?' She showed him a still from the home security footage of Stan.

He nodded. 'He did some gardening for Saul, a couple of times a week in the summer.'

'When was the last time you saw him?'

Harrison shrugged. 'Couldn't say.'

Morgan closed her notebook and slipped it back into her bag. She stood up. 'Thanks, Harrison. I'll leave you be now. Do you need a lift home?'

'No, thank you, I have my car.'

She left him still sitting at the table digesting the shocking information she'd just shared with him.

Stan had a legitimate reason to be at the Potters' house if he did odd jobs for them. He could have fallen and scratched his face. As much as she disliked him and his lousy parenting, she didn't think he would stoop to murder, no matter how desperate he was. Gary or Greg was definitely another person that needed speaking to. What did it mean if he was there more than Saul? Was he sleeping with Olivia? Did that give him motive to kill her and her family?

She was keen to get back to pass this onto Ben and to get back to working on the cold case in her new office.

CHAPTER TWENTY-EIGHT

Morgan parked in the only empty space outside the front of the station in the visitors' car park and hoped no one noticed. There was an older woman sitting in the car beside her; her red-rimmed eyes were brimming with unshed tears. Her hair, which had started the day in a French pleat, was almost loose, more strands of hair dangling on her shoulders than were pinned up. Her knuckles were white she was gripping the steering wheel so hard. Unsure what to do, Morgan tried to catch her attention. The woman's gaze never wavered or looked in her direction she was so fixed on the front of the police station.

Morgan let out a sigh. She couldn't ignore her despite knowing full well she should continue inside and leave her to it. Dan would have dragged her away; his favourite saying was 'Don't make eye contact with anyone unless you have to.' Morgan had never been able to get her head around his coldness at times. She'd joined the police to help people.

Getting out of her car, she slammed the door; the woman's gaze never faltered. Morgan knocked on the glass and saw her shoulders jerk at the sudden noise.

Her head finally turned.

'Are you okay?'

She just stared at her as if in a complete daze.

Morgan shouted again through the glass. 'Are you okay, can I help you with anything?' She tugged the lanyard from underneath her shirt, holding her warrant card up so she could see she was a police officer and not some random person.

The woman's head moved from side to side. Then she turned back to continue staring at the front doors. Morgan shrugged; some people didn't want help. Huge black clouds were rolling in from the top of the patchwork, bracken-covered slopes of Skiddaw which overlooked the valley Rydal Falls had been built in. Having no jacket, she hurried towards the entrance. Lake District weather was temperamental and it had its own unique system which often defied the Met Office. She almost made it inside when she heard a car door slam behind her. Pausing, she turned around. The dishevelled woman was rushing towards her.

'Wait, are you a police officer?'

'Yes. Can I help you?'

She shrugged. 'Probably not, I just needed to talk to someone about what's happening.'

'With what?'

And then the tears began to flow, silent at first as she blinked furiously to hold them back, but it was as if the dam had been broken and a loud heart-wrenching sob erupted from the woman, startling Morgan. A huge rain drop landed on Morgan's nose, followed by a succession of them, getting heavier by the second. She gently took hold of the woman's arm, leading her inside the building, but not before both of them were damp. As they stepped inside, the heavens opened and the loud drumming of the rain as it rattled against the glass made her difficult to understand.

Brenda came out of the front office to see what was happening. She pointed towards one of the side rooms. Morgan led the woman across towards it. As the door swung inwards, Brenda mouthed 'Are you okay?' She nodded, for now they were, pointing to a seat. The woman sat down and buried her head in her hands; tears were still flowing.

'Brenda, would you get...?' She realised she had no idea who she was talking to. 'What's your name?'

'Helen, Helen Taylor.'

'Could you please get Helen a cup of tea?'

She disappeared and Morgan waited for Helen to compose herself. There was a box of tissues on the table, and she pulled a handful out, passing them to her.

'Thank you, I'm sorry.'

'No need to apologise, but do you want to tell me what's wrong?' She expected her to say her husband had been cheating on her and taken all her money or her partner had beaten her. She never expected what came out.

'I don't know where to begin. My family, they're dead. I've lost them and I didn't even get to say goodbye.'

'Helen, who are your family?' she asked, but already knew the answer. Entire families dying wasn't a regular occurrence around here.

'My daughter, Olivia, the children – oh God, my beautiful grandchildren – and Saul.'

Morgan reached out, clasping her hand in hers. 'I'm so sorry for your loss, Helen. I know how upset you must be, but Bronte is still okay, isn't she?' She wondered if the girl had died and she hadn't been notified.

'How do you know Bronte? Yes, she's on life support, but she may as well be dead. Her poor head. When I spoke to the doctor on the phone he said she'd suffered possible life-changing injuries. She is such a pretty, clever thing. Her everything has been stolen from her and I don't know what to do.'

Morgan wished with all her heart that Dan was here beside her. He was pretty good at dealing with distraught relatives, his lack of empathy making him give calm, sensible advice. All Morgan wanted to do was to bawl along with the poor woman whose entire life had been ripped to pieces. Ben would be even better; he'd had years of experience. The door opened and Brenda came in with two steaming mugs of tea and a couple of packets of sugar. She put them on the table.

'Thank you, please could you ring Ben or Amy? Anyone from upstairs will do.'

She nodded and left them.

'I know some things; I need to tell someone about them. Can I talk to you?'

'Of course, I was the officer who found your family, Helen. I was first on scene for Olivia, then Saul and the girls. I found Bronte and called for the ambulance and I'm now investigating their murders.'

There was silence between them as Helen picked up the mug of tea and began to sip it. Morgan didn't interrupt her, but waited for her to speak.

After dabbing her eyes and blowing her nose, Helen looked at her.

'I'm sorry, I'm a mess. I've done nothing but cry since I found out.'

'Have you been to visit Bronte? That might help. I'm sure she'd love a cuddle from her...' she paused, not sure whether the well-spoken woman would be a grandma or nanna.

'Nannie, that's what the girls call me. I'm not old enough to be a grandma, horrible thought.'

Morgan smiled. She had no idea how old Helen Taylor was, but she imagined the day before she found out her family had been brutally murdered she'd looked a lot younger and less haggard than she did now.

Helen stared at Morgan, making her feel like squirming.

'You found them? You're so young, that must have been a terrible shock for you too.'

She nodded. 'It was my first day on independent patrol.'

'You poor girl, thank you. I'm glad it was you, you seem like a nice person.'

Morgan squeezed Helen's hand. 'Did you want to tell me something? We desperately want to find out who did this and if you know something that might help the investigation...'

'I loved her very much despite our differences. Do you get on with your mum?'

She decided that honesty was the best policy. 'Yes, I did, I loved her very much. She died when I was eighteen.'

'Oh my dear, then I'm sorry too.'

'Thank you, I still miss her. It's hard not being able to ring her when everything is going wrong or right. Did you and Olivia have a rocky relationship then?'

Helen let out a small laugh. 'Something like that. I'm afraid I used to stick my nose in a little too much. Not to be awful, I thought I was helping. Olivia hated being told what to do, a bit like her father. I should have kept quiet, but I couldn't. It was too much this time, too blatant.'

'What was?' Morgan was sitting straight, wondering what she was going to be told.

'Her lack of morals, her disregard for other people's feelings. The fact that she cared about herself a lot more than those beautiful girls or Saul.'

Every image Morgan had of Olivia Potter had just been blown into pieces. In her mind she had pictured her as a wholesome family woman who doted on her children and husband, and now she had just been told the woman could possibly have been a narcissist.

'My daughter was having an affair. It wasn't the first by any means; I have no idea how Saul put up with her wretched behaviour. He was a far better man than she deserved.'

'You mean she was involved with another man until a few days ago? Did Saul know about it?'

Helen nodded. 'Poor man, he did. He came to me a few days before, asking what he should do. He said he couldn't take any more.'

A shiver ran down Morgan's spine. 'What advice did you give to him?'

'To sort it out for good, to stop letting her walk all over him. To tell her to leave, get out of his house. I mean she's my flesh and blood, but I didn't condone her carrying on like that. I'm terrified he took my words to heart and killed them all. How would I ever live with myself?' Her voice broke; it was barely a whisper.

Fresh tears began to trickle from her eyes.

'Helen, we don't believe that Saul killed his family. His injuries were as severe as everyone else's, and there was no evidence at the scene to suggest that was a possibility. We believe he was killed.'

'Then what about my daughter? Did she kill them in a fit of rage and kill herself because she couldn't live with what she'd done?'

Morgan didn't know; it was a possibility. Where was Ben or Amy? She stared towards the door, realising that no one was coming to help her out. She was going to have to sort this out herself.

'Do you know who she was seeing, Helen? We'll need to speak to them urgently.'

'I'm sorry, she never told me names. I heard a rumour he was a councillor, but you know what this place is like. For all I know it could have been the postman or the gardener.'

Morgan's heart almost jumped from her chest at the mention of the gardener.

'Did they have a regular gardener, do you know?' Her fingers were crossed under the table. She was hoping they employed another gardener.

'Yes, they did. I'm not accusing him though, he's a bit too old and I shouldn't imagine he had anything about him that Olivia would find attractive. She liked wealthy, powerful men and I think he's a bit of a drinker. You can tell them, can't you?'

Morgan stopped herself from responding. 'Do you know his name?'

'Stan, he seems like a nice enough man and Saul had a soft spot for him. Saul was such a good man; he was a very loyal man, which is why he probably put up with Olivia all these years. He doted on those girls.'

'Saul seemed like a good guy.'

'He was.' She sniffed.

'What about the girls, did they get on well with their mum and dad?'

'Bea is an angel, such a quiet girl. She always has her head in a book. She rarely argues with either Saul or Olivia. I can't say the same for Bronte. She's very much like her mum. Feisty and likes the boys far more than she should. I don't know what to do?' Her eyes pleaded with Morgan's for answers she couldn't give.

'Why don't you go and visit Bronte? It might make you feel better to see her and it will be lovely for her to know you're there. The only visitors she's had are the police and Harrison.'

Helen shook her head and blew her nose. 'Dear God, this is a complete mess.' She stood up. 'Thank you for being so kind. I needed to get that off my chest. I can't say I feel better, but I feel as if a load has been lifted. You'll let me know, won't you, if you arrest someone? I don't care what time of day or night it is. I can't sleep anyway. I think you're right. I'll go and visit my granddaughter. She needs me more than ever.'

Morgan passed her notebook and pen across the table.

'Of course I will; can you give me your number?'

Helen jotted it down and Morgan stood up. She opened the door for her and followed her outside. The rain had stopped as abruptly as it had started. There was the fading remains of a rainbow over the fells and she paused for a moment to take in its beauty.

Helen Taylor lifted her hand and waved to her as she drove away, and Morgan went inside to find someone to share her latest discovery with.

*

Upstairs she passed Amy in the corridor.

'Did they find Stan?'

Amy nodded. 'Ben and Abigail are talking to him now. How's the girl?'

'Still hanging on, they're going to reduce her anaesthetic later. See if there's any reaction.'

'Ben said to let you know you can get off if you want. He said you had an early start.'

'I'm okay, thanks. I've just had an interesting conversation with Olivia Potter's mum. Apparently Olivia wasn't quite the perfect wife; she was having an affair right up until her death, which Saul knew about. Harrison also said Saul had been in the process of setting up a business with a partner that fell through: he is either called Gary or Greg.'

'That is interesting. We need to confirm who her lover was and speak to him and no, you won't be okay if you spend every spare minute here. Trust me, you need to go home and chill for a bit, everything is in hand. I'll let the boss know about the boyfriend and the business partner. You're supposed to be working the cold case, by the way. Well done, though, I'm impressed and Ben will be too when I tell him.'

Morgan didn't want to argue with her. She nodded and turned to walk back to her office. She slipped inside and grabbed the files she'd placed on the makeshift desk. She could go home and read them, make her notes ready to get started researching and tracing anyone who was involved with the original murders.

CHAPTER TWENTY-NINE

Ben kept his gaze on Stan, who was sitting opposite. Abigail was taking notes. She let Ben lead the interview.

'Did you know the O'Brien family who used to live in the Potters' house a long time ago?'

Stan nodded. 'Yes.' He kept Ben's gaze. 'I used to do a bit of gardening for them too. They were a lovely family. It was terrible what happened to them.'

'Don't you think it's a bit of a coincidence that you worked for two families who have both been murdered in that house?'

Stan slammed the palm of his hand against the table. 'I know what you're saying, what you're trying to do. I had nothing to do with either of them. I didn't do it.'

'Do what, Stan?'

Stan shook his head. 'Kill them. I liked the O'Briens and I liked the Potters even more. They were kind, decent people. I may not be a model citizen but I'm not a killer.'

His hands were waving in the air and he was very animated. Ben liked to think that he was pretty good at reading people and Stan's body language seemed to be telling the truth. He had kept a consistent rhythm of blinking the whole time. When people were lying they often kept their eyes wide and didn't blink; they also kept very still. Stan had been moving around all over the place.

Ben glanced at Abigail, who nodded once and stood up. She excused herself, leaving them alone.

'Right, Stan, you're free to go for now. We won't be pressing charges or setting any bail conditions.'

'Good, I should think so.' Stan stood up. He looked less agitated than when he'd been brought in.

'There's just one more thing. I work with your daughter, Morgan, and I happened to call at her flat last night on my way home from work. Do you know what I found?'

He shook his head; what little colour was in his cheeks left his face.

'I think you do; you ransacked your own daughter's flat after she took pity on you and let you stop there. That's a pretty bloody lowlife thing to do. Where's her necklace?'

'I don't know what you're talking about, what necklace?'

Ben stood up; he towered over him. 'The necklace you stole from her. She doesn't want to press charges, despite my advising her to do so. But unless you get that necklace back to me, I will, so you'd better go to whoever you sold it to and get it back. I'll give you twenty-four hours, and then I'll bring you in for burglary, and I can promise you this: I will give you a list of bail conditions to make your life a misery.'

He opened the door for Stan to walk out.

'Have a good evening and don't you dare go back to Morgan's.'

Stan rushed out as fast as he could.

Ben would have liked to give him a shake, but he was much older than him and he didn't want to risk him having a heart attack. He had no idea if he'd be able to get the necklace back; it might be better for him to check the second-hand shops himself than rely on Stan's good nature, which was seriously lacking in morals.

As he passed the room he'd relocated Morgan to, he pushed open the door to update her. It was in darkness and her handbag had gone. He looked at his watch: it was almost seven. He wasn't ready to call it a day yet but was glad to see she'd gone. When he went into the office Amy was mid-conversation, her phone stuck to her ear. She passed him a yellow Post-it note with a name scribbled across it: 'Gary or Greg Barker or Ryder possible business partner, and the wife had a lover – no name as yet.' She whispered, 'Ring Morgan, she said you'd want to know about it. I sent her home, she looked knackered.'

He was taken aback by this kind gesture. Amy normally didn't give a shit about anyone.

'Oh, and you don't look too hot either, you should call it a day as well.'

He waved his hand. Going into his office, he began to search for a combination of names on the intelligence system, to see if he was known to them. The business partner would be a good person to speak to.

A page loaded with a record of a person called Greg Barker with no photograph and a few lines about some dodgy dealings back in 2009. They also needed to find out the name of Olivia's lover. He wondered if the two were connected. It was a bad idea to mix sex and business.

He realised he didn't have Morgan's phone number to ask; it would have to wait until tomorrow.

He looked at the calendar on his desk and felt his heart sink. It was three years to the day that Cindy had died, and he had been too busy all day to even think about it, he realised. Deflated, he grabbed his overcoat, stuffed his phone into his pocket and left.

Too many memories began rushing back into his mind. He'd worked later than he should have that day as well, and he hadn't even needed to. When he'd gone home, she was dead, had been for some time. If he'd finished at the right time, he could have made the difference; he could have saved her life. Instead he'd failed her spectacularly and would shoulder that particular guilt the rest of his life.

He didn't say goodbye to Amy like he normally would; he went down the back stairs where he wouldn't pass anyone and have to speak to them. He wasn't in the mood for polite conversation. He needed to stop off at the supermarket and buy a bunch of white roses to put in the bathroom where he'd found her. As well as a large bottle of whisky. He'd sit on the bathroom floor and toast his dead wife, because what else could he do for her now? He'd failed her in life and was still failing her in death. A decent husband would have known what date it was and taken a nice bunch of flowers up to the cemetery to lay on her grave.

All thoughts of the Potter family were pushed from his mind as he began to wallow in the self-hatred he thought he deserved.

*

When he parked the car outside the house they'd shared, he realised he'd rather not go in there. He should have packed everything up and put it into storage after it happened. Moved to a smaller place; a flat like Morgan's would be more than sufficient for him and a lot cheaper than the mortgage on this monstrosity full of memories he'd rather forget.

Throwing his coat into the hall closet, he kicked his shoes in there too. He went into the messy kitchen with a couple of days' worth of pots stacked by the sink. He was a terrible housekeeper and always had been. Tidiness was not one of his traits; he didn't see the point when there was only him.

Taking the same small, square glass from the back of the cupboard that Cindy had left on the side of the sink that night, he grabbed the bottle of whisky and the flowers. The whole house was cloaked in a heavy feeling of sadness, or was it just him: did houses have feelings? He thought that they probably did. How could they not soak up the atmosphere of the people who resided within them?

Loosening his tie and the top two buttons of his shirt, he trudged up the steps. He often wondered if he would get to the bathroom and see it all play out again. What would he do differently if he had the chance to save her? Going into the bedroom, he unzipped his trousers and let them fall to the floor. Stepping out of them, he continued to the bathroom in his shirt, socks and boxers.

The door was closed; he always kept it closed. Pushing it open, he expected to see her there, her voluptuous, naked lifeless body in the bath. Pressing the light switch, he didn't open his eyes until the room flooded with bright light. The breath he'd been holding released when he saw it was empty, messy and no ghost of his dead wife waiting for him. He placed the flowers on the side of the bath, then sat on the floor. His back pressing against the wooden panel they'd chosen together in B&Q one rainy Sunday afternoon. He'd wanted wood, she'd wanted plastic and they'd argued there in the shop not caring who was listening, until they'd come to an agreement. He could have a wooden panel; she could choose the colour scheme and she had. He looked at the rubber-duck covered walls and smiled; they were garish and completely Cindy.

Unscrewing the cap on the bottle, he poured enough to almost fill the small glass, lifted it to his lips and swallowed it in one gulp. It burnt the back of his throat and he began to cough as it warmed up his insides. Refilling it, he held the glass up: *to you, Cindy, wherever you are. I miss you and I'm sorry I messed everything up.*

Tears flowed freely down his cheeks now; pent-up months of sadness, guilt and grief poured out of him. He drank again and again, not caring that he might pass out and end up sleeping semi-naked on the floor. All he wanted was to forget it all. The last two years he'd finished up sitting at the kitchen table, every pill from every pot lying across it in a long line. He'd stared at them, willing himself to do it. To take them one by one until he overdosed and sank into unconsciousness; every year he'd failed, waking up in the morning usually to find them strewn across the floor.

He was a lot of things, but brave enough to take his own life on his darkest days, no, he couldn't even do that.

CHAPTER THIRTY

Morgan dragged the cushions off the chair onto the floor, then she opened the file she'd brought home with her. It crossed her mind that she probably shouldn't have brought it home with her. But then again, she'd been the one to spend the best part of an hour in a pigeon-shit-filled attic searching for it. It was hers for the time being. She was in charge of looking into this case so who was going to shout at her? She had a large glass of wine and a bag of chilli Doritos, perfect supper. She also had a notebook and pen. Taking the small packet of photographs out first, she began to flick through them. They were bad, worse than the Potters' crime scene. The house looked a lot different, old-fashioned despite it being a relatively new build.

She'd done a search and found that it had been built in the early seventies. The previous house had been a tiny stone cottage that was falling to pieces. The O'Briens had bought the land, demolished the original and built their much bigger property in its place. She sipped the wine, as she studied each photo. Since her early teenage years she'd wanted to be a cop, well a detective, and had loved the US TV shows that used to play. When she'd applied to be an officer, she'd been told it would be a long, hard slog to make a detective. She hadn't even completed her first week and here she was up to her neck in violent murders and trying to solve cold cases.

She laid the photographs into what she assumed was the order they'd been taken in. A shot of the house from outside, nothing out of the ordinary, just a nice house in a peaceful part of England.

Inside the entrance hall again it looked normal, no tell-tale sign of what the photographer was about to uncover. The stairs had dark streaks on the walls, though, that went all the way to the top. There was a picture of the hallway, where the first body lay. Then a close-up of that body. It had a piece of heavily bloodstained cloth covering the face. She sat up straight, her spine rigid and stared at the photograph. The cloth looked almost identical to the ones used to cover the Potters' faces. Whoever killed the Potters knew about the O'Briens' murders and was copying their crime scene. She knew this body was a man by the striped, button-down pyjamas. One leather moccasin slipper was on the right foot; the left foot was bare, with drops of blood on it. There was a trail of blood along the wall here, as if whoever had done this had put their hands in it and smeared it along the pristine, white walls for effect. She scribbled in her notebook: *dramatic scene, blood handprints all along the white walls. Why?*

The next photograph was of a bedroom. It was painted a pale yellow and on first glance it looked as if the walls had been speckled with a dark red paint. She held the picture closer; it wasn't paint. It was blood. The next one showed the bodies of two children on the floor, their heads caved in. The same cloths covered their faces. Morgan let out a small gasp. They looked so small and helpless; what an awful way to die. She stared in horror at the images that were forever burned into her mind. How did you get used to this? she wondered, and if you did, what kind of a person did that make you? Forcing herself to put the picture down, she put that one to the side, just out of view.

The rest of the upstairs was normal or as normal as it could be considering an entire family had been murdered in cold blood. Had Jason O'Brien died trying to defend his daughters, she wondered or did the killer let him see them lying there smashed to pieces before killing him? She shuddered; it was too horrid to contemplate. More photos of the downstairs: the lounge, dining room, an office were all intact, until it got to the kitchen which was another total bloodbath. This must be Jennifer, wife and mother. Again her head was severely beaten and there was a large pool of blood on the white, tiled floor.

She glanced at the other two photos of the bodies. They were lying on thick carpet so the blood didn't look as horrific on those. It would have soaked into the pile. The tiled floors made it look as if a small lake of blood had flowed from Jennifer's head. Her face was covered like the rest of her family. Morgan found her fingers reaching up for her beloved necklace, which was her source of comfort whenever things got too much for her and realised it was gone. *Fuck you, Stan, I hope to God you choke to death on the vomit from the alcohol you bought with my necklace.*

She did the next best thing and downed the rest of the wine. She put the picture with the ones of her children and husband. Picked up her notebook and wrote *WHY?* in capital letters. Why had someone killed this family? Why had another family been killed in the same manner, and in the same house, forty-five years later? Could it be the same killer? She began scribbling furiously.

Are the families connected?
What did Jason and Saul do for a living?
Murder weapons?
Meaning of cloths on face, same material in both sets of murders?
What is the significance of the house?
Motive?
Both families had two daughters, any significance?

Picking up the photos of the house that weren't actually gory, she studied them carefully, looking for something. On the one of the landing there was a large, built-in cupboard, and the door was slightly ajar as if it hadn't been closed properly. She scanned the other photos to see if any other doors weren't shut properly. Every single one was closed; even the kitchen cupboards and drawers were shut tight. She stared at that cupboard. It was large enough for a person to hide in. The perfect place for a killer to lie in wait for their victims to come home and catch them unaware. She double-checked: all of the victims were in their nightwear, ready for bed. At their most vulnerable and unprepared for an attack.

Was that cupboard still there? She couldn't remember, and if it was, maybe they could still get evidence from it. She needed to speak to Ben. She had no doubt he would want to know about the similarities. If she was in charge she would. Grabbing her phone, she rang him, but it went straight to voicemail; instead she rang the station. No one answered in the office either, which left her with one option.

She phoned the control room at headquarters and asked for Ben's address, telling them she had an urgent file to deliver to him. They looked it up and in minutes she pulled a hoody over the top of her pyjamas, slipped on a pair of battered Nike trainers and was in the car typing his postcode into the sat nav. She was glad she'd only had the one glass of wine and not finished the bottle before she had this brainwave. It did cross her mind that it was the wine making her act so impulsively, but she dismissed it. She was on a mission to find a killer and this was important.

CHAPTER THIRTY-ONE

She parked outside the large Victorian detached house her sat nav had directed her to and nodded in admiration. It was a bit unloved for all its promise, though; the garden was overgrown and the gate looked as if it would fall to bits if you pushed it too hard. It was wedged open. She made her way up the tiled path to the front door and rang the bell. It echoed around the inside but she didn't hear footsteps. Ben's car was parked on the drive so he was home. Maybe he'd gone to bed, but it wasn't that late.

She peered through the bay window into an empty room. The only thing inside was a Chesterfield sofa. She knocked on the door, there was still no answer. Opening the letterbox, she saw a light on at the far end of the hall. He must be at the back of the house. She slipped through the side gate and walked around to the rear. This garden was huge and even more overgrown than the front. It was the perfect family home; she'd love a house like this. Renovating it would be a dream.

As she looked through the large window, she could see Ben sitting at the kitchen table., she stepped back. He had an almost empty bottle of whisky in front of him and a row of white tablets. Her heart began to race and she felt bad for intruding. No idea what was wrong with him or why he'd be looking at the pills, she hammered on the back door, he didn't answer so she knocked on the window.

His face appeared at the glass, looking out into the darkness and she realised he might not be able to see her. He must have seen something, though, because she heard his muffled voice through the glass as he shouted: 'Piss off.' Then pulled the blind down.

Morgan felt the fear inside her turn to a fiery ball of anger. How dare he? She only wanted to speak to him. She pushed the kitchen door handle; it didn't move. She had a deep-seated fear that he was going to do something stupid, so she ran around the front and tried that handle too. It didn't budge.

Unsure what to do, but knowing she'd better do something, she looked for something to throw at the window and spied a crumbling house brick. Picking it up, she raced around the back again.

'It's Morgan, open the door.'

No answer. She didn't want to ring for backup to come and help her. Ben would kill her and wouldn't thank her for the intrusion. Taking a step back, she pulled her arm back and launched it at the smallest pane of glass in the kitchen window. The sound of cracking filled the air followed by the Ben's voice.

'Are you fucking nuts?'

His face appeared at the window and she bent down to pick up a loose rock. She clutched it in her hand.

'I might well be. Let me in or I'll smash another window.'

'Go away, Morgan, before I call the police.'

'I am the police, you idiot, let me in.'

He stared at her and his face broke into a smile as he began to laugh. He moved away and she heard the back door being unlocked. He threw open the door.

'Drop the rock or you're not coming in.'

She dropped it and pushed her way inside.

'Sorry about the window, but I looked in and saw you sitting there. I got scared.'

He was bending down, trying to pick up the pieces of broken glass.

'Yeah, thanks for your concern. Who bloody tutored you by the way?'

'Dan, why?'

'He taught you to do this?'

She shrugged. 'Not really, well maybe a little. I didn't need a tutor to show me how to be a decent human being.'

'What do you want anyway? What's so important you had to break my window to get into my house? You're not some crazy stalker, are you?'

'You should be so lucky. I needed to talk to you about the case.'

'Morgan, take a look around you. Where are we?'

'At your house.'

'Correct. Therefore, that means on the rare occasion that I'm not in the station or at a crime scene then I'm off duty. Although technically my kitchen now resembles a crime scene. I need you to convince me why I shouldn't arrest you for criminal damage.'

'It was a concern for welfare, under section seventeen of PACE to save life and limb.'

He grinned at her. 'You know you're pretty good, crazy but good. I like you.'

He flopped down onto the chair, using his arm to swipe the tablets to one side. Morgan spied a dustpan and brush next to the overflowing bin and grabbed it. She began to sweep up the broken glass.

'Want a whisky? I haven't got anything to go with it, though, I drink it neat.'

She shook her head, emptied the pan full of glass shards into the bin and turned around, taking the bottle from him.

'No, thanks and you don't need any more. I'll make you a coffee.'

'What? Are you my mother?'

She ignored him, filled the kettle and began searching the cupboards for coffee and mugs. When she had two steaming mugs of strong coffee, she sat opposite him, sliding one across the table.

'No, I'm your colleague. I'd like to think we could be friends. I have no idea what's going on in your life, but I care about you so maybe you could tell me.'

They sat in silence, sipping their drinks, looking at each other. Eventually he reached across the table and patted her hand.

'That's the nicest thing anyone has said to me in a long time. Thank you, I am still pissed at you for breaking my window though.'

She laughed. 'Sorry, I'll pay for the damage.'

'No, you won't. I'm having a bad day. Cindy died three years ago tonight and I'd forgotten because I was busy and because I'm a shit husband. I wasn't going to kill myself; I haven't got the guts. I'm supposed to be on tablets for diabetes and I forget to take them.'

She felt her face begin to burn. 'I'm sorry.'

'You're forgiven. I should have opened the door, but too much alcohol on an empty stomach and feeling sorry for myself. Well, you know how it is. Anyway, what was so important you needed to speak to me about?'

'It doesn't matter, it can wait until tomorrow.'

'I'm—' He pointed to the stairs. 'Toilet, be back in a min.'

He pushed himself up and stumbled out into the hallway. She heard his heavy footsteps and began picking up discarded tablets. She looked at them and saw 'paracetamol' stamped on each one. Blimey, he'd tried to make light of it. Who was she to embarrass him further? She put them in the bin and dragged the bag out. Knotting it, she carried it outside to the wheelie bin and dropped it inside. Then she went back in and began to tidy around. Washing the mountain of pots and stacking them on the draining board, she realised he hadn't come back down and a prickle of fear ran down her spine. Ever since her mum had overdosed, she had this fear of people doing the same. Standing at the bottom of the stairs, she listened and heard a loud snore. She looked around; it wouldn't hurt her to check on him. Make sure he was okay, then she could let herself out.

She ran upstairs, following the snoring to a small bedroom at the bottom of the hall. The door was ajar and Ben lay across the top of the single bed in his shirt and boxers; the duvet was scrunched up on the floor. Picking it up, she threw it over him and left. After locking the front door and pushing the key through the letterbox, she then drove home.

He was right, everything could wait a few more hours. Before she knew it she'd be awake and back in work.

*

Exhausted, she opened the communal front door and slipped inside. She spun around as a loud crack echoed around the gardens. It sounded like a branch snapping. She couldn't see anyone it was so dark . Her heart racing, she slammed the front door shut and let herself into her flat, locking the door behind her. If Stan was hanging around she wasn't letting him in tonight; she was exhausted, even though she knew she was going to have to confront him with a whole host of questions that had been forming inside her mind since she'd spoken to Helen Taylor. Tomorrow she would find him and have the most adult conversation of their lives, but until then she was going to sleep.

CHAPTER THIRTY-TWO

She arrived at work a little later than the last two days, despite waking up at the same time. She had showered and then read through all the crime scene notes for the O'Briens. As Morgan passed the CID office, Amy shouted: 'Morgan, the boss wants to see you.'

Stepping inside, she looked towards his office, surprised to see him sitting in there so early; she thought he'd be a hungover mess. 'Why?'

'No idea, but he's in a bad mood and has been stomping around since he got in. What did you do?'

Amy had her chin resting in her hands and a big smile across her face.

'Nothing much.'

'Well, if it wasn't much, you'll be okay.'

She thought about sneaking back out, but it was too late. He'd already spied her and banged on the glass, beckoning her towards him.

'Shit.'

'Good luck; at least he's eaten most of his sausage and egg muffin. Ten minutes earlier and he'd have eaten you.'

Amy burst out laughing at her own joke, which Morgan didn't find the least bit funny. She trudged towards the closed door, and he knocked it open as she walked inside.

'I wouldn't dare not open a door to you again. These floor-to-ceiling windows are very expensive. My budget can't afford to replace them.'

He began to close his blinds so the rest of the team, who were all staring and whispering, couldn't see inside. 'Now, what was all that about last night?'

He sat down and pointed to the chair. She followed suit, clasping her hands in her lap.

'I spoke to Olivia Potter's mum yesterday, and she told me some things about Olivia which kind of threw me. Did Amy tell you?'

He nodded. 'Yeah, seems like Olivia was quite the woman. I've asked Amy to concentrate on her for now. Was that what was so important? I mean yes, it's very important but not window-smashing urgent.'

She shook her head. 'No, when I went home I was looking at the cold case photos and the victims all had similar white cloths covering their faces. Also, the pictures taken inside of the house show there was a built-in wardrobe on the landing. I wondered if it was still there, I can't remember. I think the killer could have hidden inside it and waited for them to come home.'

Ben logged onto his laptop and brought up the recent photographs. As he turned it around to face her, she could see the hall cupboard.

'Did CSI check inside it?'

'I would assume so.'

'I need to go back to the house. I want to take a look inside it. The first set of crime scene photos are far worse than these ones. I want to see if there's a possibility of any evidence inside that cupboard that we could have missed. Maybe even something from the first murders.'

'Like what? It's been, what? Forty-five years.'

'I don't know; a loft hatch to hide a weapon in. Carpet fibres, bloodstains, fingerprints.'

He picked up the phone. 'Wendy, when you did a sweep of the house did you check inside the upstairs landing cupboard? Some new information has come to light.'

He listened to what she told him then put the phone down.

'Photos were taken of the inside, nothing looked disturbed, so it was left.' He shoved the remaining piece of his muffin into his mouth. 'Come on then, let's go. If we find anything I'll get CSI to come back.'

He had his jacket on and opened the door for her. She followed him, glancing across at Amy, who made a swiping motion across her throat with her finger. Morgan shook her head, then chased after Ben, who was already on his way down the stairs.

The drive to Easdale Road was breathtaking. Morgan enjoyed looking out at the fells and lakes. A gentle breeze blew in through the open windows; neither of them spoke, but it wasn't awkward. Morgan felt as if their relationship had moved more towards friends than colleagues and she was happy with that. It seemed like the pair of them were loners with a small social circle; maybe their working together was meant to be.

The house no longer had a PCSO guarding the scene, though the blue and white crime scene tape was still fastened across the drive.

'Well if that isn't a signal for every burglar in the area to come in and ransack the place while it's empty, I don't know what is.'

He stopped the car, got out, ripped it down and screwed it up, throwing it into the back seat.

Morgan spoke. 'I thought it would still be under guard.'

'So did I, but we're short-staffed and it's secluded so the DCI decided to take the scene guard away. Big mistake if you ask me, but what would I know?'

He parked outside the front and they got out. Morgan turned to take a look at the backdrop of the fells. The lush green hills and trees that covered them soothed her nerves. Helvellyn, the third highest mountain in England, stood majestically in the background. A river ran along the end of the garden and there was a densely wooded area on the opposite bank; it was beautiful.

She let out a screech and Ben turned to see what she was screaming at. Her heart racing almost as fast as she was running, she pelted towards the tree, horror etched across her face; this couldn't be happening again. It was like she was stuck in some bad movie and she had no control over it whatsoever. Lying at the base of the same oak tree where she'd found Olivia Potter was the lifeless body of Harrison Wright.

She reached him in seconds, pressing two fingers to his neck and relief flooded over her: she could feel a pulse. There was a noose around his neck, but luckily for him the rope had snapped. She heard Ben's breathless voice as he jogged towards her; he was on the radio calling for urgent assistance. He requested an ambulance and a patrol.

'Harrison, Harrison, can you hear me?' He didn't stir. 'He's breathing, but unconscious.'

Ben relayed the information on to the control room operator. Taking his jacket off, he covered Harrison with it.

Morgan looked at Ben. 'Do you think he did this himself or someone else did it?'

'Only he can tell us that. After the events this week I don't even want to hazard a guess.'

Morgan did not know what was going on, but she'd never envisaged anything like this in her wildest dreams. She had expected her first few months to be a bit of an anti-climax after her time spent in company with Dan. He'd answered every immediate response job whenever they were on shift and every sudden death, to make sure she got plenty of experience. A feeling of overwhelming sadness filled her; how had it all gone so wrong between them? She thought they were friends and it hurt her that he had turned against her the way he had.

Feeling sorry for herself, she looked down at Harrison. Her fingers reaching out, she stroked his head. He was a teenage boy who should be thinking about nothing but having fun and what he was going to do with the rest of his life. Yet he was lying here on the ground of an empty house, lucky he was still breathing. His life would have been over before it began, just like Bea's and Bronte's. It made her so sad and even more determined to find out what had happened here. Maybe she could talk it through with Dan, tell him she hadn't asked for the attachment in CID, that it had been pure luck she'd been in the right place. It wasn't helping things that he'd been hoping for the opportunity for a long time.

They waited for what seemed like forever until finally a siren could be heard in the distance. Ben went to wait at the entrance to the drive to flag them down. The ambulance manoeuvred up the drive and parked behind Ben's car. The two paramedics got out and raced across to where they were. She stood up to let them get near him and realised one of them was Luke.

'What is it with this place? Hello again, I was here on Friday.'

She smiled. 'I remember; hello, Luke. No idea, but I wouldn't live here if they gave it to me for free.'

She stopped speaking, realising how bad it sounded. Stepping back, Morgan and Ben both watched the paramedics assess the boy. He murmured and groaned a little while they began to ask him questions and take his vital signs; the air was fraught with tension and sadness. Finally, they loaded him into the back of the ambulance.

'Where's he going?'

'Westmorland General A & E is closed at the moment, so it will be RLI.'

Morgan wondered if he'd wanted to be close to Bronte. Had he done this because he wanted to be with her or had he done it because he had a guilty conscience? A patrol arrived, Dan got out and Ben began explaining the circumstances of what had happened to Harrison. Dan didn't say much; he didn't even look Morgan's way. He couldn't ignore Ben because he was his superior, but when she turned away from him she could feel his eyes burning into the back of her head. A couple of grunts later and he reversed out of the drive to let the ambulance out, then followed it. Morgan stared after him. He walked back to where she was standing, staring after Luke. Realising he was watching her, she snapped out of it.

'Where's he going?'

'Hospital to keep an eye on Harrison. I'm not entirely convinced this was a serious attempt, although it wasn't as if he knew anyone was coming this morning to rescue him. He was either very lucky that the branch snapped, and we turned up or…'

'But he's unconscious. Or what?'

'Paramedic seemed to think he might be putting a little bit too much effort into acting as though he was. There's only a slight reddening around his neck where the rope was.'

'Oh, why would he do that?'

Ben shrugged. 'Maybe he wanted some sympathy; at the moment everything is focusing on the Potters. He was the one who found Olivia and his girlfriend was beaten half to death; no one seems too bothered about him. Maybe he was getting a little jealous of the attention they were getting. We get people like this all the time, desperate for attention, you'll see.'

Morgan stared at him. 'What, you think he did this for attention? Not because he's broken-hearted or maybe guilty.'

'Now you're thinking straight. Yes, he could quite easily have used a rope that he knew would snap. But maybe he is guilty, who knows? Come on, let's get the inside of this place checked out so you can see if your theory has some substance to it. Either way we need to find some solid evidence that might link whoever did this to the crime scene, and then we can arrest them. Then everyone can get on with their lives, the boss will sleep better, and the locals won't be terrified of going to bed. There are all sorts of rumours going around that there's a serial killer on the loose. We need to put an end to those and fast; this is Rydal Falls, not Yorkshire.'

As they reached the front door, Morgan paused for a moment and looked up at the house. Could a house be evil? Or maybe it was unlucky. She watched as Ben fished the keys from his pocket and opened the door. Her heart beating a little faster than it normally did, she tried to stay calm as she followed him inside. The photographs she'd studied last night flashed into her mind. Staring at the stairs, she took a deep breath and paused at the bottom.

'Stop! Get out now!'

She felt as if she was going to pass out as every bit of colour drained from her face. She didn't need telling twice as she retraced her footsteps out of the door.

'I'm an *idiot*, that kid threw me off-guard. We need to get suited and booted, just in case there is some evidence.'

'Is that it?'

'What do you mean?'

'Jesus, you scared me. I thought you meant there was someone in there.'

He laughed. 'Sorry, I wondered why you went white.'

They walked back to his car and began to dress in protective clothing.

Morgan couldn't help stealing a glance back at the house. She had the distinct feeling that someone was watching her and it was giving her the creeps.

CHAPTER THIRTY-THREE

Jamie Stone walked into the council meeting late, like always, and Greg lifted his arm and looked at his wristwatch like he always did whenever this happened. Jamie shrugged, held up a hand and began to squeeze in next to Jackie and Steph, the two local councillors who seemed to idolise him. Greg felt the first tiny flames of anger ignite inside his chest and he had to flex his knuckles. He didn't know why he let Jamie upset him this way, he just did. His ex-wife would say it was jealousy, that he was envious of the attention the man seemed to command whenever he walked into a room. Which was bullshit; he just didn't like the smarmy bastard. He realised everyone was staring at him, waiting for him to continue, and he didn't have a clue what he'd been talking about. He glanced down at his notepad.

'Where was I before we were rudely interrupted? Oh yes, the terrible tragedy on Easdale Road.'

Jamie spoke up. 'Terrible yes, but it wasn't some tragic accident, was it? Almost an entire family has been murdered in cold blood and the police haven't got anyone in custody for it yet. Do we know what's going on and if they have any viable suspects?'

'Not that I'm aware of, but isn't this your department? You usually know far more than me. What's the matter, have they given the media a blackout?'

He let out a laugh that echoed around the room. The look of surprise on all their faces at his reaction made him realise everyone was horrified by his words and he stopped abruptly.

'Sorry, totally inappropriate. It's not funny at all, I'm not saying it is. We need to reassure local residents that everything is okay and they're safe in their homes. There are a lot of older people who live in this area, we don't want to be scaring the living daylights out of them. Perhaps that's why the police press office isn't telling you anything, Jamie. We all know the reputation that paper you're responsible for has, sensational headlines that are never factually correct, to sell papers. I sometimes wonder how it hasn't been shut down, the amount of complaints you must get.'

Jamie leant forward on his elbows. 'Say it as it is, Greg, don't hold back, will you. How can you say people are safe in their own homes? That's rubbish, no one is safe until they have the killer behind bars. We don't know why he killed a family. Who's to say he isn't out there now choosing the next? We could have the next Yorkshire Ripper on our doorstep. It happens, Greg; just because we live in a rural county it doesn't mean people don't do stuff like that.'

Jackie spoke up. 'I thought the oldest daughter survived and was in hospital, have I missed something? Bless her, is she dead?'

Jamie turned to her. 'No, sorry. She isn't, but my source said it's not looking very promising for her. She's suffered terrible head injuries.'

'Poor girl, I taught her in year six. Such a lovely family, her younger sister was a delight to teach as well. I just can't believe it.' Jackie sniffed and Steph passed her a tissue from her handbag.

Greg wanted to tell her to snap out of it. She was always so dramatic; there was just no need. He didn't though. 'So, then what are we to do? I think we need to ask for more rural patrols and get the Chief Super to make an announcement. I'll ring him tomorrow.' He caught the eye roll Jamie gave to Steph.

'Right, well, has anyone got any other business? No? Let's call it a day.' He stood up, eager to get out of the room away from them all. They knew nothing, he knew nothing. He wanted to leave before Jamie cornered him and almost made it to the bottom of the stairs before he heard his name being called.

'Greg, hang on.'

Stopping, he turned to face him. 'What?'

'You do know the history of that house, right?'

'Of course I do.'

'Well don't you think it's a bit of a coincidence that two families have been murdered in the same house? Didn't you know the first family as well? I know you were friends with Saul and Olivia Potter; there have been a fair few photos of you all snapped at various charity events.'

'What are you insinuating? That I know more about this tragedy than I'm letting on?'

Jamie shrugged.

'I did know the O'Briens; in fact I worked with Jason for a few years. They were a lovely family and he was a good friend. I was devastated when they were murdered, just as I'm devastated by the loss of the Potters.'

'You have to admit it's weird though. It's as if that house is cursed or something. I've got a reporter looking into the history of it. You know it was empty for years before the Potters bought it to renovate. I'm going back to do some in-depth research, look through the archives at the paper and pull everything that's ever been printed about what's happened at that house. Who knows, perhaps your name will crop up once or twice. Once I've got my story and sold lots of papers, I'll hand it all over to the cops.'

The smile which spread across his face made Greg want to hit him, hard, but he couldn't; it would make him look guilty.

'We live in a small area, of course people know each other. What do you want me to say, that I killed them all?'

'I don't know, is that a confession, Greg? Did you?'

'No, it bloody well isn't, and is this blackmail, Jamie? You must be desperate if this is all you can come up with. If you so much as print any of that on the pages of that rag, I'll take you and the paper to court for defamation of character. I'll sue you for so much that you'll have to sell your house, car and shitty business to pay me. Now piss off and leave me alone before I phone the cops and tell them you're harassing me.'

He strode out of the building, towards his car. He had to get away from here before he did something he'd regret for the rest of his life.

CHAPTER THIRTY-FOUR

Morgan entered the house on Easdale Road for the fourth time in as many days; this time she walked behind Ben. He pointed upstairs and she followed him. At the top they paused.

'Did you bring the original crime scene photos with you?'

She nodded, pulling the packet out of her pocket and passing it to him. She had put them in order of the bodies found. She looked at the photograph he held in his hand of Jason O'Brien. He would have been lying just in front of where they were standing now.

'The plaster on the walls is new, it's all been replaced.'

'So is the flooring.'

Ben glanced at the polished hardwood flooring. There was thick carpet on the original. He pointed to the cupboard. It was still there; the doors and handles were new.

'You were right, it is a fair old size.' He opened the double doors wide. It was floor-to-ceiling height and there was shelving on one side full of board games, jigsaws, DVDs that were probably no longer used. There was also a space big enough for someone to hide in.

Morgan lifted a rolled-up duvet off the floor. 'Look, that looks like the carpet in the photo.'

There was the smallest square of carpet sticking out from underneath the shelves. 'Maybe the killer left something behind from all those years ago. It's worth a shot: this and the duvet need to go to the lab to be tested.'

Ben smiled. 'Thanks, boss, I'll bear it in mind.'

'Sorry, not telling you what to do. Just thinking out loud, and there is a loft hatch, look.'

Ben stared up at the small square in the ceiling. 'Not a very big hatch, is it?'

'Bet I could get through it.'

'Well you can try, but first we need to bag this stuff up. Do you want to go get the evidence sacks out of the car while I photograph it?'

'What about Wendy?'

'If you find anything up there, we'll ask her to come out and take over.'

She rushed to get the bags. When she got back Ben was taking an assortment of photos and videoing the cupboard on his work phone. She held the bags open, and he stuffed the duvet inside one. She opened another, he bent down and tugged the small carpet square from the floor, dropping it inside.

'Ladder?'

'There's one in the garage.'

Morgan went to retrieve the stepladder and carried it back. She was out of breath. The paper suit she was wearing was like a mini sauna and she could feel her blouse sticking to her back.

Ben positioned it, handed her a torch and said: 'You're on, there's no way I'll fit through that hole.'

She began to climb the ladder, her palms slick with perspiration and her heart beating too fast. She needed to stop watching ghost-hunting programmes if they were turning her into a nervous wreck. Trying not to let Ben see how scared she was, she forced herself to continue until she reached the hatch.

'Can you see any prints on it?'

'Nothing obvious.'

Her throat was dry, so she nodded. Then pushed the hatch. It swung upwards and landed with a loud bang on the attic floorboards. The space up there was blacker than she'd expected. Pressing the button on the torch, she stepped onto the final rung of the ladder, putting her head and shoulders through the opening. Lifting an arm, she shone the torch around and let out her breath. There was no homicidal maniac waiting with a sledgehammer to bash her brains in.

'Boxes, it's just cardboard boxes.' She said this to herself, calming her nerves.

'Take a good look around. Can you get up there? Is the floor boarded? If it's not, don't put yourself at risk.'

Pulling herself up, she clambered inside. The floor was boarded and felt pretty secure. It was a big space. Her heart was still racing but she took a step inside. Shining the torch around, the beam landed on a wooden baseball bat propped in the far corner, leaning against the side of the roof. As she lowered the beam she realised the end of it was dark brown; stepping closer she saw strands of hair stuck in the brown stuff and realised it was blood.

Rushing back to the hatch, she shouted down to Ben.

'I've found it; I think I've found the Potters' murder weapon.'

'Bloody hell, well done. I'll phone Wendy now; I need you to retrace your steps and get out of there without disturbing anything.'

Morgan didn't need to be told twice. Lowering herself back onto the ladder, she began to climb down as fast as she could. Ben grabbed her waist, lifting her off the bottom. She turned around and he high fived her.

'Well done, we'll make a detective out of you yet.'

Smiling, she didn't say anything. She couldn't tell him how scared she'd been up there in the dark on her own. She left him standing outside the cupboard on the phone to the CSI department and went outside. She needed fresh air. She felt as if she was suffocating in this paper suit which was now drenched with fear-filled sweat.

Stepping out of the door, she tugged off the hood, unzipped the top and pulled it off. Her hair was stuck to her head and her blouse was damp.

The huge oak tree where Olivia, and now Harrison, had hanged themselves from was the first thing her eyes fell on. Above her head was the CCTV camera and she looked up at it; there was a loose wire coming from it. There was the answer why no footage recorded the day of the murders. She found herself walking towards the oak tree. How had they both managed to get up there with no ladder? Unless someone removed it after they'd jumped. She dashed back towards the house, up to Ben.

'The ladder, we need to check that for prints. If someone killed Olivia and tried to kill Harrison, they'd have used it to hang their bodies from the tree and the external camera, it looks as if it's been tampered with.'

Ben nodded. Ending his phone call, he looked at her. 'At this rate you're going to be putting me out of a job and running my department. Good call, Brookes, we'll get it taken to the lab along with the other samples.'

'Worth a shot.'

'Always. Keep the ideas coming; with a bit of luck you'll have this mess solved by teatime and we can go back to chasing burglars and drug dealers.'

She went back downstairs. Even though she didn't think either of them had climbed the tree unaided, she was going to give it a go. She'd rather be outside in the fresh air than cooped up in that house. Just knowing so many people had died such violent deaths in there scared her more than she'd ever admit.

Scaling the tree was more difficult than she'd anticipated, but she did manage to get up to the branch that seemed to be the strongest and from where both Olivia and Harrison had tied their nooses. She looked across the rest of the garden and saw a thin trail of black smoke rising into the air above the trees that bordered the edge of the property. Someone was out there and had lit a fire.

Clambering back down, she headed in that direction, her interest piqued.

CHAPTER THIRTY-FIVE

There was a dry-stone wall running alongside the grounds of the house, separating it from the woods on the other side. It was high, but Morgan knew she'd be able to clamber over. Looking back over her shoulder, she made sure Ben wasn't watching her; it wouldn't look very ladylike. She grabbed hold and pulled herself up then jumped down onto the other side, surprised at how big a drop there was, as the ground was much lower on this side. The scent of burning woodsmoke filled the air, mingling with the smell of damp leaves, and she walked along the tiny path through the canopy of whispering trees towards where she thought it was coming from. The woods were peaceful; the sound of the splashing water as it bubbled along the stream in the background was soothing. She hadn't even known these woods existed. Forests, beaches and woods had been her favourite places to be when she was younger; they stirred something inside her chest that always made her feel at ease. Following the path, she turned a corner and saw a tiny stone cottage, smoke billowing from the chimney. She looked around, wondering if she was daydreaming, because it was like something out of a fairy tale.

An older woman came out of the lilac-painted front door, her arms folded across her chest, and stared at her.

'Can I help you?'

'Maybe. I'm a police officer and we're investigating a serious crime at the house which backs onto these woods. I saw the smoke and wondered if you might have seen or heard anything on Friday.'

The woman beckoned her to come inside the house.

Morgan looked around; she should have told Ben where she was going. No one knew where she was, and she couldn't see the house from here. Still, she opened the gate and walked along the path, ducking under the low doorway to step inside the cottage. It was light and airy inside, not at all what she'd been expecting. It was tiny but the kitchen and living room were all one room. The walls of the kitchen were lined with jars and bottles filled with all sorts of dried herbs and liquids. She wondered if she'd just stepped inside the witch from Hansel and Gretel's cottage.

'Would you like some tea? You look as if you could do with some.'

'What sort of tea?' Morgan was half expecting her to say a special blend, freshly foraged from the forest floor.

'Yorkshire. I only drink that, for my sins.'

She laughed. 'Yes, please, that would be nice. I'm Morgan by the way, Morgan Brookes.'

'I'm Ester Jackson, but everyone calls me Ettie. Sit down, I'll make your tea and we can discuss that terrible tragedy.'

Morgan realised that Ester knew exactly what had happened. Why wouldn't she, it was public knowledge. It didn't mean the woman was involved, of course. Just because she lived in this secluded little house it didn't mean she didn't use a computer or smartphone.

Ettie carried over a wooden tray with two mugs and a plate of biscuits. She set it down on a large, battered pine trunk, with an assortment of candles in the middle, that served as a coffee table. She passed a mug to Morgan.

Morgan realised she hadn't told her how she liked her tea, but it looked perfect.

'Thank you. Can I ask, did you know the Potters very well?'

'I knew Olivia, lovely woman. She introduced herself when they moved in, even brought the girls to visit a couple of times. They weren't interested, of course, they're teenagers; who wants to visit elderly neighbours when you can be doing far more exciting stuff?

They seemed like nice girls, though, especially the younger one. Very polite; the older one had a bit of an attitude, but you get that at her age. I didn't know her husband, saw him a couple of times. He'd wave, but never actually spoke to him.'

'Do you know what happened?'

'I heard they were murdered, and Olivia was found hanging which is ridiculous. There is no way that woman would hang herself. You need to ask yourself why whoever did this hung her that way. If you ask me, she was already dead when they did that. Awful thing to do, vile. It's like killing her twice; once wasn't enough so they did it all over again.'

'Did you see anyone in the area the day or night of the murders?'

She smiled. 'Honey, look out of my windows. I can see trees and that's it, that's why I choose to live here. I like the peace and quiet. I couldn't wait to move out of the village into my little cottage. I don't hold well with the village gossips. I would never partake in their vicious rumours they so enjoy spreading. No, I did not see anyone or hear anything; if I had I'd have phoned the police.'

'You know it's not the first time that house had suffered such a terrible tragedy.'

'I know, the O'Brien family were murdered there in '75. Another lovely family. I don't know why they built that house. Some places are not meant to be lived in.'

'What do you mean?'

'Come now, you might be young but don't tell me you haven't watched your fair share of horror films over the years. Tainted land, curses, that kind of stuff.'

'You think the land is cursed? You live on it.'

'No, I don't live on the same land. The river and woodland separate them. I don't really know if it's cursed, but it's certainly bad luck. I wouldn't live in that house if someone gave it to me and said Merry Christmas.'

Morgan was a little taken aback by the passion in Ettie's voice.

'Did you know that Olivia was having an affair? Did you ever see her with another man?'

'I don't like to speak ill of the dead. She was, from my experience, a nice woman with a few issues. Being faithful was one, but that was none of my business. I did see her walking through the woods on several occasions with a man, but it was from a distance. It may have been her husband, it may not. I couldn't tell you one way or the other. I'm pretty sure the village post office will have an opinion on her love life. You could ask them.'

'Thanks, I will. Can I ask, what are in all those jars?'

Ettie stared at her for a few moments and Morgan got the feeling she was deciding if she should tell her the truth or not.

'Herbs, the medicinal kind. I'm a natural healer; people come to me when they've tried everything else and it hasn't worked. I've always loved working in the garden and the kitchen. Sometimes I read their tea leaves or tarot cards.'

'You remind me of my mum, she was the same.'

'Was she? How lovely, I knew there was something about you I liked. I don't usually invite strangers into my house you know, I make them wait at the garden gate. People come to see me when they're looking for answers buried deep inside their souls. All this modern technology, yet people are lonelier than ever.'

'What do you do to help them?'

'Not much, give them a bottle of lavender or rosemary oil. Tell them to meditate and sprinkle a few drops over their pillows.'

'Does it work?'

'No idea, I bulk buy it off eBay and don't really care too much.' She began to laugh, startling Morgan.

'Then why all this?' She pointed at the jars.

'It's what I was brought up with. My grandmother and mother were the same, it's the way we are. I only do it if I have to.'

Morgan finished her tea then stood up, realising Ben would be worrying where she was. 'Thank you, sorry to have bothered you.'

'Wait.' Ettie went to the shelves and began rooting through the jars. Pulling a small one out, she handed it to Morgan.

'Here, mix a teaspoon of this in with your loose tea before bed. It won't work with tea bags. No more, mind you, it's quite potent.'

She laughed. 'An eBay special?'

'No, it's to help you sleep and stop those bad dreams you have every night that wake you before morning. You've been through some hard times when you were younger and they're haunting your unconscious memory. You need to put them behind you and focus on your future. This is a special recipe, none of that cheap, chemical crap.'

Morgan took the jar from her, staring at it, wondering what on earth was going on and what the contents inside it were.

'Oh, and you should get yourself some better crystals than the ones you have now. Amethyst, prehnite, lapis lazuli are an excellent combination. Put them under your pillow and those you *can* buy off eBay, just make sure they're genuine crystals.' She winked at Morgan, who was speechless. 'When you find this killer, I imagine you'll sleep better without the hocus pocus; until then, what harm can it do to give it a try?'

'Thank you.'

'You're welcome, you might find yourself drawn back here and that's okay. I don't usually like visitors, but for some reason I like you, Morgan, so you're welcome to come back if you need to or want to.'

Ettie held the door open for her, and Morgan smiled and left the cottage.

Turning around, she looked at the small woman, her long, wispy grey hair piled in a bun on the top of her head. She seemed so familiar, yet she knew she had never set eyes on her before. Maybe it was the similarity to her mum's love of all things herbal.

Her phone began to vibrate, and she answered it.

'Where the hell are you? Did you decide to walk back to the police station? Was I boring you?'

She pushed the small jar of loose herbs into her pocket. 'I'm coming, there's a cottage in the woods. I went to see if they knew anything.'

'Did they?'

How could she answer that Ettie seemed to know an awful lot about her indeed?

'No, not much. Knew the family, said Olivia visited. Didn't know Saul and didn't see anything the night of the murders.'

'Worth a try, I suppose. CSI are here.'

'See you in a couple of mins.'

She walked the path back towards the house. The woods were eerily silent; the birds had stopped singing. When she reached the wall, she remembered it was much higher than she'd thought. Looking for a place where there were a couple of footholds to boost herself up, she finally found a piece with bits of missing and chipped stones. Clambering up, she was careful not to break the jar, not sure if she was brave enough to even try it. She had no idea what was in it, might be poisonous for all she knew. Landing on the other side, she peered over the wall, and she felt as if she'd stumbled into some alternative reality.

'Morgan.'

Ben's voice bellowed at her from the front door of the house, bringing her back to earth with a jolt. She turned and waved, deciding not to share with him that Ettie had given her a jar of what could be ground-up cannabis for all she knew. That would definitely help her sleep and soothe her bad dreams. The only thing was she never remembered what she'd been dreaming about.

She thought about what Ettie and Helen Taylor had said: maybe Olivia was the key to all of this.

Why had someone killed her then hung her to make it look like a suicide?

It didn't cross her mind that this wasn't public knowledge, or how Ettie could have known about it.

CHAPTER THIRTY-SIX

Jamie went into the old records room at the newspaper offices, where he wanted to see if he could find any more information pertaining to the murders in 1975. That prick Greg had connections to both families, and he wanted to know if the police had ever interviewed him or thought of him as a suspect. Just because he thought he ran the local villages it didn't mean he was above the law. Everyone had left now and there was only him. The building was old and often when he worked late alone he heard noises. It didn't bother him; he didn't believe in the supernatural. Old buildings creaked and groaned. The two reporters who worked full time for the paper refused to work alone there once it grew dark, and it both amused him and made him despair at their lack of courage.

He was elbow deep in boxes of files when he thought he heard footsteps along the wooden hallway which led to the records room. Pausing, he listened to see if they were heading in his direction, but they stopped. Someone must have come back for something. He carried on rifling through the files, distracted and also determined to find something on Greg, anything; there must be some gossip, dirt, accusations thrown in his direction over the years. There was no way he was the pillar of the community that he pretended to be. No one was that perfect, including himself. He had taken a few bribes in the past to discredit people he shouldn't have for a few grand and upset a few of the local business owners in the process.

He pulled out a faded green folder marked 'O'Brien Murders' and smiled. Opening it, he flicked through. The newspaper clippings, and original handwritten notes by whoever had been reporting the story at the time, were all there and he couldn't wait to read them. Tucking everything back inside, he was going to take it home to read with a large glass of red wine then figure out what and how he could use it. If there was anything that genuinely hinted at the murderer, he would obviously hand it over to the police, but not before he'd had the chance to make Greg's life a misery.

He had almost made it to the front door of the building, he could see it only a few steps away, but he stopped. The feeling of being watched settled over him like a heavy weight, and the tiny hairs on the back of his neck began to prickle. This was stupid, completely ridiculous. What was he thinking about to be scared? A voice inside his head whispered *get out now*. He shrugged, rolling his shoulders back, trying to make himself appear calm.

But someone was standing behind him, he was positive.

All he had to do was walk the six, seven steps to the front door and leave, that's all there was to it. He didn't need to turn around, had no reason to look behind him. Yet his shoulders began to turn, as if to prove to himself that he wasn't a coward. His head looked behind and he let out a scream so loud it echoed around the building. There was a dark figure standing perfectly still behind him, his face covered by a rubber mask. In his hand, a huge butcher's knife. Jamie didn't know if this was some sick joke, but his insides turned to ice and he felt a hot stream of liquid run down his left leg as he urinated himself.

Seven steps.

That was all he had to take to get to freedom. He turned, forcing himself to move and ran towards the door. His hand reached the handle and he grabbed it, pressing it down so hard he felt the metal bend. A sharp, burning pain between his shoulder blades took his breath away and he opened his mouth to scream again. He felt the blade penetrate his neck, cutting off his airway mid-shout.

Lifting his fingers to his neck, he felt the hot spray of blood as it spurted out from the pulsating wound. His knees gave way and he fell forwards, slumping against the door, a gurgling sound coming from the large, ragged wound in his neck.

The man bent down, plucking the file from his fingers. Then stepped over him to open the door. Tugging the mask off, he pushed it into his pocket.

Jamie blinked; he recognised the back of the head, he'd know it anywhere. He could tell the police exactly who it was.

On that thought, he sank into unconsciousness.

Laura Grainger was early to work the next morning. She'd much rather turn in first and get her work done. She was surprised to see Jamie's car already parked outside; he must have been in a hurry because he had abandoned it across the double-yellow lines. That was typical of him. She'd never worked for anyone so self-absorbed. Walking up the steps, she pushed her key into the door and opened it, but the door moved an inch and no more. Frowning, she pushed it again; it still didn't move.

Pushing her mouth against the gap, she yelled: 'Let me in, the door's stuck.'

A rich, earthy smell filled her nostrils and she let out a small grunt of disgust. A cold chill settled over her as she shouted: 'Jamie?'

This time she leant forwards, put her shoulder against the door and shoved it as hard as she could. It scraped open a few more inches, enough for her to peer through the gap. That was when she saw Jamie's crumpled body, collapsed onto the floor.

Stepping back, she ran towards the post office next door, hammering on the door until it opened and she saw Mr Riley looking at her as if she'd gone mad.

'Oh my God, I think he might be dead. I don't want to go inside. Can you phone an ambulance?'

'Who?'

She pointed at Jamie's car.

'Where is he?'

'Inside the doorway to the office. He's on the floor and I can't get in.'

'Susan, Susan.' Mr Riley called to his wife. 'Ring an ambulance now. Come on, you'd better show me.'

Laura led the way and let Mr Riley try to get inside. He pushed the door, managing to get it open just enough to squeeze in. She didn't follow, didn't want to see what was waiting on the other side. Moments later he pushed his way out, his usually ruddy cheeks devoid of all colour.

'He's dead. There's blood everywhere. Jesus, I've never seen anything like this in my life.'

He landed heavily as he sat down onto the stone steps, his face between his hands. Laura didn't know what to do, so she patted his back.

Susan came running out of the post office, her phone pushed against her ear.

'I don't know, hang on.'

She looked at her husband, then spoke to Laura.

'Is the casualty conscious and breathing?'

'We don't think so. There's a lot of blood.'

'No, probably not, there's blood all over. Right, well I'm not a doctor, am I? Please hurry.'

She ended the call and looked at them both. 'Jesus, what a way to start your day. Police and ambulance are on their way.'

Laura sat next to Mr Riley; there was nothing any of them could do now except wait for help to arrive.

CHAPTER THIRTY-SEVEN

Morgan had brewed a cup of tea before bed and used some of the mixed herbs that Ettie had given her. She'd still woken at 04.25 a.m., but felt unusually rested, almost like she could go back to sleep. Before she'd left for work, she'd been tempted to bag some up and ask Wendy to take a look at them. Sniffing the bag, it hadn't smelt like cannabis, but she didn't want to turn up to work high.

She took her large latte and bagel into the small office which was now hers and flicked all the lights on. Today she would hopefully get to grips with this case. Sipping her coffee, she began to read through the case notes. The list of possible suspects was small to say the least. A small, black MG sports car had been seen leaving the O'Briens' house earlier on the day of the murders. Police enquiries had been unable to trace it or the owner. As she read down the list of witness statements, her eyes fixed on the name Stanley Brookes – gardener. Underneath it was a comment that his alibi had been corroborated, and she released the breath she'd been holding. As horrible as he was, she couldn't see him as a killer. What would he have to gain from killing the people who bothered to employ him? There was no motive; it wouldn't make sense.

Her finger stopped on the last name on the list; she knew that name, not the person, but she'd heard of him. Gregory Barker was the local mayor. He'd known the O'Briens quite well according to this, and she was sure his name had also come up in connection with the Potters. He must be the Gary or Greg that Harrison had told her about. He was definitely someone she wanted to talk to.

Typing his name into the intelligence system, she waited to see if there were any hits. He was on there but only as a victim of a burglary. Scribbling down his address, she decided to catch him early.

Grabbing her coffee and bag, she headed out of the door.

'Morgan, are you busy?'

Turning, she saw Ben and Amy walking out of the CID office, both wearing coats.

'Just off out to do some enquiries.'

'Can they wait? They've found a body at the *Cumbrian News* offices.'

She nodded and followed them out to the car park, getting in the back seat of the unmarked car.

Amy got into the driver's seat.

'How many bodies can we have in a week, boss? This is getting out of hand.'

Ben was staring out of the window. 'The world's gone mad. At this rate we're going to put tourists off coming here for life.'

Morgan didn't speak. She wasn't sure if she had quite expected to be exposed to so many dead people in one go. In some ways it was what she'd always dreamed of, yet it was quite unsettling. Seeing people who'd been murdered in reality was a lot more shocking than it ever looked on the Netflix documentaries she binge-watched on her days off.

They reached the main street, which had been cordoned off at each end with police tape, a PCSO guarding the entrance. Amy parked up and they got out. When they were suited and ready to assess the scene, they signed themselves into the scene guard book the PCSO was holding. Morgan hadn't known whether she was to go in or not and had hung back. Ben, who'd been talking on his phone the whole time, ducked under the tape. Realising she wasn't with them, he pointed to the boot of the car and she realised he was telling her to put protective clothing on.

As she dressed, she could hear loud sobs coming from the post office doorway. Turning to look, she saw a woman watching them and crying into a tissue. Dan was standing next to her, but she realised that he wasn't paying the sobbing woman any attention because he was too busy glaring at her. Trying not to, but unable to control it, her cheeks flushed red. How had they gone from colleagues to him hating her this much? As much as she disliked him, she didn't hate him, but there was no mistaking the anger etched across his face.

Turning away from him, she signed herself into the scene and followed Ben's footsteps. The whole street was eerily quiet considering it was mid-morning and usually a bustling hive of activity. There were plenty of people pretending not to be watching from shop doorways and windows when in reality they were.

Ben and Amy were already at the entrance to the building which housed the *Cumbrian News*. The door was ajar. Parked outside, on the double-yellow lines, was the blue BMW that had been parked outside the Potters' drive the other day. Morgan crossed towards it, looking inside to see if the keys were still in the ignition. She didn't think that the three of them needed to go in there. For some strange reason her pulse was racing, yet she had no idea why and wondered if it was the fear of the unknown. Of not knowing what she was going to find behind that door. Neither Ben nor Amy stepped through the door, just peered into the gap in turn.

She heard a whistle and turned to see Ben waving her over. Her feet betraying her feelings, she trudged towards the steps where he was waiting for her at a snail's pace. If he noticed her reluctance he didn't comment.

'Did you just whistle at me like I was a dog?'

'No, sorry. Absolutely not, I was trying to catch your attention.'

She smiled at him and his shoulders relaxed, making her feel mean and wonder if he always felt this tense around her. Maybe she needed to give him a break and not be so feisty around him.

He was really a nice guy and had enough of his own problems without her adding to them.

'Take a look, but don't step inside because CSI will have our backsides if we go in before they do.'

She paused before forcing herself to squeeze in the gap between him and Amy. Her eyes locked on the bloodied mess on the tiled floor in front of her. Blood, there was so much blood. It filtered into her nose and she made the mistake of inhaling the bitter, coppery scent, which hit the back of her throat so hard she could taste it. A loud gagging noise came out of her mouth as it filled with a rush of hot water and she cupped a hand over it. She felt a hand on her arm, dragging her backwards. Almost falling down the two steps, somehow, she managed to keep her balance and was pulled away from the entrance to the crime scene. Back towards the cordon, where a grinning PCSO was holding the tape up for her. She was surprised at Ben being so rough, then realised she could still see him standing on the top step.

When she was beside the car they'd arrived in, Amy opened the driver's door and for the second time this week gently pushed her inside.

'First rules of murder: you must never, ever puke in the crime scene or surrounding areas. No matter how bad it is you hold it in.'

Morgan stared at her, horrified. 'Sorry, I—'

'You don't need to apologise, we've all been there and done that. Some affect you worse than others. It happens, for me it's kids. Are you okay?'

'Yes, I hate the smell of blood. It didn't smell that bad at the Potters'.'

'The heating is on in that hallway, it's stifling, and it also speeds up the smell of decay and bodily fluids.'

'Ben's going to think I'm so childish.'

Amy crouched down. 'No, he's not. He'll be relieved you didn't offload your breakfast all over his feet. Anyway, I don't know what it is about you, but he seems to have a bit of a soft spot for you which is literally unheard of. He's usually a grumpy, miserable bastard but I have the utmost respect for him as my boss, so if he likes you then I like you. You're okay, Morgan. To be fair I think you've done amazing this week, considering you should only be out herding sheep back into fields, giving tourists directions and dealing with the odd road traffic accident. Don't be too hard on yourself. Why don't you wait here for a bit? At least until CSI have been; trust me, you don't want to piss Wendy off. When you feel okay you can start to speak to the shopkeepers either side, see if they have any CCTV or saw anything. You know the drill.'

She nodded, grateful for the chance to compose herself and not totally blow it.

'Thanks, Amy, I will.'

Amy began to walk back towards Ben, paused then turned back.

'Hey, don't tell anyone I was nice to you. It will ruin my image.'

She winked at her and Morgan smiled.

A couple of minutes and she'd be good to go. Inhaling the air inside the car, she noticed it smelt of stale curry. It was still lingering from someone's takeaway the night before, but it was a whole lot fresher than inside that doorway.

CHAPTER THIRTY-EIGHT

Morgan walked across to the post office, where she assumed it was the owners standing outside watching everything.

'Hi, can I have a word?'

The guy nodded. His face was devoid of colour and he was nursing a mug of tea. He had a wedding ring on his ring finger. A woman standing behind him with a matching mug and ring smiled at her.

'I'm Susan Riley. This is awful, what's the world coming to? Although he was a bit of a pain in the arse, wasn't he, Mick?'

Mick nodded once more.

'Who?'

'Jamie Stone, the guy that ran the paper. Wouldn't wish that on him, though, wouldn't wish it on anyone.'

'Did you see anything? Do you have CCTV?'

They shook their heads in unison. 'No, we keep saying we should get some.'

'Did you know the Potters?'

'Yes, we did. Lovely family, such a terrible shame. Olivia used to come in a couple of times a week. She usually had parcels to return.'

Morgan wondered if she was doing the right thing and decided that yes, she was. They needed answers and as much information as possible. If she was going against protocol then it was for a good reason.

'Did you ever hear about Olivia having an affair?'

Mick, who still hadn't spoken, shook his head again. Susan pointed to the shop. Turning, she walked inside and Morgan followed. The door closed behind her. It was dark inside and she had to blink a couple of times so her eyes adjusted to the gloom.

'I don't want to say anything in front of Mick; he's upset about Saul. Used to drink with him in the pub now and again. I did see her a couple of times with another man, not in the village; it's too small for that.'

'Where then?'

'There's a little pub a few miles away, The Grain, do you know it?'

'No.'

'Well, I go there twice a month to meet a couple of my friends on a Friday for a bite to eat and glass of fizz. I saw them together, leaving, as I parked, then again a couple of weeks later. This time they were arguing as I went in. She looked pretty mad at him. Nothing to do with me. I went inside.'

'Who was it?'

'Greg Barker, our esteemed mayor. He's a creep if you ask me. He was like a dog on heat. I have no idea what she saw in him. Saul was far better looking and much nicer.'

'Thank you.'

She walked out of the shop with a renewed passion to go and speak to Greg Barker about the O'Briens. She couldn't speak to him about the Potters, though, that wasn't her place. Ben would do that; but she had to speak to him first, because once he was brought in for questioning she had a feeling he wouldn't tell them anything. But it was certainly interesting to know that this man now had connections to both dead families.

*

Ben was busy on his phone, CSI were processing the scene and she felt a little like a spare part. She crossed to where Ben was leaning on the bonnet of the CSI van and waited for him to end his call.

'Boss, no one saw anything. The only CCTV is on the Co-op on the corner, but staff don't know how to access it. The manager is in at twelve and will sort it out then. What should I do now?'

'Please can you go to the hospital? I need you to speak to Harrison Wright; check he's okay and see why he did that yesterday. You could also check in on Bronte. That was Declan on the phone. He fast-tracked the toxicology samples and there's been a hit. All three of them had traces of GHB in their blood.'

She nodded. She'd heard of GHB; it was a date-rape drug and could knock a person out with only a few drops. Which would explain how the killer managed to take out an entire family without a fight.

'If they were drugged then it had to be someone who knew them or had access to their food or drink.'

'Yes, which is why I want you to speak to Harrison. It's the kind of drug used by partygoers trying to chase a high. If he's well enough to be discharged, can you ask him if he can come in to the station. Tell him it's just a friendly chat with me; there's a couple of things I forgot to ask about the family. Is that okay?'

The relief flooding through her entire body at the thought of escaping this scene was palpable.

'Yes, of course it is.'

'Good, whatever you do try not to make him feel as if he's under suspicion for anything. We have no concrete evidence, it's all circumstantial.'

He passed her the car keys.

'Thanks, I won't.'

Then he walked away and she was relieved he hadn't asked if she was okay and had finished freaking out, because the way she felt she'd probably burst into tears of embarrassment and feel even more of a fool than she already did.

She had a nightmare trying to find a parking space outside the hospital. The car parks were full and the on-street parking was mainly for blue badge holders. On her fourth attempt a car's reverse lights came on and she stopped to let it out, waving thank you enthusiastically at them even though they couldn't see her. As she walked into the main part of the hospital she realised she had no idea which ward Harrison would be on, so she went to the desk and showed her warrant card explaining she needed to speak to him. The receptionist eyed her up and down, and Morgan realised that she looked different; in the picture she was wearing full uniform. Today she was wearing a pair of black linen trousers and a white shirt.

'Hang on, why do you need to see him?'

'It's more of a welfare check. I found him yesterday when he attempted suicide. I wanted to see if he was okay and have a chat about an investigation he's helping me with.'

The receptionist raised an eyebrow and Morgan smiled. She knew it sounded crazy, but what was she supposed to say?

'Harrison Wright, yeah?'

She nodded.

'Second floor, Ward 12, you'd better clear it with the ward manager before you go walking straight in there.'

'Thank you, I will.'

Morgan walked along the long corridor to the bank of lifts, knowing she should really take the stairs but couldn't be bothered. She felt drained. It seemed like hours ago since she'd had her breakfast; her stomach was grumbling. She might see if Harrison wanted to go to the canteen again; the cake was pretty good for a hospital. More corridors that stretched on forever and she finally found the one which said 'Ward 12'. There was a cluster of nurses all wearing different coloured uniforms standing around for handover. A man typing on a computer smiled at her.

'Can I help you?'

'Yes, I'm Police Officer Morgan Brookes. I wanted to check in on Harrison Wright. See how he is.'

He didn't bother asking for ID. He smiled at her. 'Bay eight, right at the bottom of this corridor.'

'Thank you.'

She walked towards the bay. Inside there were ten beds but only one was occupied by an elderly man. She looked around and saw the bed near to where she was standing had crumpled sheets, and on the whiteboard above it said 'Harrison Wright'. Morgan took a seat in the chair; he must have gone to the bathroom.

The old man looked at her.

'Can you take me home, miss?'

'I can't, sorry.'

He nodded. 'No one can, this place is keeping me against my will. He had the right idea.'

'Who did?'

'Young chap in that bed. He got up and walked out.'

Morgan stood up. 'Do you know how long ago that was?'

He shrugged. 'A couple of days ago.'

'Thank you.'

She hurried back to the desk.

'He's not there; the man by the window said he'd left.'

The nurse who'd been looking after him turned around. 'He was there last time I looked. Don't take too much notice of Frank; he gets a bit confused. I'll check the bathrooms.'

Two of them hurried off to check the bathrooms, while Morgan dashed back to see if his clothes were still in the locker next to the bed. It was empty.

She pulled out her phone and dialled Ben's number.

'He's gone.'

'Who, the kid? Where's he gone?'

'It looks as if he's walked out. His clothes are missing.'

'Shit. I'll get someone to go and do an address check. Please can you go and talk to Bronte's doctor? I'll ask Lancs if they can send officers to check the bus and train stations. He'll be on foot; he can't have got too far.'

The line went dead.

Morgan turned to the nurses. 'We'll put a missing person's report on the system. Can someone phone up 101 and give them the details, please?'

Then she left them to it, making her way to the intensive care unit.

CHAPTER THIRTY-NINE

The intensive care unit was still busy; there were no free beds. The officer had been removed from Bronte's bedside, and Morgan could understand why. She was on a secure ward; access was only given by the nurses and visitors were restricted. She was in full view of the nurses' station and it seemed a waste of resources to have an officer here full time. She approached the desk in the middle of the room. The nurses here were busy, all working on patients, and she waited until one was free to speak to her.

Kimberley, the nurse from the other day, waved at her, leaving Bronte to come and see her.

'How is she?'

'Holding her own; she was taken off the ventilator and is breathing unaided, which is great. There's been some involuntary movements of her fingers and toes.'

'Has her boyfriend been in today?'

She shook her head. 'No, he hasn't been here since the day before yesterday. I sent him home, told him he was no use to her if he was exhausted. I thought he'd have been back before now though.'

Morgan wondered how much information she was permitted to share with the woman, and then wondered how she could protect Bronte if she didn't know what was happening. She would take the flak for it if needed, she decided. She leant forward and lowered her voice.

'He tried to kill himself yesterday and was on Ward 12, but he's discharged himself and I'm worried about him.'

The nurse's hand lifted to her mouth. 'Oh no, is it because I sent him home?'

Morgan shook her head. 'No, I wouldn't think so. Did you speak to him much?'

'Not really, he wasn't the talking type. He spent most of his time staring at his phone and taking selfies.'

'What of? Him in here?'

'Mostly, a few times I caught him crouched next to Bronte's bed. I don't want to sound mean, though, and I know that's what all kids do now. They live their lives on their phones and forever take pictures, but it made me a bit uncomfortable of the ones he took with Bronte. I mean, the girl is in a bad way and there he is spending twenty minutes making sure his hair looked right before taking photos of them both. Another thing as well, he never looked sad on them; he always had this big grin with his white teeth showing.'

'That's odd, I'd feel uncomfortable too. Did you ever ask him why he was taking them?'

'I did, once, he said they were so Bronte could see how poorly she was and how he'd always been there for her when she did wake up. He started crying and I felt mean, so I left him to it. I hope to God he wasn't putting them on Snapchat or Instagram.'

Morgan was starting to get a really bad feeling about Harrison Wright. What if Ben was right and he was loving all the attention and drama? Maybe he wasn't so innocent in all of this.

'My sergeant wanted me to ask if Bronte had full blood work done when she was admitted.'

The nurse nodded. 'All patients in a serious condition do.'

'Would they have run toxicology tests?'

'Given the circumstances I would have assumed so, let me check her notes.'

They walked into the room. It was much quieter in here without the ventilator. Morgan reached out, gently taking hold of the girl's hand.

'Hi, Bronte, it's me, Morgan, from the police. Glad to see you're fighting. Keep going, we're all rooting for you.' Tears welled in her eyes and she lifted her sleeve to brush them away. This was so hard; that poor girl didn't deserve any of this.

The nurse smiled at her. 'You're pretty nice for a copper. I take it you haven't been one very long.'

'Why?'

'Oh, just a guess. You'll get used to it eventually, although not always. I've been working in here for nine years and most days I can go home and try to switch off, you have to, or it would send you insane. But occasionally someone will end up in here and they're far too young and didn't deserve it. Those days it can be difficult to leave it all behind. Yes, here we go. There were no traces of anything unusual.'

'Oh, right. Thank you, I just need to check in with my boss.'

She left and went in search of the canteen. She needed something to eat and coffee. Ben didn't answer so she left him a voicemail. Taking her latte and slice of Victoria sponge, she went and sat at the table she'd shared with Harrison. Pulling a notepad out of her bag, she began to scribble notes inside of everything she'd been told since she got here. It occurred to her she could go and speak to the pathologist while she was here. He may be able to help. As she left the dining room, she stopped a porter.

'Please can you tell me how to get to the mortuary?'

He pointed to the far end of the corridor. 'Down there, turn right, straight on then first left.'

'Thank you.'

She headed in that direction and hoped that Declan would speak to her. She didn't want to go back to Ben without anything of value.

*

Turning into the corridor that led to the mortuary, she noticed the dark green paint on the walls was peeling and chipped. It badly needed painting to brighten it up; a few more lights wouldn't go amiss either. Compared to the rest of the hospital it was as if they didn't pay the electric bill down here. Morgan wished she had her jacket and hadn't left it in the car. She shivered in the cool breeze flowing along the corridor. She felt as if she was going downhill into a gloomy, damp tunnel rather than walking along a hospital corridor. She supposed it made sense for it to run down; easier to push the trolleys that carried the dead.

She stopped in her tracks, a feeling of unease spreading over her. Footsteps not too far behind made the hair on the back of her neck stand on end. A porter came into view and she screeched.

'Blimey, love, sorry. I didn't mean to scare you. I was just coming to make sure you'd found it all right.'

Realising it was the man she'd asked for directions, she let out a loud laugh.

'Oh, my God. I'm so sorry, I got a little freaked out.'

He grinned. 'I believe you. I probably should have sent you out to go via the main entrance instead of down here into the depths of hell.'

'It is a bit like that, isn't it? I watch too many ghost-hunting programmes on television.'

He caught up with her and carried on walking towards the double doors in the distance.

'I realised you wouldn't get in without a card.' He waved his pass at her. 'This place is ancient, but the security is pretty good. I don't suppose the board want visitors stumbling into the mortuary. It's not the nicest place to be.'

'No, I don't suppose it is.'

They reached the doors and he pressed his card onto the small electronic reader, then pushed the door, holding it open for her. She was right in the thick of the mortuary. Next to her was a bank of fridges that filled an entire wall along with a couple of examination tables.

'Lucky for you the doc isn't in the middle of a PM.'

The tall, blonde man she recognised as Declan, wearing a pair of blue scrubs, walked in, a clipboard under his arm and a pen tucked behind his wavy hair.

'Lee, what you doing bringing people into my humble abode without an invitation?'

Morgan really wished she'd come the front way.

'Sorry, Declan, she was looking for you. I didn't think.'

Declan stared at her. 'And you are?'

'Morgan.' She coughed. 'PC Morgan Brookes; I'm working with Ben Matthews on the Potter murders. I was here the other day.'

She hoped she sounded more professional than she felt.

'Ah, so you were, Morgan. I've a terrible memory for faces. Names, now, they always stick in my head. Cool.' Turning to Lee, he waved. 'You're all forgiven, we're good.'

Lee gave him a thumbs up and went back out the doors they'd just entered through.

'How can I help?'

Declan led her out of the air-conditioned room which was so cold she was sure her fingers had frostbite. She followed him as they went into an office and he pointed to a chair which had seen better days. She sank down into it, realising it was actually quite comfy.

'Ben said the tox reports showed GHB in the Potters' results. I've just visited the girl who survived in ICU, and the nurse checked her notes; nothing showed up for her. I wondered if you knew why?'

'Good question, Morgan, basically GHB is broken down by the body really fast. The detection window is short; it's only detectable in the blood for up to eight hours and twelve hours in urine. It's a central nervous system depressant also known as a date-rape drug, but you already know that bit, I imagine?'

She nodded; she knew some of it.

'It's highly potent and can be slipped into a drink or food unnoticed, which is why it's so dangerous. The effects usually kick in after ten minutes of ingesting it and can last quite a few hours.'

'So more than enough time to murder an entire family if they'd been given enough to render them unconscious?'

'Absolutely.'

'I still don't understand how you found it in the Potters then. They weren't found for at least twenty-four hours and Olivia's post-mortem wasn't until the next day.'

'I took samples of femoral blood and vitreous humour, which came back positive. I can also send hair samples to be analysed, but the results were conclusive without the need for that.'

'Wow, that's clever. Does that mean if we take a sample of Bronte's hair you could send that off to be tested to see if it was administered to her?'

'I can, yes. Though it would have to be taken by a CSI and submitted to protect the chain of evidence. I would imagine if her family were given it then she would as well.'

'Unless you killed them or were an accomplice to their murder, but the murderer turned on you... Sorry, just thinking out loud. Thank you, Declan, this is great. I'll let Ben know.'

She stood up. When she reached the door she turned around. 'Are you really good friends with Ben?'

'I'd like to think so, why?'

Was this any of her business? Probably not and she didn't know whether to divulge the information or not. Ben might be angry with her.

'I don't know him very well, but the other night—'

'He got hammered and thought about taking an overdose. How do you know?'

'How do you know?'

'You first?' Declan smiled at her.

'I needed to talk to him about this case and I went to his house; it was quite late. He was sitting at the kitchen table with a row of tablets in front of him. He said it was the anniversary of his wife's death.'

'Shit, I forgot all about Cindy's anniversary. I usually take him to the pub, he tells me how he's going to do it and I tell him not to bother because having to do his post-mortem is way beyond the realms of our friendship.'

'Oh, so he wouldn't have?'

'I like to think not. He was devasted to find Cindy dead and blames himself, but he knows suicide won't help anyone. Look how it's left him.'

'She killed herself. Oh God, I thought she'd died accidentally.'

'No, it would have been better for Ben if she had. He wouldn't be shouldering the guilt like he is. I'll give him a ring. Thank you for reminding me.'

'Please don't tell him I told you. I don't want him to think I'm interfering or gossiping.'

He smiled. 'I won't, it's not interfering when you're concerned. I can't believe I didn't remember; it was the day the Potters turned up. No excuse, but it was busier than it's been in here in a very long time. I'll let you out the main entrance.'

Leading her to the door she came through with Ben the other day, he held one open. 'You take care, Morgan.'

'Thanks, I will. You too.' She walked back to her car, a whirlwind of emotions blowing in her mind.

CHAPTER FORTY

Ben stood in front of the briefing room, which was full. As he looked around, the only person missing was Morgan. Dan was sitting next to Abigail at the front, his legs crossed, staring at his phone, and just looking at him made Ben want to take the phone from him and slap him with it. He'd never known anyone irritate him as much as he did.

'Right, we are in what I would say is a bit of a mess. You already know about the Potter family; we are progressing that investigation. I still need a lot of work doing in regard to that case and several of you are going to be tasked with enquiries, so hang on after this finishes. Amy will go through what I need you to do. This morning a male was found brutally murdered at the offices of the *Cumbrian News*. We believe this male to be Jamie Stone, the editor in chief of the paper.'

There were murmurs around the room; everyone knew him. Most people disliked him and the way he ran the paper. He loved to write stories that slated the local police and officers. Ben waited for them to quiet.

'He hasn't been formally identified yet, although the co-worker who found the body thinks it might have been him. I'm also pretty sure it is after a bit of a run-in with him outside the Potters' the other day. She didn't look long enough to make a positive ID. However, his car was parked outside on the double yellows and the engine was cold, so it had been there some time. No one else was in the building, so it's highly likely to be him. Dan, can you go check out the home address and any other addresses on the list I'll give you just to make sure he's not in bed nursing a hangover?'

Dan rolled his eyes. Ben clenched his knuckles under the podium he was leaning against. The door opened and Morgan slipped through it, mouthing 'sorry'. He nodded and continued, but not before noticing the look of contempt Dan threw her way. He was going to have to speak to the little git at some point and remind him about his attitude.

'Send Morgan, I have some urgent enquiries.'

Ben stared at Dan, not quite believing what he was hearing. 'Morgan is tied up.'

'Yeah, I bet she is.' Dan sniggered and a few of the others joined in.

Ben couldn't look at her. He could sense she was trying to squeeze further into the corner she'd already backed herself into.

'I've already cleared it with the duty sergeant, she said it was fine.'

Dan shook his head, and Ben had to turn his attention away from him before he launched himself across the room and dragged him outside.

'Harrison Wright is currently missing; he is also top wanted. For anyone who doesn't know he is the boyfriend of the girl who survived. He tried to hang himself yesterday and failed. I need him locating, not only for a welfare check, but also I want to speak to him again in regards to some new evidence which has come to light. Do not tell him this before he's been cuffed. I don't want to scare him off; ask him nicely to come in. That's it for now, thank you.'

He walked out, beckoning Morgan to follow and she did. They went upstairs to his office.

'I seriously worry for his health, that Dan is such an idiot. Thank God he didn't get sent up here to help out, I'd be suspended by now.'

'Was he going to?'

'He was next on the list, yes; he would have been given the opportunity.'

'No wonder he's so mad with me. I didn't understand what was going on. I know he's been wanting to work in CID for ages. He kept telling me he was coming up here eventually. I should apologise to him.'

'For what? He's the one with a problem. If he wasn't so difficult then he could have come up here.'

'Is that why you asked me? Not because you think I'd make a good detective or because I have potential but because you think Dan's an arse?'

Ben realised he was digging himself into a deeper hole. 'No, of course not.' He couldn't look her in the eyes, though, because technically it was, and he didn't want to make her any angrier. He could tell by the way she was standing with her feet apart, jaw clenched and the deep furrows on her forehead as she almost sneered the words at him, she was raging.

'What, did you feel sorry for me or something? Because I don't need you or anyone to feel sorry for me. I just want to do the job I signed up for without any of this bullshit.'

With that she turned and strode out of his office, straight down the stairs.

Turning, he looked out of the window down onto the car park and saw her exit the building, striding towards the car. In less than sixty seconds she was gone. Ben was left with a strange feeling of guilt as Amy walked in.

'Phew, she's feisty that one. What have you done now?' She began to laugh. 'I tell you what, though, it's great entertainment watching you get your arse chewed by a kid. I've never had so much fun at work.'

'Piss off, Amy. She's not a kid, she's an adult and I probably deserved it.'

'Aww, next time you get on my nerves and I tell you to do one we'll see if you're as understanding. I think you like her a lot more than you ever anticipated.'

'What do you mean by that?'

'Well you must because you've been different since she came up here, which is not a bad thing because I was fed up of your moping around.'

He glared at her.

'Anyway, I gave Dan the worst jobs on the list to keep him busy, thought you'd like that. I'm going to get something to eat, are you hungry?'

He sat down, not remembering the last time he'd eaten. 'Yeah, please. Whatever you're having is fine.'

She left him to it.

He stared out of the window, wondering if he was getting too involved and if he needed to back off. He realised that for the first time since Cindy his life had begun to have some meaning, and if that was in the form of Morgan's friendship then he was thankful. He had to figure out what part she played; was it as a colleague, a student or a friend? After her concern the other night, he decided that a friend was nice, but he didn't want to make her life awkward or difficult. He probably also needed to apologise to her, for upsetting her even though he hadn't meant to.

His phone rang and Declan's name flashed across the screen. 'What's up?'

'I'm sorry, I missed Cindy's anniversary. I shouldn't have.'

Ben laughed. 'You shouldn't have, I shouldn't have, but I did until it was almost over. Thanks, Declan, but I think we were all a bit overworked that day. No need to apologise.'

'Well, you know where I am. I've told you that before, anytime you need me. Oh your colleague was here before, have you had the chance to speak to her?'

'Sort of, why?' Ben couldn't hide the surprise in his voice.

'She came up with a brilliant idea; she wanted me to test the surviving girl to see if she had traces of GHB in her system. Apparently, she checked her notes and nothing showed. She's been down here to see if I could take a sample of her hair for analysis.'

'And can you?'

'I can't, but your CSI can. Just thought you should know she's pretty good for a newbie, so don't be too hard on her.'

'Why do you think I'm hard on her?'

'Because you're a self-serving miserable git and sometimes you can't see what's in front of your face for looking. She's not bad on the eyes, either, is she?'

'Morgan?'

'Who else?'

'I didn't really notice.'

'Get away with you, even you must have noticed.' He stopped himself. *'Sorry, not very professional. She's clever, smart and pretty – not a bad combination. Maybe you should smarten yourself up a little, have a shave, cut down on the takeaways, buy yourself some new threads.'*

'Cheers, are you saying I look like a slob?'

'Your words, not mine. See you.'

The line went dead and Ben tried to look at his reflection in the glass window. He had let himself go. Maybe it was time to make an effort, not because of Morgan but because he felt like life was beginning to be worth living again.

CHAPTER FORTY-ONE

Morgan glanced down at her notebook to check Gregory Barker's address. She knew the area where he lived, and it wasn't too far from Easdale Road. As she drove along the quiet country roads, the late afternoon sun felt warm on her face, and with both front passenger windows open the breeze flowing through was lovely. She parked outside the huge double gates at the entrance to Gregory Barker's home and realised he must have more money than she'd imagined.

She got out of the car and pressed the intercom; it crackled to life.

'Hi, I'm Morgan Brookes from the police, I'm here to speak with Mr Barker.'

There was a slight pause. 'Drive through.'

She got in the car and watched as the gates slid seamlessly open. The drive up to the house was tree lined and long. When the house came into view she sighed. If she'd thought the Potters' house was her dream house then this was her ultimate fantasy. It was the size of a small hotel, built in the grey slate of a lot of Lake District properties. A tall, grey-haired man was waiting for her on the front steps, his hands tucked into the pockets of his coral-coloured chinos. The smile on his lips didn't reach his eyes. She parked the car and got out, crossing the gravel and admiring the huge stone lions which flanked either side of his front door.

'Mr Barker?'

He stretched out his hand. 'Indeed. You're Officer Brookes? If you don't mind me saying you look awfully young. Or am I just getting old?'

He laughed at his own joke, and Morgan found herself taking an instant dislike to him. She shook his hand, gripping it firmly.

'I'm here to ask you a few questions relating to the murders on Easdale Road, if that's all right?'

He nodded. 'Of course, come inside. It's a terrible tragedy, such a lovely family.'

He led her inside the grand entrance, down the hallway and into the biggest kitchen she'd ever seen. It was beautiful, everything was pristine; pale grey hand-painted cabinets filled the room with a huge island in the middle. The sparkling white granite worktops were clear of any kitchen appliances; it didn't look as if anyone used them to prepare food. He pointed to a row of stools one side of the island.

'Please, take a seat.'

'Thanks, do you live here alone?'

'For the time being I do, my ex left me some time ago. Can I offer you a drink?'

She shook her head. 'I'm good, thanks.'

He didn't sit down but stood across from her. 'Those kids were so lovely, it's just terrible what's happened. So were Olivia and Saul. You couldn't have met a nicer couple. It's so hard to believe it.'

'I believe they were and yes, it's beyond tragic. Did you know the Potters well?'

'Yes, quite. We met through the mayor's charity fundraising ball; they were very supportive.'

Morgan smiled. 'Actually, I wanted to talk about the previous family that were murdered there.'

He stared at her, his lips parting slightly.

'Why the O'Briens? That was a very long time ago. I don't understand.'

'I've been tasked with looking into their cold case. No one was ever brought to justice for the slaughter of the O'Briens. You have to admit it's very strange to have two families murdered in the same property. I think there may be some connection between the two murders.'

She smiled at him, and noticed there was a faint flush of redness creeping up his neck. She could see it through the open buttons on his white Armani shirt.

'I guess there could, I didn't think about that.'

'When I was looking through the notes from the first murders your name cropped up a few times. Could you tell me how you knew the O'Briens?'

Morgan had no idea if she was overstepping her boundaries or not; she was totally winging it.

'Am I being questioned here? Am I under suspicion?'

She shook her head. 'No, not at all. I'm trying to get as much background information about the O'Briens as I can, to form a picture of them. What they were like, what kind of lifestyle they led. At the moment you're the best link I have to them. It really is just helping me with enquiries.'

His shoulders relaxed. Taking a glass from the cupboard, he pressed it under the ice dispenser of the American-style fridge. The clanking as the chips of ice hit the glass seemed to echo around the room. He then took a bottle of whisky from the cupboard and filled the glass half full. He walked back to look at Morgan and took a large gulp.

'Cheers, don't mind me. It's been a long time since I've thought about Jason and his family. It's a bit of a jolt to the old system.'

'Sorry to bring up bad memories.'

He pulled up a stool and sat opposite her.

'They were a nice family. We owned a construction company, Jason and I. He was a very good friend and I thought a lot of Jennifer and the girls. It was a hell of a shock when I heard the news that they were all dead. I mean who does something like that?'

'Hard to imagine why or who could do that. Did Jason have any enemies, fall out with anyone?'

'No, he was a good guy.'

'I read in the notes that you both had a bit of a falling out?'

His eyes narrowed and the redness on his neck began to spread to his cheeks. 'We didn't fall out exactly, it was more of a disagreement. Running a business is hard at the best of times. Things weren't going too well. I wanted to sell up and cash in while we had the chance. Jason didn't; he thought we should stick it out.'

'What happened?'

'Well he got killed, so it ended that discussion. I sold up, invested the money, and here I am.'

'Yes, very impressive. When you found out about the Potters did it not cross your mind to speak to the police and tell them about the O'Briens?'

'Look, Ms Brookes, I don't like the way you keep making accusations yet saying they're not. What are you trying to insinuate? Do you know who I am? I have friends in the police, high-ranking friends, and the police commissioner is an acquaintance. I'm going to have to ask you to leave now. I'm not answering any further questions unless it's with a solicitor present.'

He began to stride towards the front door. Morgan stood up, taking one last look around. He had all of this because the O'Briens had died and he'd been able to sell the business that Jason had wanted to keep. Money and greed were as good a motive for murder as any. She followed him and stepped out into the fading sunlight. Determined not to let him think he had the upper hand, she stared him in the eyes.

'It worked out pretty well for you, didn't it, Jason O'Brien dying. It meant you got the business, the money. I mean look at this house. Yeah, it really did.'

She got into the car, slamming the door shut before he could answer her. She knew she'd gone too far, but couldn't help it. All she wanted was to discover the truth and get justice for Bronte, her family and the O'Briens.

CHAPTER FORTY-TWO

Morgan took the police car back and swapped it for her own. She didn't bother going upstairs. She had nothing to say to Ben. She'd emailed Wendy in the car and told her to speak to Ben about taking a sample of Bronte's hair. Inside her flat, she kicked her shoes off. She was hot, tired and could still taste the overpowering scent of blood from this morning every time she closed her eyes. After a quick shower she curled up into a ball on her chair, her damp hair still wrapped in a towel, she closed her eyes. Just for ten minutes, she wanted to go back to last week where she was still on speaking terms with Dan. Still had him to rely upon when they went to jobs for advice; for all his being an idiot he was a very good copper.

A loud crack on the window made her jump off the chair, the towel falling from her head as her wet hair hung down over her eyes. Brushing it back, her heart racing, she stepped towards the glass, pressing her face against it. She couldn't see anyone or anything out in the dark. What the hell was that? Was someone trying to scare her? She turned off the lamp then looked outside once more. For a fleeting second she thought a dark figure slipped behind the huge oak tree in the garden and a cold shiver made her body shudder. Maybe it was Stan? But she knew that running away wasn't his style; he hadn't the last time. Drawing the curtains closed, she rushed to the front door to make sure it was locked, then she went into the bathroom and bedroom double-checking the windows were secured and closing the blinds. Her hands were shaking; it was different when she was at work. Until this week she wore a uniform, had equipment to protect herself with and backup. When you were home alone, in your pyjamas, half asleep, it was a whole different situation.

Realising she couldn't do anything, she dressed in her black leggings and roll-neck jumper, and tugged on her Nikes. She had to check out the garden and communal entrance to the flats. Anyone could be out there, and she wouldn't settle for hiding inside. She looked around for a suitable weapon if the need to defend herself should arise. The only thing of any use was the wooden rolling pin in the drawer. Tucking her phone into her bra, she gripped the makeshift baton in her right hand. Pressing her ear against her front door, she listened to see if she could hear anyone out in the hallway. The only sound was her pounding heart which seemed to fill her mind. She peered through the spyhole; it looked okay. There wasn't really anywhere to hide out there except for the cleaning cupboard, which was usually kept locked. She hoped it still was.

Opening the door, she slipped into the hallway. Tiptoeing across to the cupboard, she gripped the handle and pushed it down. It didn't budge. The stairs that led up to the first and second floors were all in darkness. That was good; they had motion-sensor lights which fired up the minute someone put a foot on the first step, so no one could be up there. She locked her door behind her and tucked the key into her left shoe. With trembling legs she waited for the sensor light to turn off in the hall then pulled open the front door just enough to squeeze through.

Outside, she pressed her back against the wall, blending in to the shadows so she could sneak up on whoever might be hiding. The whole time she was scanning the gardens where she thought she saw the figure disappear. If they were still there, they were doing well keeping so still. Her fear was now turning to anger. What had she done to deserve this? Nothing! Whoever was trying to scare her would regret it. Gripping the rolling pin harder, she walked along the wall, thinking she'd go around the outside and

sneak up from the front drive. The oak tree was a few metres away
from her. She crept closer.

'What are you doing?'

Morgan let out a screech so loud Ben jumped back and covered
his ears. She raised the rolling pin and he lifted up his hands.

'Bloody hell, it's me, Ben. What's up?'

Clutching her heart, she lowered her arm, but kept tight hold
of the rolling pin.

'Jesus you scared me. What are you doing here? Sneaking around
in the dark; do you think you're funny, is this some kind of joke to
you? What is it, revenge for breaking your window?'

Her tone was accusatory, and Ben looked puzzled.

'Hang on, what are you talking about? I've only just got here.
Amy dropped me off; my car wouldn't start. I wanted to see if you
were okay. What's going on?'

She stared at his face, trying to decide if he was telling the truth
or bullshitting her.

'Morgan, why are you dressed in black and sneaking around
your garden holding a rolling pin?'

Her shoulders dropped. 'I heard someone outside, saw someone
run behind this tree. Then you turn up, it's a bit of a coincidence.'

'Can we go inside? You're shivering.'

Morgan was torn; what if it had been him hiding? She realised
that she'd been watching the tree the entire time since she'd come
outside, and he hadn't come from that direction. She nodded and
turned, walking back to her flat. Ben followed, his hands tucked
into his trouser pockets.

'Look Morgan, I don't know what's going on here. But you're
shaking and your face is white. Sit down, I'll get you a drink and
you can tell me what happened.'

She sat down, the rolling pin still in her hand. He began to open
her cupboards and found two glasses. 'Do you have any alcohol?'

'Vodka in the freezer.'

He opened the fridge and smiled. 'I see you're as interested in cooking as I am.'

She shrugged. 'I actually like cooking, I haven't had time to shop.'

Pulling the vodka out of the freezer compartment, he said, 'You're a girl after my own heart. I always keep my vodka in the freezer.'

Pouring out two measures, he carried one over and passed it to her. She threw her head back and downed it.

'Nice.'

He did the same; it went down the wrong way and he ended up coughing into his sleeve. For the first time since he'd arrived, she smiled at him.

'Better?'

'A little.'

'Good, what happened?'

She filled him in on the last fifteen minutes and he stood up. 'I'll go and check outside.'

'No point, whoever it is has gone.'

'Who do you think it was?'

'Stan, maybe? Although he's usually too drunk at this time of night to stand straight, never mind hide behind a tree and stay perfectly still. You?'

'Morgan, it's not me. I have no reason to try and scare the life out of you. Why would I want to do that?'

She knew he was telling the truth. 'Sorry, it was just a bit weird you turning up at the same time.'

He looked down at the empty glass in his hands. 'I was worried about you. I felt bad. I've totally pushed you in to the deep end for your first week. Then when you didn't come back, I couldn't settle, and thought I'd better check in on you. I might be an arsehole, but I'm a caring one.'

A laugh escaped her lips and she felt better. She pushed the rolling pin down the side of her chair.

'I also had a phone call from Declan. He said you'd been to see him and made some excellent observations. He thinks you're okay and believe me he doesn't like many people. Wendy has been to the hospital and took samples of Bronte's hair. They're on the way to the forensic lab in Chorley as we speak.'

'That's great.' She stood up; her legs didn't feel as wobbly. 'Would you like another drink?'

He passed her his glass and she refilled both of them.

'I'd better call a cab.'

'You can sleep here if you want, the chair is really comfy. I don't have a spare bed, but I do have spare bedding. I'll drop you off at yours in the morning so you can shower then we can both go to work. Save you messing around with taxis.'

'Thank you, that's really kind of you but I'm a bit old to be sleeping on chairs. My back will be breaking by the morning. I'll ring for a taxi.'

Morgan had to stop herself from blurting out that he could sleep in her bed. He'd think she was too forward.

'No worries, I can still pick you up in the morning. Do you want some food before you leave?'

'No offence, I'm starving but your fridge contents leave a lot to be desired.'

'Ah, but you haven't seen my store cupboard. I can rustle up a tuna pasta bake and there's a garlic bread in the freezer.'

Ben laughed and nodded. 'All right, sounds perfect.'

She didn't tell him she had an ulterior motive and was trying her best to keep him here as long as possible. She didn't want him to go; she liked his company and there was no way she was telling him she was scared to be alone.

CHAPTER FORTY-THREE

Greg Barker was pacing up and down the front office of the police station. He'd been waiting fifteen minutes and his blood pressure was rising by the second. The sliding doors opened and in walked that cheeky bitch who'd come into his house yesterday and all but accused him of murder. If that got out, he'd be finished; it didn't matter if it wasn't true. He stared at her and the much older man next to her. She smiled at him and he couldn't stop himself.

'I want to make a formal complaint about you.' He stepped too close to her. He knew he was out of order, but the tight ball of anger inside his chest didn't care.

The woman stepped away from him, still smiling. In a polite but firm voice she answered him. 'I'm sorry, Mr Barker; if you take a seat I'll speak to you.'

'Take a seat? Are you having a laugh? I've been here fifteen minutes already, waiting for someone. I'm a very busy man.'

The older man stepped in front of him. 'I'm Detective Sergeant Ben Matthews, I'll take your complaint. Just let me get in and you can come into that interview room over there.'

Greg nodded. 'Don't be long, I'm not waiting.'

He watched as they buzzed themselves through the double doors leading into the station. Christ, he was furious. He'd lain awake all night thinking about her accusations, then got up with the worst indigestion he'd ever had.

The door opened and he stepped in. The woman wasn't anywhere in sight, thank God.

'Please, have a seat and tell me what this is about?'

'Ms Brookes.'

'Officer Brookes?'

'Whatever. She came to my house to ask me questions about the murders yesterday afternoon. I didn't like the tone of her voice or the way she spoke to me. You do know who I am, right? I have friends in high places.'

'What's your name again? I missed it the first time.'

Greg knew his game; well, two could play that.

'Mayor Gregory Barker.'

'Date of birth, Mayor?'

'Mayor is my title not my name, and what has my date of birth got to do with anything?'

'Whenever we, and by we, I mean the entire police force, have to speak to someone and take their details we have to make sure they're correct, to put on our system.'

'Why are you putting me on your system?' His voice was incredulous.

'If you want to log a complaint it will have to be submitted on our system, and I need your full details, sir: name, date of birth, address. It's standard procedure.'

Greg felt his chest tighten. 'Twenty-second of May 1950. Look, I want her spoken to; she had no right turning up at my house like that.'

'I'm afraid Detective Brookes had every right, sir. This is a serious murder investigation; your name has come up in our enquiries, therefore we are duty bound by the law to ask you questions in relation to the case. It wouldn't matter if you were my boss, the rules apply to everyone. How else would we solve crimes?'

Greg pushed back his chair and stood up, leaning over the desk, waving his fist. 'You're all in this together. You lot are a pack of wankers and I'll see you pay for this.'

He watched in slow motion as the man in front of him slammed his hand against a red button on the wall. The door behind him burst open and in rushed three coppers. Before he knew it he was pushed face first against the wall and in handcuffs.

'What are you doing? Get off me, you morons. I'll sue you all.'

'Mr Barker, you are under arrest for an offence under Section Four of the Public Order Act. You do not have to say anything, but it may harm your defence…'

Barker let out a roar as he began to grapple with the two officers holding him. He didn't hear the rest of the caution the copper was reading out because he was too busy trying to throw them off.

There was a hiss and he heard a shout of 'PAVA deployed'. The next thing his eyes were watering and stinging so much he buckled to his knees, screaming. He felt himself being dragged out of the small room. His legs were dragging along the carpet, but he didn't care because his eyeballs were burning out of his skull and he couldn't see for the tears pouring down his cheeks.

CHAPTER FORTY-FOUR

Morgan watched, open-mouthed, as Gregory Barker was dragged screaming and in handcuffs down to the custody suite. Ben came out of the interview room, his eyes watering.

'Christ that stuff goes everywhere in a small space.'

'What happened?'

'Our esteemed mayor lost his shit, so I arrested him.'

She started to laugh and Ben joined in. Both of them were almost bent double with laughter when Tom came striding towards them.

'Am I interrupting?'

Ben stopped laughing. 'No, boss.'

'Care to tell me what the hell just happened and why Gregory Barker is in custody having his eyes rinsed by a nurse?'

'He was angry and aggressive towards me, and I feared for my safety. He's been arrested under Section Four.'

'Jesus, you're having me on. Why couldn't you have sorted this out amicably?'

'Boss, the man is an idiot. Just because he's the mayor doesn't give him the right to threaten me or my team.'

'No, it doesn't but it sure as shit makes my life difficult. I'll have to talk to him, smooth things over a bit.'

'Tell him if he drops his ridiculous accusations, I'll drop my charges. I still want to talk to him in connection with these murders, so you can break that news to him. He can either come back a little later when he's calmed down or get it over with now. His call.'

'Jesus.'

Tom stormed off towards custody and Ben looked at Morgan. 'Come on, let's grab a coffee and you can fill me in on why you went to talk to him alone. I hate lecturing people, but that was risky. Especially with people like him. They have a way of using their connections to make their life easy and everyone else's difficult. You saw how he kicked off. What if he'd done that to you and no one knew where you were?'

Her cheeks began to burn. 'Sorry, I thought I was helping.'

'You were.'

Morgan followed him to the office where Amy and a couple of others were mid-conversation. She went to switch the kettle on.

'Anyone?'

Everyone held their hands up. Three mugs of tea and two coffees later she was sitting opposite Ben in his office. The others were watching, and she felt a little awkward. It was as if she was the entertainment factor of CID.

'So?'

'He knew the O'Briens very well; he also knew the Potters. When I asked him if I could talk to him about the murders, he didn't even mention the O'Briens. If you knew two families that had been murdered in the same house, wouldn't you mention it? He got really cagey and told me to leave when I asked about his business partnership with Jason O'Brien.'

'Very odd. I'm going to have to keep you out of anything to do with him now though. Even though he won't make a formal complaint, it's easier that way.'

'A formal complaint?'

'Look, one thing you need to be ready for in this job is the complaints. It doesn't matter how good you are or whether you didn't do anything wrong. People don't like being accused or arrested. They sometimes get arsy and will blame everyone but themselves. It's usually the arresting officer. Most of them get dropped before they even start, so don't worry about it. But next time make sure you don't go on your own. For your own safety.'

'I won't.'

She took her mug of coffee and walked down to the office she now called home. She still didn't know who had banged on her window last night, but in the clear light of day she reasoned that it could have just been teenagers, messing around. But what if it was Stan? The thought brought her back to the whole Stan situation. She had to speak to him. She wanted to know what he had done with her necklace and what he might be able to tell her about the Potters. She doubted he would have opened up to Ben about them. Stan had a long-standing hatred of the police due to various run-ins with them over the years, further fuelled by her decision to become one. Maybe it was time they had their first adult conversation of her life. Before she disappeared through the door, she turned around.

'Can I go to the library?'

'If you need to, I don't think you'll get in any trouble there.'

Ben winked at her and she smiled. She wanted to get the newspaper reports from the O'Briens' murders. How would the person who killed the Potters know about the cloths on their faces and the killer hiding in the cupboard if it wasn't them? There was some kind of connection she had to figure out. And when she'd finished there, she'd hunt down Stan. It wouldn't hurt to visit The Grain either.

The small library wasn't even open when Morgan arrived. Deciding to grab herself a coffee, she wandered down the high street to the small coffee shop she favoured. Taking her latte with her, she was glad to see the librarian opening the doors.

'Morning.'

She smiled back at her. 'Morning, I was wondering if you kept copies of old newspapers.'

'How old?'

'The seventies.' Morgan was praying they did; she needed to find something to warrant her interest in Barker.

'We do, although most of them have been scanned onto the computer. That's a popular decade.'

She smiled.

'Come in and take a seat at one of the computers in the corner, I'll come and get them up for you in a minute.'

'Thank you.'

Morgan walked in and felt her whole body relax. She was instantly transported back to her childhood. The library had been her favourite place to hang out; she loved reading more than anything. She sat down, the worries and stresses of the last few days pushed to the back of her mind. Tonight, she'd be taking her baton and cuffs home with her, maybe even her police radio. Better to be prepared should whoever the idiot who was messing around come back. She scanned the paperbacks; it had been ages since she'd lost herself in a book. The last six months had all been nonfiction books about law and order while she'd been in training.

'Right, let me see.' The older woman leant over her shoulder and began typing in the search bar. Within a minute she was on the archive pages.

'Was there any particular year, date you were looking for?'

'Yes, the murders on Easdale Road in 1975.'

The woman stared at her. 'What are you, a reporter?'

Morgan shook her head. 'No, definitely not. I'm a police officer.'

'Oh, well I hope there's something here that can help you. If you type it in the search bar it should bring everything up. Shout me if you need anything else.'

'Thank you.'

The woman walked away to sort out the large pile of books on the desk, leaving her to it. Morgan waited for the articles to load and lost herself reading them, scribbling down notes as she read. Greg Barker's name was mentioned a few times; there were pictures of him looking haggard despite his youth. A lot of pictures of him: visiting the house to lay flowers at the entrance to the drive; at the funeral,

wearing dark glasses and a long black woollen coat, looking more like
a Mafia boss than a friend. She finally found what she was looking
for in a small column. A police source had confirmed they believed
the murderer had lain in wait for the family to come home from an
evening celebrating at a restaurant for Jennifer O'Brien's birthday.
The reporter on this case had an inside source; there was no doubt
about it. There were pictures from inside the house and on one of
them the hall cupboard with the caption 'Waiting to Slaughter'.
These headlines were repeated not only in the *Cumbrian News*, but
the reporter had sold them on to the nationals as well. There were
several articles stating that close family friend and business associ-
ate Gregory Barker had been helping police with their enquiries.
Nothing about being a suspect or arrested, and no other suspects
had been singled out either. After an hour of reading everything
there was, she slipped her notepad into her handbag and finished
her now cold coffee. Standing up, she heard a voice.

'Did you find what you were looking for?'

'I did, thank you.'

'That seems to be the hot topic at the moment.'

'It is unfortunately.' She walked to the door then turned back.
'What did you mean when you said it was a popular decade?'

'A slight exaggeration on my part. You're only the second person
to ask to look at them.' She laughed.

'Do you remember who the first was?' Morgan crossed her
fingers, excited at the thought of there being some connection.

'I do, it was a teenager. He said he was doing research for a
college project. Strange research if you ask me, but it's not my job
to judge. I just loaded them up for him like I did for you.'

'Do you have his name?'

Morgan felt her stomach begin to churn with excitement; the
thought of someone coming here to look up the first murders was
a huge coincidence and would explain how they knew about the
cupboard.

'I don't, sorry, I didn't ask.'

Her excitement was short-lived. 'Can you remember when he came in?'

'About a fortnight ago.'

'Do you remember what he looked like, was wearing?'

'He was a little taller than you, smartly dressed for a teenager. He had nice hair, though, he was forever running his hand through it. I'm pretty sure he had a girl waiting outside. She was on her phone chatting rather loudly to her friend.'

Morgan rushed back to the computer and brought up Instagram and searched for Harrison Wright's page. After scrolling through the list, she found him. The woman came over and stared at the screen.

'Looks like him, but I couldn't be a hundred per cent sure of it.'

She found a picture of Harrison and Bronte. 'What about her, did you see her?'

'Hard to say, she's similar but I wouldn't want to say for definite. I've been off for ten days. This is my first day back in work, and my memory isn't as good as it used to be. To be honest, after all the gin and tonics I consumed, half of my brain cells are probably dead. Sorry, I'm not much help, am I?'

Morgan smiled. 'No, you've been very helpful. Thank you.'

She walked back to her car. She'd pass all this on to Ben as soon as she'd hunted down Stan.

CHAPTER FORTY-FIVE

Morgan drove at a snail's pace through Rydal Falls, keeping an eye open for Stan. With his drunken shuffle he wouldn't be too hard to find. Turning into Harrison Street, she stopped outside Carol's terraced house. She'd been here twice in four years and it had been twice too many, but needs must. This wasn't about her and Stan, it was about the O'Briens and the Potters. She owed it to both families to try and figure out what the hell went wrong and why so many people had died in the same house.

Opening the rusted gate, she walked along the short path and knocked on the broken front door. A dog began to bark inside; she could see it through the yellowing net curtains as it tried to jump at the window to get to her. It was an ugly thing that looked like some kind of pug crossed with a bulldog. She heard the click-clacking of Carol's heels as she tottered towards the front door. Morgan stepped back, unsure what kind of mood the woman was going to be in or whether her ugly dog would come pounding out of the front door.

The door opened a couple of inches and one of Carol's eyes stared at her through the crack.

'Oh, it's you. What do you want?'

'Is Stan here?'

'Piss off, Spot.' Carol screamed at the dog so loud Morgan thought her eardrums had burst.

'Mangy dog, it never shuts up barking. Always the same whenever he's not here.'

'Who, Stan?'

There was a bang as the front door slammed shut, what sounded like a full-on scrap from inside and then another loud slam as a door inside was closed. The front door opened a lot wider this time and Carol smiled at her. Morgan smiled back.

'Christ, sorry about that. I can't hear myself think with its constant yapping. Where were we? Oh yeah, Stan. He's got a nerve your dad, he thinks he can do what he wants whenever he wants.'

Morgan nodded, and thought to herself *same old Stan*. 'Is he here though?'

'Sorry, love, I've had enough of him. Chucked him and his stuff out a few days ago. I tried, you know, to put up with him. But there's only so much lying and stealing I can take. Is it important?'

'Yes, I need to speak to him urgently about a work matter.'

'Oooh, finally got himself in trouble with the cops, has he? I'm amazed it's taken this long to be honest.'

'He's not in trouble, I just need to find him.'

'Try the pubs along the high street. He was spending more time in that little crappy one, The Kings, that's full of the heavy drinkers like him, than he was anywhere else. If not, I don't know where else to suggest really; the homeless shelter maybe? If they'll have him that is.'

'Thanks, Carol, I will.'

Carol slammed the door shut, no 'goodbye' or 'take care'. Morgan turned and walked out of the gate. The dog was still barking and slobbering all over the already filthy net curtains.

*

The Kings was next on her list.

She walked inside, and her stomach churned at the lingering smell of stale lager that hung in the air. She looked around, couldn't see Stan and was about to walk out when the barman shouted: 'What's up, who you looking for?'

She walked towards him. 'Stan Brookes, do you know him?'

He nodded. 'Reckon I do, what's he done to get in trouble this time with the law? If he carries on, I'm going to have to ban him. He's bad for my business all these coppers turning up looking for him.'

'How do you know I'm a copper?'

He arched an eyebrow at her. 'Who else would you be? No one wants to know where Stan is for anything good.'

He pointed towards the toilets. 'If you hang around, he'll be out in a minute.'

She felt her shoulders relax and perched on one of the bar stools.

'I'd offer you a drink, but have you got any ID on you? I mean you look all of about seventeen and I'm not getting caught serving underage. Sneaky bastards caught my daughter out last year. She got an eighty quid fine.'

'I'm not here to catch you out. Can I have a Coke, please, and whatever Stan drinks.'

The barman nodded. Poured out her Coke and a pint of lager, passing them to her. She handed him a fiver, but he pushed it back.

'On the house, but don't tell Stan that. It's the only free drink he's getting off me this month.'

He walked away, leaving her sipping the Coke and staring at the door to the gents. Finally it opened and Stan walked out looking much cleaner than she'd expected him to.

He stood and stared at her. She nodded her head.

'Stan, I need to talk to you.' She pointed to a table in the corner and crossed the room, holding the pint of lager towards him. She saw him glance towards the exit, then back at the drink she was holding. If he'd thought about escaping it had only been for a fleeting moment; instead he followed her and sat down opposite.

'Morgan.'

'Stan, let's not mess around. I know you worked as a gardener for the Potters and the O'Briens. Please can you tell me what you knew about them, what sort of people they were, if they had any problems we might not have been aware of? I want to find out who would kill those families; they deserve justice.'

He stared into his pint, and she tried to keep her voice calm; if she got angry then he'd clam up for definite.

'I know you don't really care about anyone except yourself but come on. Saul Potter was a good man from what I've been told about him, and he gave you work when a lot of people turned their back on you. Don't do this for me, do it for them, do it for Saul. He was murdered along with his wife and daughter. He didn't deserve that, none of them did. So if you know anything—'

'Saul was a good bloke, you're right. He never looked down his nose at me. His wife now, she wasn't such a good person.'

Morgan felt her heart skip a beat. He carried on talking.

'She was cheating on him; I saw her a few times when he was at work. Carrying on with that pompous prick, it upset me. I didn't know what to do about it, though, so I didn't do anything and look what happened.'

'What was his name?'

'Barker, Greg Barker. He's our esteemed mayor. I'm not proud of myself, you know; I wish I'd have done something, but I didn't know what to do and now they're dead.'

'It's a difficult situation to be in.'

He stared at her; she kept his gaze.

'That day you saw them, you know you're the last person we know about to have spoken to them. Can you tell me what they said, how they were with one another?'

'Saul told me to come back the next day. He said he needed a hand to cut a few of the trees back. He slipped me twenty quid. He was a bit quiet; he said to go up to the house and ask Olivia for something to eat. He was good like that, always made sure I had food when I was there.'

'He sounds great. And what was Olivia like that day? Was she okay, her usual self?'

He shook his head. 'Not really, she never liked me much. I could see the way she'd look me up and down, caught her rolling her eyes to her daughters a couple of times. That kind of thing. But she always made me a sandwich and gave me a can of pop. She looked a bit upset that day; her eyes were a bit red as if she'd been crying. Didn't say much at all, passed me a sandwich, apple, bag of crisps and a can of Vimto then shut the door. She didn't even give me the chance to say thanks.'

'Did you see the girls?'

He shook his head. 'I was about to leave when I heard her phone ring. She was shouting down it to whoever was on the other side. Said they'd ruined her life and she'd make them pay big time. I backed off; it was none of my business. I went back to Carol's and that was when she decided to throw me out, so I came to the pub and got drunk. You can ask Steve over there, behind the bar. I was here until closing time and then I went to your place. It's really dark along those lanes; I fell over into the hedgerows a couple of times. Then I realised I was the last person you'd want to see, so I sat at the edge of the drive on that big boulder. Until I was cold and plucked up the courage to knock on your door.'

Morgan had no reason to disbelieve him; he hadn't faltered once. He hadn't paused as if trying to decide what to tell her, it had come out with no hesitation.

'It's terrible. What about the O'Briens?'

'Morgan, that was a long time ago. My memory isn't what it used to be. I've drunk a lot of alcohol over the years since that happened and probably killed off more of my brain cells than I can afford to.'

'I know, but was there anything you can think of at the time that rang bells, that you thought was odd?'

He blew out a long breath. 'It's funny you know, I hadn't really thought about it much, but that Greg Barker was also always sniffing around Jennifer. He worked with her husband Jason. I just thought they were good friends, well until they fell out over money; I was a lot younger back then and had my own fair share of problems. My parents kicked me out of the house when I was seventeen, you know, and I spent a lot of years sofa surfing until I met your mum. Sylvia changed my life for the better; at least she did for a while. But it's the drink; I've always had a problem with it. I tried my best to get off it. I joined the AA and went to the meetings religiously. I was sober for almost ten years.'

'What happened?' Morgan didn't want him to stop talking. They had never had a conversation like this before.

'Sylvia, she wanted a baby so bad, it was all she talked about. But she would always lose them before she made it to three months. I prayed so hard for a miracle to happen and it did, you came along and Sylvia was in love. She was smitten with you and I got pushed to one side. Before you say anything, I know what I sound like, I was like a spoilt brat. We'd been on our own for so many years with no children, we were both almost forty when you happened. I found it a lot harder to adjust than I imagined. So instead of going home and playing happy families like I should have, like I knew Sylvia wanted, I spent more and more time in the pub. I wasn't there when she needed me, that day.'

His breath caught in the back of his throat and for the first time in forever she took a good, hard look at the man sitting opposite her. His face was full of deep grooves and lines; his greying hair was almost gone on the top it was so thin. His eyes were a piercing blue, watery with unshed tears. A lump formed in the back of her throat. She'd spent so many years hating him she couldn't remember a time when she'd loved him and that made her sad. Neither of them spoke for several minutes, and she could feel Stan's eyes on her as if he, too, was only just realising the woman sitting opposite him was his own flesh and blood. But as much as she longed to continue talking about her mum, she had to focus on the investigation.

'Stan, did you hear any rumours about the O'Briens' murders at the time? Did anyone point fingers, gossip, that kind of thing?'

'Honestly, I don't think so. I mentioned to the police that I thought Barker was involved on some level, but I didn't think they listened. They were never going to believe me over him. I'd been in a fair share of drunken fights and I got caught for petty thefts a few times. The coppers didn't like me and wouldn't take anything I said serious. I carried on minding my own business and drinking, and the house got boarded up. People eventually stopped speaking about the tragedy. The police tried to investigate but they didn't have a clue. Over the years, when no one was ever brought to justice, it all got forgotten about. The police round here were never much experienced with something of that level. It was far too serious for them to handle. An entire family were murdered in cold blood and all the locals were bothered about was if it would affect the value of their properties.'

The door opened and two men around the same age as Stan barged through it, stopped and stared at the pair of them sitting there. Morgan supposed they made an odd couple.

'What you done now, Stan? You've been in more scrapes with the coppers this week than I have my entire life.'

Stan glared at the men, his cheeks reddening. Morgan realised they had no idea who she was and Stan didn't look as if he was about to introduce her to them. She stood up, reached over and held out her hand for him to shake. He looked at her but took it firmly in his grasp.

'Thanks for your advice, Stan, I really appreciate you taking the time to talk to me. I'll see you around.'

With that she walked out of the pub, leaving him to it. He could tell his friends whatever story he wanted. She doubted it would be the truth, though; he was ashamed of her and that stung, a lot more than she'd ever admit to anyone. She'd wanted to ask him about the necklace, but missed the chance when those two had walked in.

As she sat inside her car staring at the pub in the distance, she thought about her mum and a sharp stabbing pain filled her chest. Sylvia had wanted her so much; they had been so close. Yet Morgan had no idea why she'd killed herself. Now that Stan had actually spoken to Morgan she wondered if he'd open up about the circumstances surrounding her death. After it had happened he'd clammed up and barely spoken to her. She had blamed him for everything. Maybe she was being a little unfair. She now knew after working this job that people could snap out of the blue.

CHAPTER FORTY-SIX

Morgan knew she needed something concrete to give to Ben, some kind of hard evidence of Barker's involvement with Olivia. The woman from the post office had mentioned a pub she'd seen them at, The Grain. Might as well visit that as well, see if anyone there had anything to say. At least Ben would know she was trying her best to help. The drive to the small country pub took her past Thirlmere. Hot, tired and fed up of getting nowhere fast, she stopped in a small lay-by and got out of the car. She walked to the dry-stone wall which formed a barrier between the steep drop to the huge reservoir and the car park. The sun was trying its best to peek through the dark clouds that were forming above the Helvellyn mountain ridge to the east. The rugged beauty of where she lived and worked was never lost on her. Though the warmer weather brought swarms of tourists to the area, if you knew where to look there were still plenty of places to escape to while most people flocked to Lake Windermere, Coniston Water or Tarn Hows. The conifer-clad banks of Thirlmere were still a good place to escape to and a couple of times she'd hiked the ten-mile walk around it. Her mind felt heavy, so much responsibility felt like a dead weight around her neck. She wanted to prove her capability as a detective to Ben on her own merit. If she could just find something to move this case along, it would prove to him he'd made the right decision.

The Grain was definitely a hard place to find. She drove past the lane which led to it a few times, having to do the tightest five-point turns on the narrow lanes. Eventually she turned into the secluded car park. Baskets, tubs and window boxes overflowing with geraniums, petunias, trailing nasturtium and bacopa, against the backdrop of the white-washed walls, made the outside look so pretty. There were a few picnic benches and a small fenced-off play area. Hers was the only car and she wondered if anyone was in. The front door was ajar, and she knocked.

A voice shouted: 'Come in.'

Morgan stepped inside her second pub of the day. This one smelt far better than the one before. Inside it was much brighter and modern as well. There was a woman behind the bar, polishing the woodwork.

'Morning, lovey, we're not open yet.'

'Morning. Oh, that's okay, I'm not a customer. I'm from the police. I wondered if I could ask you a few questions about an investigation.'

'Yes, of course. You'd better come and sit down; would you like a tea or coffee?'

'If it's no trouble, a coffee would be amazing. Thank you.'

'No trouble at all, I was going to make myself one anyway. I'm Elaine, I run this place with my partner Simone. You've just missed her; she's gone into Rydal to get some shopping.'

Elaine disappeared for a few minutes and came back with two mugs of coffee; passing one to Morgan, she sat down.

'What can I help you with?'

'I'm part of the team investigating the murder of the Potter family. Are you aware of it?'

She nodded. 'Terrible tragedy, yes. I am very aware of it.'

'Did you know the Potters? Did they ever come here?'

'I'm not one for gossip, but I knew something bad was going to come out of it.'

'What?'

'That woman's blatant lack of morals. She used to come here now and again with her husband. He was such a nice guy. Then she stopped bringing him and brought another man instead. It was obvious what they were up to. They'd be holding hands under the table. I tried not to look, but you could see him stroking her thigh. I'm not a prude at all, but it was the total disregard for her family which upset me. I thought they'd split up and it wouldn't have been so bad if they had, then I saw her the day after in town with her husband, her arm linked through his. He looked so happy and it made me feel sick. Simone told me to forget about it, not to let it bother me, that it wasn't any of my business and she was right, it wasn't.'

Morgan felt so sad for Saul; they say the partner is always the last to know.

'Who was the man she came with, do you know?'

'Greg Barker, you'll know him, he's the mayor.'

She smiled; she knew him very well. Looking up, she spotted a domed CCTV camera by the bar.

'You wouldn't have any footage of the pair of them together, would you?'

Elaine let out a laugh. 'Do I? Yes, I do, only it's more like a pornographic video. I didn't know what to do with it. Simone told me I should destroy it, but I didn't. I just had a bad feeling about it. I guess I realised it was all going to go to shit before it actually did. Truth be told, I'll be glad to be rid of it. I've kept it in the safe, not sure why I did but you are very welcome to it. If I never have to look at it again that would suit me just fine.'

She stood up and disappeared behind the bar for a second time. Morgan's stomach was churning; she wanted to know what was on the footage and prayed to God it was enough evidence to keep Barker in custody. Elaine came back clutching a pen drive in her hand and passed it to her.

'There you go.'

'Thank you, I really appreciate it.'

'You're welcome, I hope he never darkens my door again. He's a vile man. God knows who voted him in as mayor, because most of the people I know can't abide him either.'

Excited to go back and see what was on the pen drive, Morgan headed back to the station to view the footage and tell Ben.

CHAPTER FORTY-SEVEN

Ben was waiting for Tom to give him the all-clear to speak to Greg Barker in custody when Morgan came rushing down the stairs, breathless.

'Boss, you need to come and look at this footage which was handed to me at The Grain.'

'I'm about to go into interview.'

She was shaking her head. 'No, like now.'

He followed her up to the office, where she had an image paused on her computer monitor. He perched on the desk behind her and she played the short clip for him. He watched as CCTV footage began to play of a couple walking out of a pub. Judging by the way the woman was walking in front and the distance between them, they'd fallen out. The footage was clear and Ben realised he was watching Olivia Potter; the male behind her wasn't her husband. It was Greg Barker. Morgan paused it again, turning to look at him.

'Bloody hell, this is good. What were they doing? Is she with any of her family?'

'I hope not because it gets better in a terrible sort of way.' She pressed play again and they watched as Barker jogged to catch up with her. He grabbed hold of her elbow and pulled her back towards him. She pushed him away, but he gently tugged her forwards. The next minute they were kissing, and not just a peck on the cheek: it was full-on. The car park was deserted. The only two cars there must have belonged to the pair of them. The next minute he was pushing her against the bonnet of a car, his hands running up her thighs, lifting her skirt.

'Jesus, does he bang her there in a car park?'

Morgan nodded. 'At least you can have him for public indecency if all else fails.'

They watched in silence as the couple on the screen had the quickest sex Ben had ever seen, in full view of the outside camera. When it was over he shook his head.

'Blimey, my eyes are burning.'

Morgan nodded. 'Mine too, and that's the second time I've had to sit through it.'

'Where did it come from?'

'The landlady at a small pub, The Grain. When I spoke to the couple who own the post office she told me she'd seen Olivia and Barker together a couple of times at the pub. I thought I'd go and speak to them.'

'Brilliant, absolutely brilliant, Morgan. This gives my little chat with Barker a whole new perspective. He has motive, he knew the Potters, well Olivia, a lot more than he's been letting on and he knew the O'Briens very well. He's the right age to have committed the first murders.'

'What are you going to do?'

'Play him his debut into film-making and see what he has to say for himself. The sly old fox, just goes to prove you're never too old to do anything when you put your mind to it. It's not enough to charge him, though, we need forensics to tie him to one or both cases. You know what the CPS is like; they won't take this anywhere unless we have concrete evidence.'

'What about Jamie Stone? Do you think there's a connection between him and Greg Barker? I don't believe we have that many murderers running around Rydal Falls.'

'You and Amy can focus on Jamie Stone, and his associates. If they were acquainted and how well they knew each other. As the mayor and editor of the newspaper they were bound to move in the same circles. Attend the same functions. Maybe Stone knew about the video and was going to expose Barker. He's certainly angry enough to have the balls to kill someone. Go and interview the staff at the paper, see if there was any talk of a big exposure.'

'Or even blackmail?'

'Maybe, depends how much Jamie Stone knew about Barker's affairs. If it comes back to Barker, though, then we have motive.'

He left her, smiling to himself. Things were picking up now. His main focus was the Potters' and Stone's murders. They were the ones he was most likely to get a conviction for; the evidence was fresh. He wasn't discounting getting justice for the O'Briens. They'd certainly waited long enough, and he hoped that he could link Barker to both sets of murders, but he had to focus on the now. Grabbing his laptop from his office, he was looking forward to seeing Barker's face when he played the short clip for him. He'd have two officers standing at the back of the room just in case he flipped.

He was too knackered to be fighting. He hadn't been able to sleep last night when the taxi had dropped him off. He'd lain awake thinking about Morgan's offer to stop at hers, trying to figure out if she genuinely meant sleep over on the sofa or had been offering more. He liked her a lot, but for now he was happy to be friends with her and he hoped she felt the same. He didn't want to go jumping in with his size ten boots and make a fool of himself. He'd known Cindy since school; they'd been going out with each other since they were fourteen. She was all he'd known. If she'd been so unhappy with him, he would have gladly given her a divorce even though it would have broken his heart. He'd rather have let her go and find happiness somewhere else than choose dying over staying with him. All those times he'd come home late and she'd been drunk and asleep because she was lonely were too many to count. He blinked away the tears. He'd been a selfish bastard and he didn't deserve a second chance at happiness. This was his life now, forever destined to be as lonely as he'd let Cindy be. He decided it was a wise decision not to stop at Morgan's; she deserved more than he could give her and that made him sad. Taking a deep breath, he put it all to the back of his mind. His focus needed to be on doing what he knew he could do and that was catching killers.

Greg Barker was nursing a mug of tea, and there was an untouched biscuit next to it. He didn't lift his head to even acknowledge Ben or Abigail when they walked in. Tom had insisted on being present while he was interviewed, along with the solicitor who had been called out. Ben knew he was fearful of a repeat of earlier. Sitting down, he set up his laptop and turned it to face Greg with the video paused.

'Greg, I'd like to talk to you about some new information which has come to light. I need you to watch this video.'

'No comment.'

He didn't lift his head.

'Right then, I'll just play it and see if you want to make a comment after it finishes. For the benefit of the tape I'm showing Gregory Barker some footage received as evidence.'

Tom walked around until he was standing behind Greg and could see the screen. Ben pressed play. Greg lifted his head to take a look; his eyes were red and swollen from the PAVA, making him look as if he'd been crying for hours. As the video played, he sat up straight. His solicitor and Tom both squirmed. Greg's hands curled into fists. Tom waited until it finished then nodded at Ben and left the room.

'Where did you get that? I want to make a complaint, that was taken without my knowledge.'

Ben had to admit the guy had balls. He was banged up, about to be questioned about murdering at least four people and he was still playing the victim.

'We'll deal with that later.'

'Good, because it's pretty obvious, isn't it?'

'What's obvious? The only thing I can see is that you and Olivia Potter were clearly having an affair.'

'Obvious that whoever sent that is the killer. Why would I kill the woman I loved and her family?'

'You tell me, it looks to me as if she's angry with you when she's walking away from you. Was she trying to break up with you? You seem to me like a man who is used to getting what he wants. If she didn't want you maybe you decided to teach her a lesson.'

Greg was shaking. He slammed his fists down on the table in front of him, and his solicitor pushed his chair away from him.

'Calm down, Mr Barker, you're not helping yourself.'

He turned to look at his solicitor and roared, 'Get out, you useless piece of crap.'

The solicitor looked at Ben and shrugged. 'Have it your way.'

Shuffling the papers in front of him, he snapped his briefcase shut and walked out of the door.

Now it was just Ben, Abigail, Barker and the two coppers on standby behind him.

'What's it going to be, are you going to answer my questions or not? I think that was a very bad move. Do you want me to ask your solicitor to come back in?'

Barker sat back in his chair, crossed his legs and stared at Ben. 'No comment and it's going to be no comment for every single question. So, unless you have enough evidence to charge me you only have a few more hours to keep me here, then you're going to have to release me on bail. You've already screwed my entire life up, there's nothing left to lose.'

Ben smiled at him. 'Well, I'm getting paid for this so we might as well go through the motions.'

Abigail slid a clipboard across the desk to him and he began to read off his list of questions to be greeted with a 'no comment', every single time.

CHAPTER FORTY-EIGHT

Morgan waited in the office for Ben. She'd shown Amy a copy of the footage. When he finally appeared, his face was red and he'd undone the top buttons on his shirt. His tie was loosened, and he looked like he needed to go home and sleep for a week.

'How did it go?'

'Rubbish, he's not coughing to anything. Sacked his solicitor after ten minutes and went "no comment" the rest of the interview. How did you get on at the library?'

'Interesting, the librarian said someone else had been in two weeks ago to search for the exact same thing I was looking for. Said he was a teenage boy with nice hair who kept running his fingers through it.'

'Harrison Wright?'

'I think so; he had a girl with him. She waited outside.'

Ben sat down and leant forward, putting his head in his hands. 'This whole thing is a mess, it's far too complicated for my poor brain.'

Amy threw him a Snickers.

He held his hand up. 'If you say anything.'

'I'm not, I wouldn't. But you're not yourself when you're hungry.'

'Amy.'

'Sorry, couldn't help it. So, what's what and who's who?'

'I wish I knew; I think Barker has the motive, and he's definitely angry enough. I've never seen so much hostility come off a man who's supposed to be a pillar of the community. He's like a man possessed.'

'Maybe he needs a Snickers too.' Amy laughed at her own joke. Ben shook his head. Morgan stood by the whiteboard, uncapping a pen. She wrote three headings: Potters, Stone and O'Briens; underneath she wrote the families' names. Underneath Potters and O'Briens she wrote 'Gregory Barker'.

'What connections did Barker have with Stone?'

'He would have known him. He never admitted anything when I asked him just now though. I can't see how the mayor and the editor of the paper wouldn't be acquainted. We need it confirming. Write an action under Stone's name to speak to other councillors and staff at the paper, see if they knew each other.'

Morgan did. 'Harrison Wright, he knew the Potters. He's far too young to have known the O'Briens though. However, I think he did know about them. I'm pretty sure it was him who went to the library to research their murders. Why was he interested in them? Also we don't know if Bronte had a role in this. If she was with him it could have been the both of them and somehow it all went wrong.'

'We need to speak to him. I want him bringing back in for questioning ASAP. Have response officers located him yet? Write that down as an action, and when Bronte wakes up we'll question her to see if she remembers anything, but my focus would be Harrison.'

'What about Stan Brookes?'

Ben looked at her, but she didn't make eye contact with him and continued.

'Well he was the last person to see the Potters and he knew the O'Briens. He's the right age, so I don't think he can be totally discounted. I spoke to him this morning, though. I don't think he's the killer, but...'

'Put his name on the board, but somehow I don't see Stan as a viable suspect. For one thing I get the impression he hasn't got the balls and there's another.'

'What?'

'He likes to drink. The Potters' murders wasn't some unorganised spur-of-the-moment killing. It was an organised killing. Whoever did it planned it out; we know that because of the tox results. There were traces of GHB in their systems. They didn't drug themselves and it's not the kind of thing I think Stan would be into. This killer took their time in researching and planning. Why did they hang Olivia, though? She didn't have the head injuries the others did.'

There was a knock on the door and Declan walked in. 'Hope I'm not disturbing anything?'

Ben shook his head.

Morgan turned away, relieved. As much as she disliked Stan, he was still her dad. Although she owed him no loyalty, after their little chat this morning she had found the block of ice beginning to thaw whenever she thought about him. It would have been hard to come to terms with it if Ben thought he was the killer.

'I can tell you why Olivia didn't have her brains smashed in. She was already dead. The killer had given her a fatal dose of GHB; the levels in her results were much higher than the others.'

'Then why hang her if she was already dead?'

'Maybe whoever it was didn't want to think they'd killed her. It made them feel better if they remembered her hanging; they couldn't force themselves to beat her like the rest. Just a theory, by the way, but might as well throw it in there.'

Morgan was writing everything down. 'Why feel guilty about her and not the others? I don't get it. Or why not give them all a fatal dose?'

'To be honest I can't tell you that. What I can tell you is each victim had a different dosage of the drug in their system, which tells me that I don't think the person who administered it had a bloody clue what they were doing. It was hit and miss.'

'Maybe whoever it was had a burning hatred of Saul and Beatrix, yet not Olivia? And where does Bronte come into this? They didn't hit her as hard as the other two; she survived.'

Morgan shrugged. 'I think whoever did this loved Olivia far more than the others, which brings it back around to Barker. He was having an affair with her.'

Ben looked up. 'Oh, he was definitely having an affair with her. I think that CCTV footage Morgan secured proved that beyond reasonable doubt. He admitted that before he clammed up and went "no comment". Said why would he kill the woman he loved and her family. Taskforce are on the way to his house to search it and his car; hopefully they find something of forensic value.'

Declan sat on a desk next to Amy and they were whispering about something. Morgan looked away, her paranoia getting the better of her.

Ben stood up. 'Right then, we need to find Harrison Wright. He might be able to tell us a lot more about this than he's letting on, and do we have an update on Bronte? Life would be so much easier if we could talk to her.'

Declan held up his hand. 'Actually, that's why I'm here. I was passing and thought I'd give you the news.'

Morgan felt her heart drop to the bottom of her stomach; even though she didn't know the girl she didn't want her to be dead. She'd been rooting for her since she'd found her.

Declan continued. 'The hair sample tested positive for GHB and she's awake.'

Ben clapped and Amy let out a whoop of delight.

'Bad news is, she isn't speaking much. Can't remember anything about what happened from what I can gather, although her consultant can tell you more. You can thank me later. Ben, you owe me a drink or two when this is sorted.'

Ben grinned at Declan. 'I do, thank you. Come on, Amy, we need to get to the hospital and speak with Bronte.'

Morgan felt deflated. She'd wanted to be the one to speak to her and she hadn't been given the chance. She turned away from everyone and wrote the information Declan had shared on the board.

Declan was still sitting there when she turned around. Everyone else had left.

'You okay?'

'Yes, thanks. Are you?'

'Wonderful, how are you getting on with the O'Brien case?'

'I have a couple of leads, but nothing concrete.'

'Well that's good, it's not going to be easy; it's old. You're probably missing crucial evidence not to mention witnesses and suspects. Is there anything of forensic value that could be retested?'

She told him about the small square of carpet in the hall cupboard.

'That's great, it's a start. You might get trace evidence back from it or if you do get a suspect there's always a slim chance they might still have something with traces of the fibres on.

'Hey, you know he likes you a lot. But he's also a guilt-ridden, mixed-up workaholic. Give him a chance, sometimes he doesn't see what's in front of his nose. He's too busy sorting out everyone else's lives.'

Morgan laughed. 'We're not, well you know… It's strictly a professional relationship.'

Declan nodded. 'Might be better to keep it that way, at least until he comes to his senses. Not that it's anything to do with me. I'm just an old romantic. I like to see people happy and I think Ben deserves a bit of happy. Wait until you see him cleaned up, when he's had a shave and a decent haircut. He scrubs up quite well. Not sure the paunch is as easy to get rid of, but behind it he used to have a decent set of abs and plenty of muscles.'

She smiled, her face flushed pink. What had her life come to getting relationship advice from a doctor who only worked with dead people?

'Thanks, I'll remember that.'

'Anytime. I have to go; I'm not used to being around so many living souls, it's not good for my chakras.'

She laughed and he waved as he walked out of the door. She wondered about him, if he had a partner. He was funny and refreshingly caring considering she'd only met him a couple of times. Each time she'd met him he'd been kind to her; it meant a lot.

CHAPTER FORTY-NINE

The sister looked both Amy and Ben up and down. She wasn't having any of it.

'She's too poorly to be questioned.'

'She's alive though, and her entire family are dead; do you not think she'll want us to catch their killer? We need to know what she remembers; anything is good. We won't press her too hard. Please, it's very important.'

Amy nodded. 'Just a few questions.'

The sister folded her arms across her chest. 'Five minutes.'

'Does she know about her family?'

She shook her head. 'Poor thing, not yet.'

Ben didn't say it, but he was going to have to break the bad news to her and he wasn't relishing being the bastard who ruined her life for the second time. Right now, she knew she was in hospital and had been poorly and that was it.

The sister led them into the ICU and towards the room at the end. He could see her propped up in bed. She was staring at the other patients.

Amy whispered, 'This is going to be bad.'

He nodded, there was no doubt about it.

'Bronte, these are some detectives. They need to have a little chat. They won't be staying long, is that okay?'

The girl looked at Ben and Amy. One eye was swollen almost shut and that side of her face was a mass of purple and yellow bruises.

'Yes,' she croaked.

'I'll be just over there by the nurses' station. I'm watching, if you need me raise your hand, okay?'

Ben knew the nurse didn't want to be associated with any part of this. She was here to make the kid feel better not a hundred times worse. He stepped inside and smiled at her.

'I'm so glad to see you're awake, Bronte. I'm Ben and this is my colleague, Amy. She's not as scary as she looks.'

Bronte's lip turned up slightly in a half smile. He sat on the chair closest to her bed. Amy stood behind him.

'I know you feel rubbish and are in a lot of pain, but we need to ask you some questions about what happened.'

She nodded then grimaced. 'What did happen?'

Ben glanced at Amy, but she didn't speak. She was letting him take the lead and for once he wished she'd butted in like she usually did. It seemed no one had the heart to break the news to the poor girl.

'You were found with serious head injuries in the cellar of your house by a police officer and brought to the hospital. Do you remember what happened, how you got those injuries?'

She closed her eyes for a few moments then opened them.

'No, I can't remember anything. Except waking up here with the worst headache I've ever had. Where's my mum and dad? I thought they'd be here.'

Ben swallowed the lump that had formed in the back of his throat. 'The nurse is sorting that out.'

He couldn't tell her just yet because she'd dissolve in tears and he wouldn't get another thing out of her.

'Was there anything that happened that night in your house that was unusual? Did anyone turn up you weren't expecting? Any workmen, friends, neighbours?'

She paused. 'Harrison is usually at mine when he's not at work.'

'Was he there?'

She closed her eyes. 'I don't know.'

Amy got a photo of Greg Barker up on her phone and held it in front of her. 'What about him, do you know him?'

'Yeah, Greg. I know him, he comes around a bit. Usually when my dad's at work.'

Ben sat forward. 'Was he there before you got hurt?'

She shrugged. 'I can't remember anything. I'm trying to but it's like a black cloud in my mind.'

He reached out and took hold of her hand. 'It's okay, you're doing really well. Does your mum see Greg a lot?'

The question hung in the air; the girl might be injured but he could tell by the look in her eyes she wasn't stupid.

'Like are they having an affair?'

Ben nodded.

'I don't know, my dad isn't around much, and they argue a lot when he is. I want to see my mum now, please; can you get her, and Bea?'

Squeezing her hand, he took a deep breath. 'I have something terrible to tell you and it's not easy to say.'

She blinked her eyes wide, staring at him.

'You weren't the only person found in the cellar, sweetheart, your dad and Beatrix were with you.'

'Are they hurt, are they in hospital, where's Mum?'

The air in the room was suffocating and Ben wanted to run out of there and into the car park as fast as he could. He couldn't do this. He turned to look at Amy, who was shaking her head. He took a deep breath.

'Your mum, dad and Beatrix—' His voice broke and he couldn't speak.

Bronte just stared at him waiting for him to finish.

'I'm so sorry.'

'No, what are you sorry for?'

'I'm sorry to tell you that they're all dead.'

The hoarse scream filled the room and spilled out into the rest of the unit. She began to try to get out of bed. The sister and two nurses came running over and Ben let go of her hand. A nurse pushed him out of the way, bending down to hold the hysterical girl. Turning her head, she mouthed 'get out'. Amy grabbed his arm and pulled him out of the room. He let her drag him out, craning his neck around to see if Bronte was okay.

Once they were back inside the car, he looked at Amy. 'That was horrendous.'

'I thought you did okay, she had to know. Sooner or later someone was going to have to tell her; at least the nursing staff can blame you and Bronte won't hate them for it.'

'Glad to be of service. Seriously, Amy, I can't even begin to imagine what she's going through.'

'It's done.'

'Yeah, you know what, sometimes this job sucks big time. Plus, all we know is that Barker was sleeping with and visiting Olivia a lot when her dad wasn't around. I hope Taskforce have found some evidence at his house. I want to watch him squirm his way out of this one.'

They drove back in silence, Ben lost in a world of grief for Bronte Potter and her family.

CHAPTER FIFTY

Morgan arrived at the *Cumbrian News* office. There was a big CLOSED sign taped to the front window. The scene had been released late last night after Claire Williams, the murder investigation team's DCI, had visited and cleared it. She hoped to God that the specialist cleaning firm had been in first thing this morning to clean it up; surely they wouldn't have left that blood everywhere. It was a business. Her stomach lurched just thinking about the smell. She was going to find out sooner or later. She wanted to help Ben and by speaking to the staff here, she thought she might find out if there was a link between Stone and Barker.

Knocking on the door, her stomach felt like it did whenever she went on a boat. She hated sailing and even on bigger boats she still got seasick. She knocked harder; eventually the sound of footsteps could be heard on the tiled floor.

The door opened a tiny bit.

'We're closed, can't you read the sign?'

'Police, I need to speak to you.'

The door opened wide enough for her to squeeze through. She stepped in, relieved to see a sparkling clean floor and walls. The only smell which hit her nostrils was that of fresh paint.

'Mind that wall, it's still wet.'

She followed the older woman down the hall to an office. 'Take a seat. I'm Lana Wallis.'

Morgan did, and the woman sat behind the desk. 'What do you need to know?'

She didn't ask to see Morgan's credentials, which surprised her, but she looked as if she'd been in the job a long time, so could probably tell a copper from a one-mile radius. It was amazing just how many people could.

'I'm sorry for your loss. I need some background information about Jamie to help with the investigation.'

'It's sad, but he's not my loss. Truth be told he wasn't very well liked by anyone.'

'Oh.' Morgan was taken aback by her honesty; people normally loved to play grieving friends, lapping up the sympathy when someone died so brutally or unexpectedly.

'That sounds awful of me, I know it does. I'm not callous, but he didn't really care much about anyone here or his employees. He only cared about himself.'

'I take it he had a few run-ins with people then. Can you give me a list of them?'

She laughed. 'How long have you got, because it could take some time and that's only the ones I know about.'

'How about the most recent or anyone he had a particularly nasty fall-out with.'

'Let me see, he upset most of the town council. I know he had a particular dislike towards the mayor and had a fair few disagreements with him.'

'Gregory Barker?'

She nodded.

'What sort of disagreements?'

'I think Jamie was secretly jealous of Greg. God knows why, he's an arsehole as well. But the pair of them had a mutual dislike of each other. I believe they had a bit of a falling out at the town meeting a couple of nights ago.'

'Were you there? Did you see it?'

'No, my partner, Jackie, is a parish councillor and attends meetings. She told me. I have no idea why she keeps going to them, but she said she likes to give back to the community and they're entertaining.' She wrote a number on a Post-it and tore it off, passing it to Morgan. 'You can give her a call any time after five; she's also a teacher so is home most evenings if there's no afterschool clubs or staff meetings.'

'Thank you. Did you know about the family who were murdered at the same house at Easdale Road?'

'I didn't, not until Jamie mentioned it a couple of days ago. A bit weird that, isn't it? Imagine buying a house where a whole family were murdered and then it happening to you. God knows what they'll do with the place, but I can't see it being a selling point, can you? They'll probably do ghost hunts in it and sell tickets to spend a night there.'

'Did Jamie know a lot about the O'Briens? Is he, sorry, was he old enough to remember?'

'No, he's only in his late thirties. He said he was digging the old reports out, though he did mention that Greg knew both families. I told him that didn't mean much. I mean Greg was born around here and lived here his entire life. That's what happens. The ones who move away are lucky. Everyone else knows everybody else's business, there's no keeping secrets.'

'Did you know the Potters?'

'Not really, they've only been here a year or so. They're not from around here, so still a bit of a mystery to the locals, even more so now they're dead. How's the girl who survived?'

'Still hanging on. Did you ever hear any rumours of Greg and Olivia Potter having an affair?'

'Yes and no, I heard it in the post office. You wouldn't believe how much gossiping goes on in there. If you think hairdressers are bad you should stand in the queue in there for twenty minutes. I'm not one for listening to gossip, though I should because it's my job as a reporter. But there's one thing I hate more than anything and that's idle gossip.'

'Thank you, do you think I could take a look at the reports about the O'Brien murders? This isn't public knowledge, but I'm looking into them.'

'You could have them by all means, only I couldn't find them anywhere. I searched the records room where all the old papers are kept. Someone has been in there and been rooting around because the boxes are all over the place. But they're not here. I've checked all the desks including Jamie's and there's no sign of them. Did you check his car? Maybe they're inside it. I think he came back to find them, because he left before I did that day. He must have come back later on for them. Do you think that's why he was killed, because there was something in those reports the killer didn't want him to see?'

Morgan nodded. 'That would seem like a good enough motive. Please, can I ask this is between us for the time being.'

'Sure, if you need anything else give me a ring. I can't see this shithole being open much longer. We've been running by the seat of our pants for years. Jamie was the one who brought in the advertising and revenue. I suppose it was his passion. I lost my passion for this a long time ago.'

Morgan stood up and held out her hand. 'Thank you, Lana, you've been very helpful. I can see myself out.'

Morgan walked down the hall. It was hard to believe there had been a bloody, brutal murder in here a couple of days ago. Letting herself out, she made sure the door closed behind her and couldn't be opened again. Lana was alone in there and it would be awful if something happened to her as well. Although she had a feeling that Gregory Barker was the key to this whole thing: if he'd murdered the O'Briens, he wouldn't have wanted that dredging up by Jamie Stone.

Back at the station, she sat in the almost empty car park trying to gather her thoughts. She wondered how Ben and Amy were getting on with Bronte. It still hurt that she hadn't been asked to join them, but she told herself to stop acting like a spoiled child. Did she want to be there when they broke the news to the girl that her entire family were now dead? Not really; she didn't wish that on anyone. She wrote a brief draft of her conversation with Lana on the board, then phoned Ben.

Amy answered.

'He's driving. I'll put you on speaker.'

'I've been to speak to staff at the *Cumbrian News*. Well, one staff member, Lana Wallis; we had quite an interesting conversation. She said she'd heard rumours of an affair between Olivia and Greg Barker. Also said that Stone and Barker disliked each other. She thinks Stone had been digging into the old newspaper reports of the O'Brien murders. When she went to look for them, though, they were missing and she thinks that's why he came back that night. The killer must have known Stone was looking into it and taken them with him, and there's only one person who wouldn't want them dredging up.'

'Barker. That's great, thanks. So, if Taskforce turn up some newspaper clippings at Barker's house that would be the miracle we need. I'll get on to them now and see what they're up to.'

Morgan was almost through the back doors when she saw the car drive through the secure gates with Amy and Ben. She waited for them and felt bad for him; his face looked grey. No need to ask how it went: she could tell by the grim expression.

They trailed into the office one after the other to see an even grimmer-faced DCI waiting for them.

'What the hell is going on, Ben? We can't keep Barker much longer unless you get an extension. Have you got enough for an extension?'

'You saw the CCTV, he was clearly involved with Olivia Potter.'

'Yes, I did and thanks to you I'll see that for the rest of my life. It's ingrained in my memories. Have we got anything that's rock-solid evidence and not circumstantial or pornographic?'

Ben's phone rang. 'You've checked everything, the car, the attic?' There was a slight pause. He ran his hand across the stubble on his face, something Morgan noticed he did when he was stressed. It couldn't be good news. 'That's a shame. Thanks for trying.'

He ended the call and looked at Tom. 'Nothing, house and car were clean.'

'Then we have to bail him, you know the score.'

'Do you want me to do it?'

Tom shook his head. 'No, he's going to be causing enough trouble for us as it is. You need to keep away from him. For the foreseeable future.'

Ben closed his eyes and Morgan wondered if he was counting to ten.

Tom left them to it.

Amy patted his arm.

'We tried, boss, we'll nail him. It's just a matter of time. He knows we're onto him, but he's bound to slip up.'

In that small gesture of friendship between them Morgan realised how much she liked this team. She was glad Ben had taken a chance and let her come up here, even if was by default. Working alongside them, she knew she could make a difference.

'Coffee?'

They both nodded.

She left them and decided this called for proper coffee and cake. A quick walk to the coffee shop on the high street would clear her mind and give them a chance to clear theirs.

CHAPTER FIFTY-ONE

As she walked back into the station with the coffees, Barker was being escorted out of the side door. He saw her and smiled, nodding his head. The smile didn't reach his glaring eyes and she knew he was trying to intimidate her. Morgan couldn't help herself.

'Have a lovely evening, Greg.'

She hurried inside; two could play that game. He didn't scare her, despite Ben's warnings. She took the coffees upstairs to where Ben was in his office watching Barker get into his car, ready to drive away.

'Is he okay?'

Amy nodded. 'Yeah, he will be.' She opened the paper bags containing cake and whistled. 'He will be after one of those chocolate brownies anyway.' She banged on his window, waving the cake at him. He gave her a thumbs up but didn't come out straight away.

'What will happen now?'

'He's waiting for the go-ahead to put a surveillance team in place, then there will be teams of two watching the prick until he does something, and we can bring him back in. They still haven't located Harrison either.'

'It's not like on the television, is it?'

Amy spat crumbs of brownie all over herself, almost choking on the laughter which erupted.

'No, it definitely is not. We don't manage to solve the crimes in an hour.'

'That's not what I meant, it just seems so effortless and all the clues fall into place.'

'Sometimes they do, if you get someone who has committed a crime on the spur of the moment and not planned it, then yes, they tend to leave lots of forensics behind. It's much easier to catch those kinds of criminals. These killings have been well thought out, though, which makes it difficult but not impossible.' Amy looked towards Ben's office and sighed gently. 'He's a big softie under that really rough exterior. He's had an extremely shitty day. It was awful at the hospital and now this. I worry about him, but don't tell him that.'

Morgan laughed. 'I won't, I feel bad for him. Do you think he'll be all right?'

Neither of them realised Ben had come out of his office. He picked up a coffee and a slice of cake.

'Who?'

'The guy I was talking to earlier.'

Ben shrugged. 'No, idea. Thanks, this is really good.'

She watched as he demolished it in three bites.

'God you're a pig.' Amy was watching him with a look of horror on her face. 'Did you even taste that?'

Just like that the mood was lifted. He gave her the finger and washed down his cake with a huge mouthful of coffee.

'Let's call it a day, guys, there's nothing we can do at the moment. The powers that be up at headquarters are all arguing about putting a surveillance team on Barker. You know what this place is like, he'll end up killing another three people before they come to an agreement. It's been a long, crappy day. Thank you both for everything.'

'What, so we're dismissed?'

He nodded at Amy, who whooped.

'Get in, I'm going to the pub to meet Jack. Anyone coming?'

'No, thanks. I'm going home to sleep.'

Morgan declined. Realising Ben would need a lift, she waited for him.

'I'll drop you off.'

'Thank you, I forgot I didn't have a car.'

Amy was out of the door before he changed his mind.

Ben grabbed some files off his desk, stuffing them into a bag.

*

On the drive home, Morgan wanted to ask him if he was okay, as he didn't look particularly like he was. As the car idled outside his house and he opened the door, she plucked up the courage.

'Ben are you going to be all right?'

He turned to look at her. 'I am, thank you. You don't need to worry or come back later and smash another window. If you have to come back, I'll let you in, it's less messy.'

She smiled. 'I, well. If you need to talk you can ring me anytime.'

'Thank you.'

He turned away, but not before she saw the tears glistening in his eyes and it made her want to get out of the car and hug him. She didn't, in case he thought she was going a bit too far; instead she waved at him and drove away wishing she wasn't going back to her empty flat.

Deciding there was no way she was cooking, she drove to the Oriental Jade for a takeaway. Sitting in the window flipping through the pages of the latest and possibly last edition of the *Cumbrian News*, she saw a familiar figure walk past. She could tell by the walk that it was Greg Barker; he had his head bent, a woollen beanie, and a scarf wrapped around his face. She dropped the paper, and opened the door.

'I'll come back soon,' she said to the puzzled girl behind the counter.

Stepping out into the dark, she kept her distance but followed him. She didn't take him for the kind of guy who went out for late-night walks. He was heading in the direction of the Honey

Pot council estate. Her imagination was working overtime; didn't Harrison Wright live around here? What if the two of them had done it together? Ben would be furious to know they could have had him under surveillance and done this properly.

She took out her phone ready to film him if he went into someone's house. She couldn't call the police because technically she shouldn't be following him. He'd be shouting out that it was a free country and she was breaching his civil rights; but the feeling inside her gut told her he was up to no good.

He didn't go to any houses; instead he ducked into the deserted circular cul-de-sac which housed garages and lock-ups. She didn't dare to follow him inside. He would see her – it was too risky. Instead she zoomed in and tried to take some photos to show to Ben. The sound of a garage door being opened echoed around the peaceful street and she turned back. It could wait until tomorrow; she'd show Ben the footage. He could get a search team, and maybe they'd find something inside. Hurrying back the way she'd come, an eerie feeling she was being watched made her walk faster back to the Chinese.

Grabbing her takeaway, she drove the short distance home. The food smelt good and she realised how hungry she was. She went inside, her mind busy with the different scenarios she was running through her head about what was inside the lock-up Barker had gone into.

CHAPTER FIFTY-TWO

Morgan's eyes opened like clockwork. She realised she'd fallen asleep on the chair and was shivering. It was cold, the heating had gone off and she had no duvet or pillow. Getting up, she went into the bedroom and climbed into bed, under her duvet, until she felt the warmth flowing through her body. She tried to go back to sleep, was desperate to, but her mind wouldn't let her. At least she hadn't had any bad dreams. Her mind wandered to the woman who lived in the cottage in the woods, trying to remember her name. Ettie, that was it, she had seemed nice. Reminded her of her mum. She'd quite happily live in that little house. Tending the garden and brewing all sorts of teas. She might ask the landlord if she could plant a little herb garden around the back. She'd like to go and speak to her again, not for work but on a personal level. She thought about Ben's overgrown, messy garden. That would be the perfect space to plant flowers, herbs and vegetables. He didn't appreciate how lucky he was to live in that huge house. Then again it was probably more like a mausoleum to him, full of sad memories. There must have been good times, though; you don't stay married to someone for that long and not have happy memories.

She remembered seeing Barker last night and grabbed her phone. Pressing Ben's name, she waited for him to answer.

'Yeah.' His voice was gravely and she realised it wasn't even five. He was going to kill her.

'Sorry, I forgot it was so early.'

'It's okay, I'm getting used to your antisocial hours. Do you ever sleep?'

'Not much, I'll speak to you at work. Sorry again.'

'Hang on, I'm awake now. What did you want?'

'I got a Chinese last night.'

'Good for you, I'm happy for you. Was it that good you couldn't wait to share this splendid news?'

'That's not why I rang. I saw Greg Barker walking down the high street while I was waiting for it.'

There was some rustling and she realised he was throwing off his duvet and getting up. 'And?'

'Well he was walking really fast, wearing a black hat pulled down low, a scarf around his face and his hands in his pockets. He looked really suspicious.'

'Did you see where he went?'

She wondered if she should admit what she'd done, especially after his lecture the other day and realised she had to tell him.

'I followed him.'

'Jesus, Morgan. What did I tell you, he's dangerous and already on the warpath.'

'Sorry, and I know, but he didn't see me. I followed him to the Honey Pot. He went to a cul-de-sac off Macadam Street, where there's some garages and lock-ups. He went inside one.'

'Did you see which one?'

'I tried to take some photos and then I left. I didn't want him to see me. What if he's got stuff stashed in there?'

She could tell he was up and walking around.

'Can you pick me up in fifteen minutes?'

'Of course.'

'Good, you can take me there and show me. Then I'll get a search warrant. Well done, Morgan, but you shouldn't have put yourself at risk like that.'

'I know, but are you glad I did?'

'Yes, but I'm more grateful that you're okay and you didn't get hurt.'

Neither of them spoke for a moment.

'See you soon.' Her voice was barely a whisper.

*

Ben was already standing at the front gate waiting for her. There was a chill in the air this morning and he was wrapped up in a thick, padded jacket. Wearing gloves and a hat, not the usual shirts and suits she was used to seeing him in. He looked normal, but maybe that was the wrong word. Casual was better; he looked relaxed. It made him seem younger and not as conservative.

He opened the car door and grinned at her.

'I could get used to this door-to-door, chauffeur-driven service.'

'Yeah, well better not because you'll have your own car back soon.'

'Ha-ha, your green eyes pop when you're being mean. Has anyone ever told you that? They stand out against your fiery red hair?'

'Is that a compliment?'

He shrugged. 'Never was very good at them; might have been. Anyway enough small talk, breakfast is on me after this. I owe you big time, Morgan.'

She stole a glance at him and saw he was being sincere.

'I want to catch the killer as much as you do; maybe more, because he threw my life into a whole new world of hurt and sadness on my first sodding day. I want to see him locked up and the key thrown away for what he did to that family and the O'Briens.'

'Me too.'

She drove to the area where the lock-ups were situated, passing them by, then parking a few streets away.

'We'd better walk in case he's still there.'

'Good idea.'

They got out and she led the way. When they were almost at the
entrance to the cul-de-sac, they heard footsteps behind them. Ben
reached out. Grabbing hold of her hand, he pulled her close. She
didn't pull away, realising he was making it look as if they were a
couple. A minute later and the person behind them overtook. Not
even glancing their way, as they hurried on over the crest of the hill.

Ben let go and whispered, 'Sorry.'

She smiled. She wasn't giving him a hard time over that because
she'd liked the feel of his hand in hers.

They paused at the opening, Ben bending down pretending to
tie his shoelace. Morgan looked at the lock-ups; the doors were
all painted the same red colour. All of them had peeling chunks
of paint missing and a lot of graffiti. Except for one at the end; it
had a new metal shutter. Not the knackered, rotting wooden doors
the rest of them had.

She whispered, 'It's that one, it has to be.'

Ben stood up, told her to smile and snapped a photo of her with
his phone. Then slowly turned, taking several bursts of the garages
and the area. Grabbing her hand again they carried on walking,
going the long way around to get back to her car. He didn't let go
this time and she kept hold until they were back at the car.

'What do you think?'

'Why does he have a lock-up here with a secure metal shutter
when he has a big fancy house and garage at home? Something is
going on. We need to get a search warrant. Good job, Morgan, now
drive to wherever you fancy breakfast from, I'm buying.'

She looked at the clock on her dashboard. 'It's really early,
nowhere is open.'

'What time is it?'

She pointed at the clock.

'Bloody hell, I can't remember the last time I was dressed and
out of the house this early. What are you doing to me? Want to
come back to mine, I have bacon and eggs?'

'If you have bacon then yes, please.'

They drove back to Ben's. The house was much nicer in the day. She followed him in through the front door and looked around. It was lovely; everything was painted white. If anything, it was a bit sparse, lacking in the bits that would make this kind of house seem homely. Then again, who was she to talk? All she owned was an oversized chair, coffee table and a bookcase stuffed full of books. She followed him down to the kitchen, where the boarded-up window made her cheeks turn red.

'I'm so sorry, I'll replace that when I get paid.'

He turned from the fridge, from where he had taken the packet of bacon. 'No, you won't. If I hadn't been such an arse and opened the door you wouldn't have felt the need to break it. It's fine, when I get a day off I'll sort it out.'

He busied himself grilling bacon and frying eggs. Toasting thick wedges of tiger bread, he served her the best-looking breakfast buttie she'd ever seen. She squeezed ketchup on it and took a bite, egg running down her chin. Ben laughed and passed her some kitchen roll.

'I guess you're hungry.'

She nodded. 'Starving. I love food, especially when it's this good.'

He smiled, a faint blush rising up his cheeks. Making a pot of coffee, he placed it on the table and sat opposite her.

'This is nice, I've forgotten how good it is to have company. Makes this house seem a bit more alive.'

'Have you ever thought about moving into something smaller? It's a big house for one person.'

'Yes, quite a few times. I was thinking about your flat, it's nice. Something like that would be great for me, but—'

'But?'

He poured the coffee and took a sip from his mug.

'But, I love this house. We loved it; as soon as we set eyes on it we knew we wanted to live here. Wanted to raise our children here.'

'That's so sad, I'm sorry.'

'Life doesn't always work out how you want it to. It's no one's fault, it's just the way it is. Cindy couldn't conceive. We tried, God knows we tried. Then I moved to CID and began to work longer hours, deal with the terrible things we deal with. I realised that maybe it wasn't a bad thing we didn't have kids. I wasn't always around; Cindy didn't feel that way though. It drove her mad. I guess it broke her heart and I didn't notice until it was too late.'

Tears filled Morgan's eyes for Ben and Cindy, and for her own life. The similarities between Cindy and her mum were overwhelming. At least her mum had managed to have her, poor Cindy. His hand reached across the table, taking hold of hers.

'Don't cry, it's my mess of a life. I didn't want to upset you. I've never really spoken much about it except to Declan.'

She dabbed the corners of her eyes with a piece of the kitchen roll. 'I'm sorry, it's just that Cindy sounds very much like my mum; they were both good women with troubles that took away their passion for living.' She squeezed his hand back. 'Life goes on though, doesn't it? It has to; look at the difference you make.'

Letting go, she took a gulp from her mug. She was in uncharted territory. All of this was new to her, and she didn't know what she was doing.

One thing she did know was that she liked Ben Matthews even more the longer she spent in his company.

CHAPTER FIFTY-THREE

Ben knew he had to get a search warrant for that lock-up no matter what, so as soon as they arrived at the station he went to find the DCI. Knocking on his door, he walked straight in without waiting to be called.

'Morning, sir.'

'Ben, what delightful situations have you got lined up for me today?'

He smiled and Ben felt a small sense of relief wash over him; he wasn't too mad at him. That was a good start.

'It's about Gregory Barker.'

The smile disappeared from his face.

'That man's name gives me heartburn; I wish we didn't have to keep bringing him up.'

'Sorry, but new information has come to light. He was seen acting suspiciously last night and followed by one of my officers to a lock-up on the Honey Pot.'

'What would he want with one of those? Have you seen where he lives?'

'No, I haven't. But I think we need to search it. He's hiding something, it's obvious, and maybe this is where he's keeping it.'

'What if it isn't? He might have a porn stash there for all we know given his liking for sex in public places; God knows what else he gets up to in his spare time.'

'Sir, staff at the newspaper said that Jamie Stone had a file of the newspaper cuttings relating to the O'Brien murders. They are nowhere to be found and we think his killer has taken them. There must have been something in them that might incriminate him. If nothing else Barker breached his police bail: he was warned not to leave his house after 20.00 hours.'

The DCI drummed his fingers on the top of his desk, then opened the drawer and pulled out a bottle of Gaviscon. Unscrewing the cap, he drank it straight from the bottle and grimaced.

'Leave it with me, get the search team assembled. I'll get the warrant; I never liked the self-serving prick anyway.'

Ben grinned. 'Thank you.'

'How's the rookie getting on? Do you think we've pushed her further than we should?'

'Morgan is brilliant; she's an asset to the team. It was a wise decision. We wouldn't be where we are now if it weren't for her instincts and dedication. I want to put her on the detective course ASAP and make her a permanent part of the team.'

'Wow, that's some strong praise from you, Ben. Good, I'm glad.'

Ben left him making the phone calls to get the warrant they needed. He would have Barker back in custody within hours, hopefully. This time he wouldn't be leaving so soon.

Three hours later they were good to go; an arrest team was assembled to go to Barker's home address comprising Ben, Amy and two armed Taskforce officers. Morgan was to lead the search team to the lock-up and oversee the search. The briefing room was alive with electricity; adrenalin and nerves were running high. There was a lot at stake here: they needed Barker in cuffs, but first of all they needed the lock-up searched for any evidence. Anything found would give them the grounds to arrest him again. They would be waiting for the go-ahead from Morgan. Before they split off into their two respective teams, the DCI called Ben to one side.

'You're sure the rookie can handle this much responsibility on her own?'

'Morgan, she has a name. And yes, I think she is more than capable, and she's not on her own; Al and the rest of the team will be with her.'

'I suppose so.'

Morgan was watching. He could tell she was worried and he smiled at her, giving her a thumbs up. She smiled back and he felt better.

They were going to park up along the quiet country lane where Barker's house was. The two Taser-trained officers were going to go up to the house and do a bit of a recce. Once they had the all-clear they'd go in. Ben was looking forward to seeing his face when he realised he was up shit creek.

Amy whispered to him, 'What if there's nothing in the lock-up? You have thought about that, haven't you? For all we know he's leading us on a wild goose chase to piss us off for yesterday.'

'He didn't know Morgan was in the takeaway, though, did he? And we had no car following him. It doesn't matter. He's up to something. If there's nothing inside then I'll take the flak for it.'

'I hope you're right, boss. I like working for you. It would really spoil my life if you got suspended.'

He laughed. 'And mine. I'm just beginning to enjoy working with you.'

She elbowed him in the side. 'Arsehole.'

Morgan followed the search team out to their waiting van and he found himself wishing he was going with her, but it was safer for her to go to the lock-up. He was sure of it; he wanted her as far away from Barker as possible, especially after the way he behaved yesterday. The man was becoming unhinged.

*

The Honey Pot estate was eerily calm. Morgan sat in the front of the van directing the driver where to go. He stopped at the entrance to the lock-ups and blocked the narrow entrance road so no one could drive in or out. There was no sign of Barker; there was no sign of anyone. She pointed to the door and within a couple of minutes two officers dressed from head to toe in black had used a pair of bolt cutters to cut the thick, padlocked chain off the front of it. The door still didn't move. Another two took over, using the big red battering ram to break the lock. Four huge whacks and the shiny new door was bent beyond repair.

It lifted three quarters of the way up and jammed. The two officers scrambled underneath it into the darkness. They shone their lights around. Inside was a car under a protective cover, and there were various boxes stacked up. They went outside and gave Morgan a thumbs up. Dressed in protective clothing, she and Al ducked under the door. A pull string dangled down and Al tugged it, filling the space with bright, white light.

Morgan walked to the car, lifting the cover and saw a small black sports car.

Al whistled. 'Nice car, that's an MG Classic from the seventies. Doesn't look like it's been used since then either. It's immaculate; the paintwork is pristine. It must be worth a bit, that. I wonder why he's keeping it here and not at home. I'm amazed it hasn't been stolen.'

Morgan phoned Ben, who answered on the first ring. 'There's an MG sports car in here, from the seventies.' She peered inside the windows at it. 'Al's doing a PNC now.'

They all paused as the control room operator gave the results.

'Registered keeper since new is Gregory Barker of Paradise, Rydal Falls.'

'Control, when was it registered new?'

'January 1975; it's been SORN off-road since August '75.'

Morgan asked Ben, 'Did you hear that? The O'Briens were murdered in August, and on the reports a black MG sports car was seen leaving the scene but never traced. This has to be it.'

'Don't touch the car. I want a full forensic lift. Everything else is fair game.'

'Roger.'

She ended the call and began the job of searching every box, drawer, nook and cranny to find anything that might help put Barker away for life.

CHAPTER FIFTY-FOUR

Amy and Ben were leaning against the side of the white Ford Focus. Ben was fiddling with his body armour.

'I forgot how uncomfortable these are, I can't bloody breathe.'

She smiled. 'Here, loosen the Velcro side tabs.' Walking over, she began ripping the side tabs off then pressing them down, letting them out enough so he could breathe.

'Thanks, that's better. I thought I was suffocating.'

The acrid smell of smoke filtered through the air to where they were standing. 'Where's that coming from?'

One of the Taser officers came running towards them. 'He's lit a fire in one of those fancy pits.'

'Shit, he might be burning evidence. Go, go, go.'

The two officers dressed in black took off, Amy and Ben following behind. He hadn't realised how unfit he was until he began to lag behind at an embarrassing pace. He had a stitch and clutched his side, bending over, taking deep breaths. Amy was way ahead and behind the two officers. He heard shouting. Dragging himself forwards, he rounded the side of the house in time to see Barker standing next to a roaring fire. There was a smell of burning rubber; he was clutching a cardboard folder in one hand. Ben could see what he was going to do before he did it. Amy was running for the hosepipe which was attached to an outside tap. He couldn't let him burn that folder; it might have vital evidence inside.

He shouted over to Amy, 'Get that folder off him.' Then watched as Barker threw it towards the fire. Ben sprinted faster than he ever thought was possible grabbing it just as it landed on the burning pile of wood and coal. The bottom of the folder caught alight, sending a searing pain across his left hand along with the smell of burning flesh. He threw the folder onto the ground and stamped on it, an intense pain in his hand began to make it throb. The bottom of the folder was smoking and singed, but the rest of it was intact.

The two Taser officers ran at Barker. He was knocked to the ground and cuffed within seconds. Amy began to spray the water from the hose into the fire pit. As the flames extinguished, steam rose from it and they waited to see what it was that he'd thrown into it. They could see the remnants of a rubber mask and an exceptionally large butcher's knife. Barker didn't say a word.

Amy turned and read him his rights for the second time in two days. This time he wouldn't be bluffing his way out of interview. The two officers marched him down to the van. When he was out of sight, Ben began to shake his hand.

'Ouch, my hand, it's on fire. Spray that hose on it.'

He held it under the spray while she soaked it. 'Oh, that looks bad. Your skin is peeling and blistered. We'd better get an ambulance, boss.'

'We'd better not, you can drive me to the hospital, but not until we have a scene guard and a search team here.'

The pain was almost unbearable, but there was no way he was giving Barker the satisfaction of seeing him like this. He reached out for the spray gun, taking it from Amy and holding his injured hand underneath it, the cold water soothing it.

'Can you do the honours, get everyone here who needs to be,' he said through gritted teeth, and she nodded. She gave a list of instructions to the control room. He didn't dare look at his hand; he was just grateful it hadn't been his right hand. He didn't hear Amy request an ambulance for him; if he had he would have made her cancel it. He stared at the cardboard folder and prayed it was the one missing from the newspaper office. No one could touch it until

CSI got there. He wouldn't risk compromising any possible forensics. He wanted Barker behind bars for the rest of his life and then some.

His phone was vibrating in his pocket, but he couldn't answer it as his good hand was covered in water. Then Amy's phone began to ring and she walked away to speak where he couldn't hear her.

'What happened, who needs an ambulance?'

Morgan's voice was breathless and high-pitched.

'It's okay, it's Ben. He burned his hand. It's not serious. Barker is in cuffs; he was burning what looks like evidence.'

'I was so scared one of you had been hurt, then I realised it couldn't be you because you sounded okay on the radio.'

'Yeah, well he's acting all big and hard. He doesn't know I've asked for an ambulance so don't tell him it was me.'

'I won't. Thanks, Amy, I'm glad you got him and are okay.'

'See you back at the nick. Ben is going to need to go to A&E, but I'm not arguing with him. Unless you want to meet him there. You can't come here, though, because you might cross-contaminate the scene and then everything will have been a waste of time.'

Amy turned around to see that Ben was grimacing.

She walked back towards him. 'Anything I can do?'

He shook his head. 'Remind me not to be an idiot in future.'

She laughed. 'Not sure about that, for some people it comes natural.'

Sirens echoed in the distance and she turned away.

'Amy you didn't; please tell me that's not for me?'

'I didn't, it's probably for someone else.'

He could tell by the way she was avoiding eye contact that she had requested an ambulance despite his request not to. He wasn't going to tell her this, but he was relieved. He didn't want his hand to drop off and it didn't seem quite so dramatic if he hadn't asked for it.

It wasn't an ambulance but a car. The paramedic got out, grabbing the heavy kit bag from the back seat. He came walking towards him.

'So, what have we got here?'

Amy spoke for him. 'He stuck his hand in a blazing fire pit to retrieve some evidence.'

The paramedic nodded. 'Good effort, I like it. That's what you call dedication. Let me get this wrapped up; an ambulance is on its way to take you to hospital.'

'No, thanks. I mean, yes please, get it wrapped up. I'll make my own way there. I'm not wasting your time.'

'You sure? I can take you in my car if you want.'

'Positive, thanks.'

He gave him his hand, his mind wandering as he stared into the distance. Greg Barker had all this: land, a beautiful house, money and what good was it to him? None at all, because where he was going he would be lucky to ever see freedom again and that suited Ben just fine.

CHAPTER FIFTY-FIVE

Morgan wanted to go and see how Ben was, but she knew he'd be annoyed with her. Amy was with him and she would ring her if she needed her. It was late; it had been one long day. She watched as the tow-truck driver lifted the car onto the back of the low-loader to be taken to the big warehouse, where it would be stored until it was forensically examined. They hadn't turned up anything else of any evidential value and she wondered why he had come here last night. Maybe he'd come to retrieve the newspaper clippings so he could take them home and dispose of them. Whatever it was, they had him now; hopefully there was enough evidence to secure a conviction. There was nothing left for her to do. She didn't even have a lift back to the station. She'd offered to wait for the vehicle recovery to get here; the other officers hadn't had to be told twice and left her there, freezing, without a car to sit in. It had started to rain an hour ago, fine drizzle at first but it was typical that now as she set off walking it was getting heavier and she was going to be soaked through in a matter of minutes.

A car pulled up behind her. She turned around and smiled to see both Amy and Ben.

'Need a lift?'

She jumped into the back of the car.

'You okay?'

Ben turned to her and waved his bandaged hand. 'I'm fine, it's just a surface burn, more of a nuisance than anything.'

'Gee, what a hero he is. If you want to know the truth he's whinged and moaned like a child the whole time. He's only acting all tough in front of you because he wants to impress you.'

Morgan blushed and Ben quickly turned away. 'Thanks, Amy, make me out to be a baby, why don't you.'

Amy looked at Morgan in the rear-view mirror. 'Why are you stuck here without a vehicle?'

'I offered.'

Both Amy and Ben glanced at each other. It was Amy who spoke. 'Rookie mistake. Look, there are certain rules and codes of conduct that come with being a detective and working in our department. For instance, if there's a scene guard you never, ever offer to do it. Uh-uh, you just don't. Officers and PCSOs are there to scene guard. It's what they're trained to do and part of their role. You are a detective now, you're the one investigating the crimes. You pull rank; if you're too nice you'll get walked all over. Did anyone offer to come back and pick you up?'

'No.'

'See, big mistake. You're going to have to toughen up and get used to giving the orders. But on the whole, you did good, so don't let it get to you. Those idiots took advantage of your good nature.'

'Thanks. What are we doing now?'

'I'm taking you back to get your car and you're going home for a large glass of wine or whatever you drink. Then I'm taking the hero of the day back to his house and going home myself for an alcoholic beverage and a night with Jack. All three of us will have an early night, because if you thought today was long, tomorrow will be gruelling. There's a lot of work to do. Isn't that right, boss?

'Barker is claiming he's having chest pains, so will be taken under armed guard to get checked out at the hospital. Once he's given the all-clear he'll be brought back to custody for questioning. It's not going to be until tomorrow, though, at least.'

Morgan was relieved to get out of the car at the station. She felt as if she'd been told off by her aunty for being immature. As they drove away, Ben looked back at her and smiled. She drove herself home, ready to do exactly what Amy had recommended. She was tired; this week she had worked more hours than she ever imagined was possible. At least they had Barker where he belonged.

Her flat was cold; the heating must be on the blink. She checked the boiler but didn't have a clue how to get it working again. Instead she put her fluffiest pink pyjamas on and a thick pair of bed socks. Tomorrow she really had to go shopping: living off bowls of Crunchy Nut Cornflakes wasn't the healthiest of diets. Sitting cross-legged on her chair, she ate the cornflakes and tried not to think of anything remotely linked to work. She needed to switch off, relax, read a book. All week she'd been far too tired to even open one, which wasn't like her: reading was her favourite thing ever. Instead she ate her cereal and stared into the gardens; movement made her sit straight as she saw a dark figure huddled under the tree. She walked to the glass and stared at the dishevelled figure. Harrison Wright looked as if he'd been sleeping rough. His pale face had huge, black bags under his eyes. His usually perfect hair was hanging limply down over his face.

She knocked on the window. 'What do you want?'

She could barely hear his muffled voice through the glass. 'I'm freezing and starving, please let me in. I know the police are looking for me, but I'm so cold. Please, Morgan.'

He looked scared, soaked and almost hypothermic. She couldn't leave him outside; it was against her better nature.

'Hang on.' Slipping her trainers on, she put the door on the latch and went out into the communal hallway. She opened the front door; he was a dripping wreck.

'How did you know where I live and where have you been?'

'I followed you home last night. I've been hiding. I got scared but I'm too cold and I haven't eaten since yesterday. I don't know what to do any more.'

Morgan realised that her senses had been right: she'd felt uneasy and he was why. A puddle was forming around his feet.

'Come on, you can dry off and I'll feed you, though I don't really have a lot of food in.'

He followed her inside.

'Wait there while I grab some towels.'

She rushed into the bathroom, grabbing a couple of bath sheets, then passing them to him. He began to frantically rub his hair, not bothering with the rest of himself until it was towel dry.

'I have a pair of joggers and a hoodie I can lend you, if you don't mind wearing my clothes. I don't have any men's clothes here. I'm on my own.'

As she turned to go get them, a small smile played across his lips.

She took the clothes into the bathroom.

'You can get changed, pass me your stuff and I'll wash it. No dryer either; they will have to go on a radiator.'

'Thank you so much, that's great.'

As he went into the bathroom, she wondered why he hadn't gone home or to one of his friends'; maybe he wanted to get it over and done with. Although there wasn't much to ask him now Barker was in custody. They had their killer behind bars.

She put the kettle on and began opening the cupboards. There were two tins of tomatoes and the box of cornflakes; the fridge wasn't much better. Opening the freezer, she took out the emergency bottle of vodka. Pouring two shot glasses, she placed them on the counter.

Harrison came out of the bathroom looking a little bit more human, and the clothes she'd given him were black, so they didn't look too out of place.

'You look a bit warmer now.'

'Thank you so much, these are great.'

She pointed to the breakfast stool. 'Have a seat, I can rustle you up some tinned tomatoes or a bowl of Crunchy Nut. Don't take too long to decide.'

He laughed. 'To be honest, I'm so hungry I'd eat the tomatoes on the cornflakes.'

'Okay, you can have cornflakes. If you're still hungry tomatoes can be your second course.'

She turned away, poured the remaining cornflakes into the large glass mixing bowl and poured what was left of her milk on top.

She passed it to him. 'Voila, enjoy.'

'Thanks, Morgan.'

'Do you want a shot of vodka to warm you up?'

He nodded and she pointed to the one nearest to him. 'Cheers.'

Picking hers up, she tipped her head back and downed it.

'I'll eat my cornflakes first, but you're an expert; that was nicely done.'

'Drinking shots is one of my specialities. I don't have many but usually drink my friends under the table on the rare occasion I get to go out.

'Oh, Harrison, did you know Bronte is awake?'

He looked up, surprise registering on his face. Chewing the mouthful of cereal, he swallowed. 'Is she? No, I didn't. That's amazing. When?'

'Last night or early this morning. I didn't speak to her; my sergeant did when he went to visit her.'

'Did she tell you what happened?'

'Unfortunately, she couldn't remember anything, but maybe in time it will start to all come back to her.'

'I bet she couldn't. How lucky for her. I wish I couldn't and now that Greg is going to get all the glory for a crime he didn't commit.'

Morgan stared at him, open-mouthed. 'What do you mean?'

He gulped the mouthful of food down and stared at her. 'I didn't want to be the one to grass, that's why I got scared and hid.

But I don't know what to do any more and as much as I hate Greg it isn't fair.'

'Harrison, three people are dead; you're not grassing at all. What's not fair?'

He lowered his face; when he lifted it again a single tear rolled down his cheek.

'I was there that night, but I didn't do it. I couldn't stop her; she went berserk. I mean, she lost the plot completely. I've never seen anything like it, so much anger and rage.'

Morgan reached in her dressing gown pocket. Taking out her phone, but keeping it out of view, she pressed the record button and slipped it back inside.

'Who went berserk, Harrison?'

'Bronte, she killed them all.'

Morgan gasped. 'What, why?'

He didn't look at her. 'She hated it here; they used to live in Manchester and she loved it there. She found out at school about the last murders and was furious her parents had bought that house. Then Olivia started having an affair with that prick Greg.

'We used to follow them. One night we followed them to a pub. I think Olivia tried to break it off with him but ended up fucking him in a car park. Bronte was raging about that; she was so upset and angry, said she hated her dad for making them come here and her mum was a slut. She decided to do something about it, said if they were both dead, she'd get the house. Would be able to sell it, take the money and move back to the city far away from here.'

Harrison hadn't touched his vodka. He pushed it towards her. Morgan picked it up and downed it. She was so shocked. It tasted a bit funny. She looked down at the glass and wondered if she hadn't cleaned it properly.

'How did Olivia end up hanging from the tree? The cameras weren't working that day.'

'Bronte did something to them, she loosened the wires. She drugged Olivia first, but she gave her too much and she died. She wanted that arsehole Barker to think it was his fault, that Olivia had killed herself because of him. I know they'd been arguing that afternoon because I heard Olivia shouting at him on the phone that it was over and she'd make him pay.

'So we carried her out and hung her. It was so difficult; she was really heavy. Even in death she looked beautiful. I couldn't believe it was happening, it was all so weird.

'I really liked Olivia, she was so pretty and always nice to me. Much nicer than Bronte ever was. Honestly that was why I stayed with her. I liked seeing Olivia; I'd always hoped she'd like me the same way she liked Greg.'

Morgan knew she should get him to the station to give a statement, but she was scared he wouldn't talk once he was in there and she realised she'd drunk two shots of vodka. The room was beginning to spin a little; Christ, what was she doing drinking on an empty stomach? She needed a clear head for this.

'Bronte felt bad about her mum once she was dead, but it was too late: there was no going back. I think she hadn't realised the seriousness of the situation. I mean it's okay talking about this stuff and watching documentaries but when it's real... She didn't care about Bea or Saul, she hated them; she said Saul was far too weak for letting Olivia treat him the way she did. Bea was just an inconvenience; she needed her out of the way for her plan to work.'

Morgan realised that would explain the savageness of the beatings, if she felt no love towards her sibling and father. Bronte had many traits of a psychopath.

'Wow, I would never have guessed.' The words came out much slower than usual and she felt as if she was talking through a mouthful of cotton wool. She tried to ask him who had attacked Bronte, but the words didn't come out.

Harrison pulled a white iPhone out of his pocket and placed it on the breakfast bar. A picture of Saul and his two daughters smiling flashed up on the screen and fear filled her mind. Olivia's phone: she pushed herself to stand up, but her legs couldn't hold her weight.

Harrison had stopped eating and was watching her, with a huge smile on his face.

'Bronte… who?' she managed to say, before she felt her legs give way underneath her.

As she slumped to the floor in a heap, Harrison was standing over her.

'Morgan, for a copper you're so gullible. You remind me of Olivia: she was kind like you. Look where being nice has got you, though. Why did you let a killer in your flat? Who do you think did that to Bronte? Me, I did. I'll tell you why, I was furious with her. Furious with all of them.

'I thought Olivia loved me and then I saw her in that car park with him and I knew she had to pay the price. Bronte wouldn't have the nerve to have killed anyone. She was all talk. She didn't hate her family so much once she realised they were all dead, that I'd taken that decision out of her hands.'

Morgan was on the verge of passing out. She tried to get her phone out of her pocket, but her fingers wouldn't do what she wanted them to.

Harrison bent down so he was close to her, and she opened her mouth to scream. But the only noise that came out was an almost silent, 'Agh.'

CHAPTER FIFTY-SIX

Ben lay on his sofa, watching some documentary about the ancient Egyptians, trying to take his mind off Greg Barker. Something was niggling away at him and he couldn't think what. As much as he wanted a glass of something strong he hadn't touched a drop of alcohol since the night Morgan had found him in a drunken state, contemplating suicide. Instead he'd come home, showered and shaved. Rooting through the cupboards, he found an old bottle of Cindy's moisturiser and had lathered his face in that. He'd then gone downstairs for some bin bags and done what he'd been putting off for three years.

First of all he cleared everything except the anti-wrinkle cream: he kept that, God knows he needed it. All the dusty shampoo bottles, hair dyes, make-up, face wipes, sanitary towels – he binned the lot, filling two bags. He took them downstairs and put them in the garage. Next, he went into the master bedroom they used to share. It was so dusty in there he grabbed a T-shirt and wrapped it around his face. Dragging her large suitcase off the top of the wardrobe, he opened the doors and began to fill it with her clothes. There were so many it filled the case and another five bags: who needed so much shit? Then he dragged them to the garage; he would take those to a charity shop.

Going back upstairs, he'd bagged all her underwear, then her shoes. He was exhausted by the time he'd finished running up and down the stairs and sweating, his hand throbbed, but it felt good. He then set about dusting, polishing, hoovering and changing the bedding. The windows were open wide and the sound of the heavy rain lashing against the glass soothed his heart while he worked. Even as a kid he got excited when it rained; he loved it.

By the time he'd finished cleaning, the room smelt much nicer, not as stale. When his days off put in an appearance, he'd give it a coat of paint and really freshen it up. Get rid of the ugly pink and yellow flowers.

Three hours it had taken him and another shower, but now as he lay in his lounge watching the television he felt so much better. As if a weight had been lifted from his shoulders. He loved Cindy, of course he did, and he always would, but it was time to move on. He was still alive; he realised that he should be thankful. He also realised that if he ever plucked up the courage to ask anyone on a date it wouldn't be much fun bringing her back here to the shrine of Cindy. There was one more thing he needed to do though.

Standing up, he went around the house collecting the framed photos of them on various holidays and their wedding day. These he wouldn't bin. He found a large box in the garage and put them inside. He wasn't wiping out her memory; he'd never do that: he'd loved her and she'd been his entire life. They would be there on the days he wanted to remember her, but hopefully those days would get fewer and fewer as he moved on with his life.

As he walked up the stairs to go to bed he looked up at his loft hatch, thinking he could store the photos up there tomorrow. And then it hit him like a brick: the murder weapon Morgan had found was up in the loft. Through that tiny door that she'd had to squeeze through. There was no way on this earth that Barker had managed to climb up there: he wouldn't fit, he was a big guy. It was impossible. So, either he had an accomplice who could fit or he didn't kill the Potters.

He rang Morgan. It rang out, looking at his watch, he saw it wasn't that late. He tried again; this time it went to answerphone. Not once this week had she ignored his calls. A feeling of dread settled in his stomach. Something was wrong. He didn't know what but all his years in the police had taught him to trust his instinct. He ran into his bedroom and dressed, then realised he didn't have a car.

He phoned Amy.

'What now?'

'I need a lift, can you pick me up?'

'Ring a taxi.'

'Amy, now.'

He ended the call and phoned the duty sergeant's office: no answer. He thought this was probably just as well until he actually got to Morgan's to see if she was okay. He was pacing up and down his hallway waiting to hear Amy's horn blare outside; she'd kill him if it was a false alarm, but he'd rather take the risk.

Stan Brookes was suffering bad, the worst kind of affliction a man his age could have. He finished his drink, put his glass on the bar and walked out of the pub. It was late and he was the last person she would want to see, but he had to do this. For days now the guilt of being a total selfish, greedy pig had finally got the better of him. He should be proud of his daughter for choosing a life of serving the Queen and country, not ashamed. His stupid, warped, messed-up, alcohol-addled mind had screwed up his sense of loyalty. He should never have stolen her necklace; he didn't think he'd ever stooped that low in his entire life. He knew how much she cherished it and he'd taken it from her. She must hate him, but he knew she couldn't hate him as much as he hated himself.

The rain was hammering down. Good, it was what he deserved. He set off on the walk to Morgan's flat. If she wouldn't open the door then he'd apologise through the letterbox. He had to do something to lift this heavy guilt that he was carrying around with him. He thought back to the days when life was different, happier. When he'd come home from work to find Sylvia in the kitchen baking scones and cakes; Morgan would be on the sofa or the old armchair, her nose in a book. She'd been a good kid and he'd never appreciated it, just like Sylvia had been a good wife. He'd had it all and now he had nothing; it was a sobering thought.

Twenty-five minutes later he turned into the drive of the fancy house Morgan rented the ground floor flat in. She was awake because all of her lights were on; that was good. He pressed the doorbell and heard the chime echo around the communal hallway. She didn't answer. He realised it was late, and if he had credit on his phone he'd have phoned her and asked her to let him in.

Trudging around to the huge window that looked into her lounge, he pressed his face against the glass and saw a scene out of a horror film. There was a teenage boy in there, Morgan was on the floor and she looked… Oh God, his heart began to race. She wasn't moving. His hands were shaking; he couldn't get in to help her.

Pulling out his ancient Nokia, he dialled 999 – thank God that was free – and asked for police.

'You have to come, I think he's trying to kill her.'

'What's the address, sir?'

'I don't know the name, it's a large house on Singleton Park Road; it's turned into flats. You have to hurry, I can't get in to help her.' He ended the call.

The teenager was looping a length of fabric around Morgan's neck. Stan hammered on the glass, startling him, and he rushed to look outside. Stan realised it was difficult because her lights were on and he stepped to one side so he couldn't see him. The teenager drew the curtains across, blocking his view of what was happening inside and a sense of panic filled his chest. Looking around, he spied a huge rockery stone; that would do it.

The rock was slippery with the rain and coated with moss, but he managed to heave it up.

Stumbling forwards towards the window, he lifted it as high as he could and launched it at the glass. The sound as it cracked against the glass was ear-splitting and then shards of glass were flying everywhere. One embedded itself in his cheek, and he tore it out, not caring, and threw himself through the jagged, gaping hole. Landing heavily on one leg with a crash on the other side, he felt a sharp pain as another shard of glass sliced through the paper-thin flesh.

But they'd gone.

The front door was open and he pulled himself up, limping towards it.

Dripping rainwater and blood everywhere, he followed them out into the communal area.

CHAPTER FIFTY-SEVEN

Amy drove fast on a good day, but tonight she was reckless and Ben was grateful to her for getting to his in a matter of minutes. They didn't speak. His hands were shaking as he repeatedly tried to phone Morgan.

'Boss, ring it in.'

'What if it's nothing and I'm freaking out?'

'Then you have to live with the shame for a couple of days. No biggie, you've done worse.'

He dialled 999. 'It's DS Matthews, I need backup at 1 Singleton Park Road. Concern for welfare.'

'We already have a patrol on its way. We had a request a couple of minutes ago.'

'By who, the occupant?'

'A man, he hung up without giving his details.'

Amy looked at Ben, shaking her head. 'Shit.' She put her foot down and drove even faster.

Before they knew it she was speeding through the drive, gravel underneath her tyres spraying everywhere. There was a gaping hole where Morgan's huge window had been. Ben got out and ran towards it, Amy following behind. The howling wind and rain were making the curtains flap in and out of the broken window. He pushed one to the side to go in.

'Careful, boss, someone has already hurt themselves.'

He looked down to where she was pointing, to see a trail of bright red blood, and his stomach clenched so hard he thought he was going to be sick. Then he was inside, stepping around the blood. There was shouting coming from the hallway. Sirens could be heard in the background and Ben was glad he'd phoned.

As he stepped into the hall he was greeted by utter carnage. Morgan's lifeless body was hanging from the wooden balustrade leading up to the first floor, and at the bottom of the stairs a badly bleeding Stan was grappling with Harrison Wright.

Amy ran up the stairs to grab Morgan's arms and Ben put his shoulders under her feet, taking the weight off the noose around her neck. Amy deftly untied the knot and lowered her onto Ben's shoulders.

'Have you got her?'

'Yes.'

She ran down the stairs as two officers ran out of Morgan's front door. They looked at the carnage and ran to where Harrison was still trying to get away from Stan. Amy helped Ben lower Morgan to the ground. She shouted at the officers who had separated the two fighting men. 'Ambulance now.'

'On its way.'

Ben pressed two fingers against the side of Morgan's neck; she still had a pulse.

'Is she breathing?' Amy asked desperately.

He couldn't speak but gave Amy a thumbs up. Gathering Morgan up into his arms he sat on the floor cradling her.

Both Harrison and Stan were in cuffs. Stan was bleeding heavily and pulling to get to Morgan.

'Is she alive?'

Ben nodded.

Stan turned to try to get to Harrison. 'I'll kill you, you bastard.'

The officer holding Stan pulled him away from Harrison. Ben looked at them.

He pointed to Harrison. 'Get him in the cage now. And uncuff the other guy.'

'Are you sure, boss?'

'Yes, he's her dad.'

The officer mumbled an apology to Stan and released the cuffs. Stan lurched forwards, falling to his knees. He reached Morgan and tugged her necklace out of his pocket, passing it to Ben.

'Give her this when she wakes up and tell her I'm sorry, I love her.'

Amy turned away. Ben saw the tears in her eyes. More sirens and then hammering on the front door. She ran to open it, relieved to see the paramedics. Both of them rushed towards Stan and Morgan.

'You can tell her yourself you love her, Stan, you owe her that.' Ben clasped her necklace in his hand. 'But thank you.'

Stan's eyes closed and he sank back against the stairs. The paramedic requested another ambulance. One of them began to work on Stan, applying pressure pads to the deep wounds; the other began to check Morgan over. Lifting her eyelids, he slid a pulse oximeter on her finger.

Ben held her as gently as he could and didn't want to let go. He didn't want to lose her; he'd only known her for a short time and yet she'd changed his life completely. He didn't care if she didn't feel the way he felt about her; being her friend was enough for him. He could live with that; he'd settle for anything. He didn't realise he was crying until the second ambulance arrived and the paramedics brought a trolley in to lift her on to. Stan was already in the first and on his way to the hospital; Morgan would soon be following.

Amy passed him some rolled-up tissue. 'You go with her; I'll sort this mess out.'

'Thanks, Amy.'

He followed the paramedics out and climbed into the back of the ambulance. He'd stay with her until she woke up and was only leaving if she told him to.

*

Morgan had been put in a side cubicle. Despite the bruising around her neck she was breathing unaided. Ben had told them he suspected she may have been drugged and they were waiting for the results of her blood tests to come back. Despite being squeezed onto the hardest, most uncomfortable chair for the last couple of hours, he found his eyes were closing; he was desperate for sleep. As he drifted off, he heard his name being called.

'Ben.'

His eyes opened. Morgan was staring at him.

'What time is it?'

He frowned and looked at his watch.

'Four twenty-five,' they said in unison, her voice a hoarse whisper.

She smiled at him. 'Bloody insomnia; even when I'm stoned, I still wake up at that time.'

He leant forward and clasped her hand. 'I was so worried about you.'

'You were?'

He nodded. Pressing the necklace into her hand, he let go. She lifted it up and a single tear trickled from the corner of her eye.

'Where?'

'Stan came through, he brought your necklace back and saved your life.'

She tried to sit up. 'He did?'

'He did, he turned up to give it to you himself. I haven't got the whole story off him yet because he hurt himself pretty bad in the process of trying to save your life.'

'Is he okay?'

'Bruised, lost a lot of blood but yeah. He did good. I know where you get it from now.'

'What?'

'Dramatic entrances: wait until you see the state of your flat. He only went and threw a boulder through your picture windows.'

Despite the seriousness of the situation they both began to laugh, a little too loud for the emergency department, but they couldn't help it, and Ben realised he liked the sound of her laughter a lot more than anything else.

ONE WEEK LATER

Morgan stared at her reflection; she was ready to go back to work. The DCI had insisted she take some time off, but she was already bored and sitting home on her own didn't help. Apart from the couple of times she'd visited Stan in the hospital, she hadn't been out of her flat. Ben had done a good job of getting the window repaired and the flat cleaned up before she'd returned. She hadn't seen the mess or the blood because she'd been unconscious by the time Stan had made his heroic attempt to save her life. Who'd have thought it, after all this time he'd finally shown her he really did care and she was grateful to him. Her fingers reached up and touched the crescent moon necklace he'd brought back for her. It would take a lot of time to repair their fractured relationship, but at least they were both speaking to each other and she would accept that. She tugged a black roll-neck jumper over her head to hide the fading ring of bruising around her neck that was still visible. She didn't want people to stare at her. For seven days she had been forced to lie around doing nothing; she was bored beyond belief and eager to get back to work.

Inside the station she crept up the back stairs, avoiding the parade room and the officers in it. She reached the office which she'd been given and pushed the heavy wooden door open. Flipping the switch, a small 'Oh' escaped her lips. The desk and computer she'd been given were gone, along with the case notes. The realisation that she'd been moved out of Ben's team so fast stung. She leaned against the door frame; at least she could hold her head up high when she re-joined her shift downstairs. Even if she said so herself, she'd done a pretty respectable job in the short time she'd been up here. Two killers had been remanded and were behind bars thanks to her. An overwhelming feeling of sadness for the life she could have led overcame her; realising she'd been so dispensable hurt a lot more than the injuries she'd suffered. Not once when Ben had visited had he told her she was no longer needed, and she'd thought they were friends.

Determined not to let anyone see how devastated she was, she strode along the corridor. Pushing open the door that led into the CID office, about to tell him where he could shove his attachment, her mouth fell open. There in the corner on the desk she'd used a couple of times was her stuff; a foil banner was draped across the desk, the words 'Welcome Home' emblazoned across it. A bunch of blue helium balloons hovered above the computer and her whiteboard with all her notes on it had been fastened to the wall behind it. Amy, Ben and a few others began to clap and in unison shouted 'Surprise!'

For once Morgan was truly speechless. After a few moments she found her voice and looked at Ben.

'What's going on?'

He grinned. 'Is that desk okay? Sorry about the balloons, they didn't have any pink ones, but I figured you wouldn't care what colour they were. Oh, and that was the only banner they had as well, but it's the thought that counts.'

Amy shook her head. 'You're lucky he managed to find those. When Josie went on her maternity leave, he got one that said "Happy Retirement". He's not very good at this, are you, boss?'

Morgan laughed. 'I thought you'd had enough of me when I looked in my little office and saw everything gone.'

Ben shook his head. 'Definitely not. Right, enough of the fuzzy stuff. We still have a lot of work to do. Barker was charged with the murder of Jamie Stone and has been remanded for that.'

'How?'

'That folder he was about to burn had traces of blood and DNA on the papers inside that matched Jamie Stone's. The mask and knife he was burning also had traces of Jamie Stone's blood on it. Which was a miracle really, but sometimes it happens. A minute later and the whole lot would have probably been too burnt to retrieve anything of forensic value.' He waved his hand at her. 'It was worth sticking my hand in the fire for that. Barker hasn't admitted anything, but he knows he won't be coming home for an exceptionally long time, if at all.

'In the meantime, we continue to gather evidence and work on the O'Brien murders. Good news is we got a hit on the fibres from that small piece of carpet in the hall cupboard. There were similar ones in the driver's side footwell of the car you discovered in his lock-up. I'm awaiting confirmation, but Wendy thinks they'll come back as a definite match.

'Harrison Wright has been charged with the murders of Olivia, Saul and Beatrix and the attempted murder of Bronte Potter. He made a full and frank confession to them all once he realised there was no going back, and he was already going down for a long time for your attempted murder. He admitted that he wanted the media attention and us arresting Greg Barker for their murders tipped him over the edge, which is why he came after you. He also admitted that Bronte had nothing to do with any of it.'

Amy crossed towards her and patted her back. 'You did a great job. I'm pleased to tell you that starting from tomorrow you're on the intake for the detective course and you're now officially on the team. I'm your tutor, so don't worry, you've already passed as far as I'm concerned. You've covered all the good stuff, there's just the mundane to go through.'

Ben was smiling. The DCI walked in and crossed the room towards her, his hand outstretched.

'Welcome to CID, Detective Constable Morgan Brookes. We're glad to have you on board.'

Morgan took Tom's hand and shook it. 'Thank you, sir, I'm happy to be here.'

Ben nodded his approval. 'Right, enough of the niceness. Morgan, you need to catch up on what you've missed this last week. Everyone back to work.'

She sat down at her desk and stared at the banner, then she looked around the office. Everyone was already looking back at their computers; she'd had her five minutes of glory.

It was over now, time to get back to work and she had never felt happier.

A LETTER FROM HELEN

Dear reader,

I want to say a huge thank you for choosing to read *One Left Alive*. If you did enjoy it, and want to keep up to date with all my latest releases, just sign up at the following link. Your email address will never be shared and you can unsubscribe at any time.

www.bookouture.com/helen-phifer

I hope you loved *One Left Alive* and if you did I would be very grateful if you could write a review. I'd love to hear what you think, and it makes such a difference helping new readers to discover one of my books for the first time.

I love hearing from my readers – you can get in touch on my Facebook page, through Twitter, Goodreads or my website.

Thanks,
Helen Phifer xx

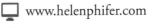 www.helenphifer.com

Helenphifer1

@helenphifer1

helenphifer

ACKNOWLEDGMENTS

First of all, I want to thank you, my wonderful readers, for choosing this book. I hope you enjoyed meeting Police Officer Morgan Brookes. I appreciate each and every one of you and thank you from the bottom of my heart. A police investigation of this magnitude would be far more in depth and be a very lengthy process. There would be many specialists brought in to assess the scene. For the purpose of this story, although as factual and true to life as I could make it, the investigation has been scaled down significantly. I hope you can understand and forgive this.

Thank you again to all the amazing book bloggers: you are so very much appreciated. I can't tell you how thankful I am that you choose to read my books and review them.

As always a huge heartfelt thank you to my editors, Jessie Botterill and Emily Gowers; your support has been amazing and you turned a rough draft into a wonderful story.

Thank you again to the fabulous Noelle Holten for her publication day support, it's truly appreciated. Thanks also go to the amazing Kim Nash for always being there. A special thank you goes to Emma Robinson for her help when I felt like throwing in the towel with my edits. The same goes to the rest of the Bookouture authors; I'm so amazed by how talented yet down to earth and supportive you all are. I feel very blessed knowing I am a part of this special group of writers.

Thank you once again to Oliver Rhodes for taking a chance and signing me; good luck for the future, you will be greatly missed.

I'm so grateful I get to work alongside the rest of the fabulous Bookouture team: same applies as last time. You guys definitely rock and you know how to party – you're my kind of people and I can't wait until we can next get together.

Thank you as always to Paul O'Neill for casting a final eye over my stories; you're definitely my lifesaver.

Thank you to my Write Romantics for always being there. Where would I be without all of your support? Jo Bartlett, Jackie Ladbury, Jessica Redland, Sharon Booth, Deirdre Palmer, Helen J. Rolfe, Lynne Davidson, Rachael Thomas and Alex Weston.

A special thank you to my book club members. I can't wait to see your lovely faces again. I've missed you all so much and our very noisy chats about books and life. Hopefully we're still allowed into Costa after Krog setting off the fire alarms last time and getting us all evacuated.

Thank you to my lovely friends, Sam and Tina. I've missed our coffee chats more than you could ever know.

A special thank you to Christine and her late husband Tom Fell.

Last, but definitely not least, a special thank you to my amazing family. I love you all more than words can say.

Helen xx

Printed in Great Britain
by Amazon